The memory  of wakefulness.

"Shh." His lips brushed her forehead as she began to weep. "Hush, sweetheart."

"Oh, Chaney. It was a nightmare."

"I know. I know." His hand stroked up and down her spine, soothing her.

She pressed the heels of her hands against her temples. What had the dream been? Not for the first time she thought if she could remember it she could put it behind her. But it was already dimming, fading into a gray fog. A name. She had spoken a name. What was it? She closed her eyes, unconsciously squinting.

"Josey," she whispered.

Chaney froze.

"A name." Her eyes popped open. "I remembered a name from the dream."

"Don't, sweetheart."

She pulled back, trying to look into his face. "But I—"

"Don't try to bring it all back."

"But—" She could feel a knot building, creasing her forehead. A headache was coming on. Instantly Chaney swung her around. He had her positioned between his thighs and began to rub her neck before she could ask him to.

He leaned against her. His breath brushed the tiny hairs behind her earlobe. "Relax," he said. His voice rumbled out of his chest, warm as honey. "Relax. Don't fight, sweetheart. You don't have to fight. You don't ever have to fight again."

She moaned her acquiescence. Even so, this time she promised herself she wouldn't forget. Concentrating despite the loosening of her body, she tried to keep the name in her mind.

"Beth Anne." His voice was deeper, a little rougher. His hand slid over her midriff. His callused fingers splayed as they angled down into the nest of curls at the top of her thighs.

Damn him for a devil. She knew where he was taking her and shivered with anticipation . . .

BOOK YOUR PLACE ON OUR WEBSITE AND MAKE THE READING CONNECTION!

We've created a customized website just for our very special readers, where you can get the inside scoop on everything that's going on with Zebra, Pinnacle and Kensington books.

When you come online, you'll have the exciting opportunity to:

- View covers of upcoming books
- Read sample chapters
- Learn about our future publishing schedule (listed by publication month *and author*)
- Find out when your favorite authors will be visiting a city near you
- Search for and order backlist books from our online catalog
- Check out author bios and background information
- Send e-mail to your favorite authors
- Meet the Kensington staff online
- Join us in weekly chats with authors, readers and other guests
- Get writing guidelines
- AND MUCH MORE!

**Visit our website at
http://www.zebrabooks.com**

TAGGART'S LADY

Deana James

Zebra Books
Kensington Publishing Corp.

http://www.zebrabooks.com

ZEBRA BOOKS are published by

Kensington Publishing Corp.
850 Third Avenue
New York, NY 10022

First Printing: April, 2000
10 9 8 7 6 5 4 3 2 1

Printed in the United States of America

For

Bob O'Brien,
who first told me about Order No. 11,
who graciously entertained me in his home
while I did research for this book,
and who went back to the library on his own
to get information I subsequently needed.

And for
Barbara O'Brien,
best friend
for more years than we care to count.

Accept this book by way of many thanks.

Chapter One

She screamed as the rifle shots dinned in her ears. They seemed to come from all directions with flashes of fire from their muzzles. She wouldn't crouch here waiting for the shots to finish her.

Even though her legs were trembling with fear, she eeled her body over the side of the wagon. The instant her feet hit the ground, an arm encircled her waist. Someone was holding her down.

She tried to throw him off. Violently, she scissored her legs. She had to get to Josey. By dint of strength she lunged away, swayed, took a staggering step, fell flat.

"Help! Josey! Help! Poppa! Poppa!"

The words wouldn't come. They reverberated from somewhere inside her skull. Her throat was too dry. And her legs wouldn't work. They kept slipping out from under her.

A deep voice called to her. "Beth Anne." Called her by name. "Beth Anne!"

"Josey? Where are you? Josey!"

She had fired her rifle. She remembered clearly. She'd already aimed and fired at the milling, galloping silhouettes. She'd seen one fall. Still she clutched the weapon, even though the singleshot wouldn't do her any good. Josey would have more cartridges. Or Poppa. If she could just get to them. She kicked out. More cloth ripped. Her foot encountered bare flesh.

Noise came from everywhere. Gunshots. Her papa's repeater thundered. Her brother's revolver cracked in her ear. Cattle bawled. Horses whinnied. Men cursed. Iron-shod hooves shook the ground.

She crawled, head down, belly to the ground. Her knees kept slipping back. Something or someone was pulling her back. She could feel the pressure on her shoulders. She opened her eyes in the darkness. Where was the house? Where was the wagon? She was cold. Her free hand scrabbled, clutched softness. A shirt? "Josey!"

"Beth Anne!"

She closed her eyes again. The ground rocked. Then she could see the silhouettes of great animals galloping toward her. Before they reached her, they rose in the air, cleared her. Their hooves were inches above her head. The ground rocked again when they came down so close to her ear that clods struck her face.

One wheeled back. She ducked her head. *Play dead!*

She pressed her cheek to the ground. The moonlight— No, the firelight picked out steel horseshoes. She couldn't tell the color of the horse, but it had white stockings. Tall white stockings, reaching above the knees. Whitish-yellow hooves tore up the ground in front of her face.

"Josey!" She flung herself across her brother's chest to protect him. Just as the horse wheeled, its rider fired a shot so close to her ear that it deafened her. Josey tumbled backward. She went with him, falling, thudding to the ground, hitting hard, rolling. She screamed from the bottom of her lungs, pushing every ounce of breath out past her vocal cords.

Fury and fear combined. She came up out of her roll with her useless singleshot aimed. She squeezed the trigger. She never heard the click. An instant later searing pain tore through her hands. A blow struck her forehead. Hot blood sprang out of the wound and flooded down her face.

She screamed again.

Powerful hands caught her wrists. A male body pinned her down. A man threw a muscular thigh across her flailing legs.

"Beth Anne!"

Her eyes flew open and the nightmare vanished.

Tonight had been worse than usual. She lay on the floor of her bedroom, looking up into the face of a three-quarter moon the color of fresh butter. Her heart pounded in her chest. The hooked rug was wadded beneath the small of her back. The polished oak boards were chill beneath her thighs. She winced and struggled to breathe under a heavy weight.

It moved, expanded. "Beth Anne?"

She relaxed. "Chaney?"

"It's me, sweetheart," he murmured. And then, "Thank You, Lord."

Her husband pushed himself off her. Without releasing his grip on her wrists, he rocked back on his knees and pulled her across his thighs. Cradling her against his chest, he pressed a kiss to her forehead. "Honeylamb."

"Oh, Chaney." Her voice broke. As always, tears were streaming down her cheeks. Fully awake now, she felt enervated. Her limbs began to tremble. Her teeth chattered as shivers of terror as well as biting cold overpowered her consciousness. The memory of the dream dissolved in the first moments of wakefulness, leaving behind only the fierce physical and emotional impact. "Oh, Chaney. Chaney."

He passed her arms around his neck and slid his own arms under her legs. She clung to him as he used the great strength of his horseman's thighs to stand straight up and lift them both onto the bed. "Shh." His lips brushed her forehead over and over as she began to weep. "Hush, sweetheart."

The dream had happened again. The horror that had seemed to lessen in the past year had come back again. "Oh, Chaney. It was the nightmare."

"I know. I know." He kissed her temple and the top of her head. His hand stroked up and down her spine, soothing her. He rocked her, repeating the two words, crooning them like a lullaby. "I know, I know, I know."

She was soaking his nightshirt front again. Disgust with herself brought her back to reality. This situation was no different from the first time she could remember. When she was a child of ten, just in this way she had tried to burrow inside Chaney's warm, solid body and leave the terrible chills behind.

Gradually, her trembling stopped. Her fighting muscles relaxed. One foot was within a hair of knotting in a painful cramp. With a sigh she stretched out both her legs, rotated her left ankle, and flexed the arch. She was wide awake now. Not even a trace of drowsiness remained.

How she hated the night!

If the sun instead of the moon had shone through the window, she would have left the bed and started her chores. Experience had taught her that hard work would make the demons scatter faster than anything else.

She sank back on her pillow. With a corner of the sheet, she wiped at the tears still wet on her cheeks.

The bed sagged as Chaney stretched out beside her with a groan. "Feeling better?"

"Yes." She wasn't really. Anger and disgust at herself had set in. If she followed the usual pattern, those emotions would give way to despair. Tonight had been worse than usual. In her terror she'd dragged Chaney out of bed onto the hardwood floor. She'd disturbed his sleep just now when he needed it most, when the hardest work of the year was before him.

How did her husband put up with her? She knew instinctively that most men wouldn't. They probably wouldn't have slept with her after about the third time. She laid her hand on his wrist, stroking the warm skin. She knew exactly what it looked like, fine-grained and deeply tanned, sprinkled with springy black hairs. "Did I hurt you?"

"Scared the fool out of me," he accused as he tried to make sense of the sheets and blankets. His voice was deep and hoarse. He yawned loudly and sniffed. He had been wakened out of sound sleep.

"And I dragged you out of bed." She hung her head. Another minute and she was going to start weeping again. "That is, I—I think we both fell."

"Pushed me, don't you mean? I was on the bottom," he grumbled. "I'm bruised on both sides."

"I'm sorry. I'm so sorry."

She sat up in the welter of covers and pressed the heels of her hands against her temples. What had the dream been? Not for the first time, she thought that if she could remember it, she could put it behind her. But it was already dimming, fading into a gray fog. She was sure that it was always the same, yet she could never remember it. A name. She had spoken a name. What was it?

"Shall I make some hot chocolate?" His deep voice interrupted her thoughts just as she dived into the shifting mists and shadows.

"Yes. Please. That would be good." He was being nice. He was always so good to her. "Thank you. I'd like some."

The springs creaked as he shifted his legs over the side of the bed. She closed her eyes, unconsciously squinting as she tried to recall the name. She'd tried and tried before with no success. With a sigh she slumped back on the pillow, letting her mind go blank. And suddenly there it was. The name. *Josey.*

"Josey," she whispered.

Chaney froze in the act of reaching for his boots. "What?"

"Josey. Josey. A name." Her eyes popped open. She lifted her head excitedly. "I remembered a name from the dream."

Chaney turned to her and all but snatched her into his arms. "Don't do that, sweetheart."

She pulled back, trying to look into his face, seeing only a white shape in the dimness. "But I—"

"Don't try to bring it all back. You're getting over these nightmares. You really are. You haven't had one of them in a long time."

"But I—" She could feel a knot building between her eyes, creasing her forehead. A headache was coming on. She rolled her head on her shoulders. Instantly, Chaney swung her around. She was like a doll in his big hands. One of the advantages of being married to a man who topped six feet by nearly four inches was his strength. He had her positioned between his thighs and began to rub her neck before she could ask him to. He had known what was about to happen before she did herself.

"Relax," he counseled. His thumbs pressed into the hard knots on either side of her spine at the base of her skull. His voice rumbled out of his chest, warm as honey, soothing as the morning sunshine. "Relax. Don't fight, sweetheart. You don't have to fight. You don't ever have to fight again."

She moaned her acquiescence. Picking up the rhythm

of his movements, she rolled her head forward and side to side.

His hands kept kneading the muscles as she slowly relaxed. Even so, this time she promised herself she wouldn't forget. Concentrating despite the loosening of her body, she tried to keep the name in her mind. *Josey*. Unfortunately, every time she remembered it, her muscles tensed again. And Chaney paused in his rubbing.

"Beth Anne?"

He didn't want her to remember. He leaned against her. His voice was deeper, a little rougher. His breath brushed the tiny hairs behind her earlobe. His lips touched, caressed.

Damn him for a devil. She knew where he was taking her and shivered with anticipation.

A minute later, her muscles tensed for an entirely different reason. Chaney chuckled. One long arm encircled her waist and guided her back against him, against the hard muscles of his belly and the harder rod that pressed against her spine. His hand slid over her midriff. His callused fingers splayed as they angled down into the nest of curls at the top of her thighs.

"Chaney Taggart, you wild man."

The chills were gone completely, replaced by delicious warmth. A different kind of trembling began in her belly and spread upward and downward into a liquid warmth that bloomed between her legs. She thrust her buttocks back against him and arched her spine, stretching, tilting her head against his shoulder, offering him her throat.

He kissed it, scored it with his teeth, nipped at her earlobe. His other hand cupped her right thigh and pulled it up over his own. Her gown rode up and she caught the tail of it impatiently and pulled it out of the way. Chaney had learned long ago that she wanted no gentle loving in the aftermath of the nightmares.

Trembling, open, wet, hot, she urged him on as he slid his fingers down across the throbbing nub of pleasure and into her body.

She caught at his wrist, writhing in an ecstasy of pleasure mixed with anticipation of more pleasure to come. "You devil, Chaney Taggart. You devil."

All his heat and all his desire were in his chuckle. Then he bit her earlobe again. "Pull your gown up, sweetheart."

She writhed, hooking her left leg over his knee, giving the lie to any protests. "It—it's up."

"No. Not high enough. Not nearly high enough."

"Oh—Chaneeeeey."

He thrust his tongue into her ear and tightened his grip around her waist. "Higher. Higher. That's it."

The night air was chill on her bare breasts. Their nipples prickled, the aureoles swelled. She twisted, rolled her head on his shoulder. "Let me—"

He knew what she wanted but denied her. His hand pulled her right thigh back tighter, increasing the stretch, exposing the private parts of her body to his knowing hands.

She writhed, panting.

"Stop that. Be still." The peremptory words gave the lie to the teasing, caressing voice that spoke them. Like soft expulsions of heat against her ear, they raised the tension in her body another notch.

"I can't." Her protest was strained. It slipped out from between her clenched teeth. She was writhing helplessly now. Gasping. Small whimpers punctuated her body's rhythms as she arched and pushed against his hand.

"No," he agreed, his lips moving against her ear. "I don't think you can." On that word he cupped her, pulling her back against him, his fingers pushing deeper into the hot wetness inside her.

She screamed and arched and thrust away from him all

in one contorting movement like a wild mare that feels the saddle for the first time.

He held her while she shuddered. Hot liquid seeped between his fingers. He pulled them out of her and laid her down, limp, at the tangled sheets and pillows. Still trembling, she watched him from beneath her lashes. In the moonlight, his broad chest and shoulders gleamed palely as he straddled her.

Then he grasped himself with the fingers wet from her body and guided himself inside her.

Her legs spread wide to accept him and locked around his waist to drag him to her. She moaned. "Damn you for a devil."

He laughed. "But you love me." He grasped her breasts, squeezing them, flicking the hard nipples. "Say you love me. I want to hear it."

Her muscles convulsed around him. "No."

"Say it." He bent to take the nipple in his teeth. "Say it."

"N-no."

He tugged it up into his mouth.

She arched and pushed her hips higher, rising with him. "No."

He bit her.

"Yes. Yes. Yesyesyes."

Her convulsions squeezed him so that his back arched and he threw back his head in ecstasy. Just before their climax came, he jerked himself out of her and spilled his seed onto the sheets.

With fumbling motions, they managed to rearrange themselves on the bed and find the pillows for their heads. Chaney covered the wet spot with a towel and settled back, already breathing deeply and evenly when Beth Anne covered him.

She sank back onto the pillows. Her eyelids were fluttering closed; then they flashed open. "Josey." No pictures. No other memories. The dream had vanished just as all the others with but one difference. She formed the word soundlessly. "Josey."

Day lilies bloomed in riotous orange and yellow on either side of the front steps. Three feet tall on pencil-thin stems, they grew wild along the creekbanks and in the ditches by the roads of southwestern Missouri.

These were Beth Anne's special joy. She'd persuaded Chaney to take her out to dig them up less than a month after they'd moved into this house. He'd done the digging while her happy tongue had run on and on about how she loved flowers and wanted them growing beside her front porch. Even without a memory, she knew.

She'd been twelve years old. At least Chaney said she was twelve. And he'd been twenty-seven. She'd already stopped thinking of him as a father.

That day she decided he was going to be her husband. She knew that many girls fell in love before they were old enough to get married. Chaney was the man for her. She was sure she could make him happy.

So the day those lilies began to bloom, she'd told Chaney they were going to get married. On that day she'd secured his promise that he'd wait for her to grow up.

For eight years those lilies had been coming back into bloom. So now she must be twenty. Eight years of lilies. She could count on them, the same way she could count on Chaney Taggart, the man who was her only family. He'd been her friend and her father. Now he was her husband.

The oak trees arched at the end of the lane. Six white oaks planted some thirty yards apart, three on each side along the road. They were old oaks. Much older than eight years. They might be as old as thirty or forty or even fifty.

Although she doubted that. Not many people had been living in this part of Missouri in 1823. It had become a state in 1821 because of the big cities of St. Louis and Independence. No one had lived in this part of the state.

One of the oaks was blighted, split by a lightning strike five years ago. One whole side of the tree had burned off. A couple of scarred barren limbs thrust skyward like skeletal arms. A white-breasted hawk perched on one of them. His eyes scanned the lush grass that rolled back toward the house. He was one of a pair that hunted that stretch of road.

Josey. Who was Josey?

She wrapped her arms around her as she stared at the hawk without really seeing it. A chill racked her that had nothing to do with the crisp air. The morning was fair. The day would warm up. She'd start in her heavy blanket coat and end in her workshirt.

Josey?

Maybe Chaney was right about her trying so hard. Maybe she shouldn't be trying to remember. Maybe she should lie back and let it come. She tried to close her eyes and think of nothing.

Nothing was what she got. Because all around her she could hear the sounds of the day beginning.

She opened her eyes and shook her head. She was upsetting herself again, trying to remember. Usually by this time, the bad dream was only a niggling shadow in her mind. What good was Josey if she couldn't remember anything else? How she wanted to remember! Maybe that was why she'd dreamed the dream again after so long. In three weeks she'd celebrate her twenty-first birthday. She hated to go into adulthood with half of her life unaccounted for.

The first of May was the date Chaney had chosen for her birthday. It was to the date nine months after she'd awakened in a strange room. Chaney, much younger, a bit frightened, a total stranger, had sat beside the bed. He'd had hold of her hand, but when she looked at him, he'd let go and risen.

Like a soldier he'd stood at attention, his face grave, his cheeks a little pale in contrast to his close-cropped black beard. A wave of black hair fell over his forehead.

She'd stared at him a long time. At first she didn't think anything at all. As if her mind were a blank page, she stared. Then thoughts began to form. *Room. Bed. Man. Chair, window, water, water, water.* "Thirsty."

Later she realized she didn't know whether she'd ever seen him before in her life, because she hadn't a single face in her memory. No mother, no father, no sisters, no brothers. No name, no home, no friends. No birthday.

For ten years it had been that way. All she was was Chaney Taggart's creation. Her new memory began from that minute and continued until now when it filled her whole life.

Until now. Josey was the first thing that was not Chaney's.

She shook herself. No time to think of it now.

The dew was evaporating from the grass. The horses were waiting in the stables. The men were already about the business of White Oak Farms—raising horses for U.S. Cavalry remounts. They were due at Fort Leavenworth, Kansas, next month. Setting her hat firmly on her head, she tightened its strings by sliding the button up tight beneath her ear.

Casting her memories aside, she strode out to work.

Chaney saw her coming from the back of a horse. Between his legs the young sorrel sweated through its paces, fighting the bit, fighting the man on its back. It was a stallion with a bad temper—a bubbling volcano waiting to erupt. Forced by Chaney's strong hands and stronger will, it followed the pressure of the reins and the bit right and left, again and again. It wheeled in a tight circle, walked back, walked forward.

When he pulled it to a halt, it grunted and tossed its head, trying to get its teeth around the bit. All its bad temper was concentrated on getting its head down between its front legs to buck. It didn't like what it was forced to do.

"Steady, son." Chaney didn't allow the horse any slack. Not one inch. Exerting all his strength, he forced it to stand like a statue, with head up, its red hide dark with sweat. White foam trickled down its chest and forelegs. Then Chaney clicked his tongue and touched the stallion with the spur. It moved forward until its nose was against the fence.

"Morning, honey. I thought you were going to sleep late."

Smiling, she approached the pair. The stallion rolled a white eye at her, but she crossed her gloved hands on the top rail and leaned against it. The horse snorted and tried to back away, but the rider held it firm. "I slept enough."

He looked at her keenly. She wouldn't look at him. Instead, she studied the stallion as if she hadn't seen him before. An uncomfortable silence fell between them. Chaney clenched his jaw. She had said a name last night. He hadn't quite heard it. But she'd said it a couple of times. She must be remembering it and feeling guilty about it. Otherwise, she'd be all smiles because the loving last night had been as good as any he could remember.

For three years he'd made love to her. She'd been a tender virgin, so small, so innocent that he'd been afraid to touch her for fear he'd hurt her more than she could bear. But even her first time she'd wrapped her legs around his waist and matched his rhythm. Over the last three years, he'd taught her all he'd ever learned or heard of. Then they'd invented caresses to try on each other. A man couldn't have a better wife than Beth Anne. He closed his eyes, savoring the memory.

The horse sidled and almost caught Chaney's leg between the saddle and the fence. He slapped its neck with the ends of the reins. "Quit that, jughead!"

"Is that what we're going to call him?"

He scowled at her too-sweet smiling face. "I'm hoping to call him Jack eventually. His papers say his name is Jack o' Diamonds. But Jughead will do until I get the kinks out of him."

The sorrel grunted and danced, fighting against the bit. Chaney leaned over to pat the horse's sweaty neck. Far from being calmed by the caress, the stallion thrust out his neck, bared his teeth and snapped at Beth Anne's hands.

She jerked back and thrust them into her pockets. A muscle jumped in the side of her jaw. "Goodness."

"Quit that!" Chaney jerked back on the reins, exerting all the force of his arms and shoulders to pull the horse's jaw back. Angrily, he ordered the animal to stand. "I'm sorry, honey." His words carried a double meaning. "Really sorry."

Beth Anne's throat worked as she swallowed resolutely. Then she looked up at him. As always, the full power of her loving eyes sent a lightning bolt through him.

A hint of uncertainty sparked in their depths. Her eyes flickered just an instant before she smiled. "Do you want me to take him, now that you've got him warmed up?"

He shook his head, relief coursing through him. She had made her choice for business as usual. As a measure of how much he mistrusted this horse, he shook his head. "Thanks for the offer, but he's still too rough. Go on around. Luther'll put your saddle on one that's a little farther along."

She nodded. They stared into each other's eyes across

the top rail of the fence. The sorrel danced and half rose, tossing his head. He came down with an angry grunt. Chaney sat him with half a mind. With the other half he watched his wife.

She grinned suddenly. Her eyelashes swept down as she tilted her head. "That was good last night."

He grinned back. "I don't know." With a shake of his head, he pretended to be considering. "I think it still needs practice."

"You could be right." Her laugh mingled with his own. With a mock salute she strode away. Over her shoulder, her voice reached him, "I'll be ready to give you another lesson tonight."

When she disappeared, relief left him weak in the saddle. The sorrel seized the opportunity to drag his head forward and kick up his hind legs. Chaney had to turn all his attention to getting the animal back under control.

Not for the first time, Chaney wondered whether this horse was a good choice. The idea of raising pleasure horses from start to finish was his dream that had been financed by buying loose stock at auction and breaking and training them for the army.

Now the dream was so close to reality. One more sale and they'd be ready for the big push—new mares, new stables, new corral to show the horses in. Oh, he had it all planned.

They'd be rich. Beth Anne wouldn't want for anything. She'd rear their children and be happy and safe for the rest of her life.

Except this horse wasn't turning out to be what he'd hoped. Jack o' Diamonds was beautiful. The sorrel had brilliant color along with perfect conformation. His colts grown up, well trained as pleasure horses, would sell themselves.

Unfortunately, the stallion was proving to be high-strung

and treacherous. Along with conformation and color, a stud passed temperament on to his get. If the sorrel couldn't be tamed, all the beauty in the world wouldn't make his colts into safe pleasure mounts for ladies and gentlemen.

Chaney tightened his legs around the horse's girth. "Let's get on with it, son," he said in his sternest, deepest voice. "Once you learn who's boss, we'll both be better off."

"Mornin', Miz Taggart." Luther Tibbets, the White Oak foreman and chief horse wrangler, touched his hat.

"Morning, Mr. Tibbets." She answered him in kind. Exaggerated formality was their little joke since her marriage. Uncle Lute had called her Bethie from the first day she'd met him. He'd been on the farm when Chaney had brought her here, sweeping off his hat, smiling, helping her down from the buckboard, pushing his little Mary Nell forward.

After Chaney had led her through the house into her very own bedroom, he'd taken her out to the stable where Luther had put her on her very own horse. After her husband, Luther was the man she trusted and loved most in the world.

He studied her critically. She put her hand to her cheek, knowing that the dark circles told him all too clearly that she hadn't had a good night. At last he put his hand on her arm. "You sure you want to ride today?"

She sighed. "Not really, but I think riding and working hard will drive it all right out of my mind."

"That's the ticket." He led the way through the shedrow out into a large pen where six horses, all sorrels like the stallion Chaney had been working, were snubbed to posts. Three were saddled. A fourth was submitting docilely while one of the White Oak riders replaced a headstall with a bridle and bit. "Take your pick."

Supplying army remounts was a big business for horse farms in this part of Missouri. In fact it was their main source of business. Railroads had long ago replaced the stagecoaches that had had to constantly replace their used-up harness stock.

Different troops in the Army of the West rode different-colored animals. White Oak sorrels, chestnuts, and red roans might be bound for troops on the Powder River in Wyoming or the Brazos in Texas. They were big horses, fifteen to sixteen hands high, and they brought in big money. Their reputation had grown as troops found them invariably good-mannered and bridlewise.

Beth Anne moved to a rangy gelding with a white race down its face. Its front feet had white stockings, one running up almost to the knee. The sight startled her. She had seen it before. Halting, she stared at the horse's hooves. Whitish-yellow.

Luther laid a hand on her shoulder. "Beth Anne?"

She sucked in a deep breath. "I'll take this one."

She went through the process of touching the horse's face, neck, and withers, talking as she did, her hands running over it until the skin on its neck stopped flinching as if it were casting off flies. When the horse was still, she swung up into the saddle and nodded to Luther.

The foreman reached to pull the reins loose.

"Luther." He looked up at her inquiringly, shading his eyes. The morning sun picked out every seam in his weathered face. "Did you ever know anyone named Josey?"

Was it her imagination, or did the cords in his neck tighten? Did his eyes twitch, or was he simply squinting more in the bright light? He lowered his hand to pass one of the reins under the horse's neck. Still not speaking, he joined it with the other and held them up to her. "Can't say as how I recall the name."

She had no choice but to nod. Turning the gelding, she tapped her heels against his sides and headed him out through the chute into the training corral. As she rode, she had an itchy feeling between her shoulderblades as if Luther's faded hazel eyes were staring into her back.

Her sorrel was mild-mannered and steady. She patted his neck when she finished with him. Some mounted infantryman or cavalryman would bless her unawares someday, when his horse wheeled with a touch on the neck and a tug on the rein rather than having to be hauled right or left with brute force.

She climbed down, pulled off the saddle, and began to rub the gelding down. Her hands in the gunnysacks moved over and over the white foreleg. Where? And when?

Finally, in disgust, she gave the mount a final pat and decided to set the whole thing aside. She stepped out of the shadow of the shedrow just as a rider rode into the yard.

From under the brim of his black hat, his eyes met hers.

Instantly, she ducked back into the opening. The response was force of habit. A woman alone didn't confront strangers. She threw a look over her shoulder. The stable was empty—of horses and men. By the rarest of coincidences, everyone was out exercising a mount.

She heard the stranger's horse stamp and snort. The saddle leather creaked as he climbed down.

Her eyes sought the varmint gun, a singleshot .22 that hung in its scabbard from a four-by-four. It might be fine for a weasel or a fox, but it wouldn't give a determined thief much trouble. If he were worse than a thief—

"Ma'am?"

The voice was deep and gentle. But thieves seldom rode in cursing and ranting. Some of them even smiled and thanked their victims kindly after they'd robbed them. Or as they shot them down.

She waited, gathering her courage. Inwardly, she scolded herself. She should have faced him confidently as if she had all manner of hired hands close by in the stable. She should have ordered him off before he dismounted.

"Ma'am, I'm looking for work."

No figure filled the doorway.

Well, of course not.

He hadn't come any closer. He was smart. Very smart. Coming out of bright sunlight would blind him inside the shedrow. She opened her mouth to give a holler.

Then she stopped. She was almost twenty-one. White Oaks was her farm as well as Chaney's. She was being silly. If he tried anything, she'd have plenty of time to scream then. She wasn't exactly alone on the place.

Wrapping her dignity as Taggart's wife around her, she stepped out into the sunlight.

Chapter Two

The stranger was shorter than she'd expected. Of course, all men looked taller on a horse. His shoulders and chest were thin as if he were a youth who hadn't filled out yet, but the lines around his mouth and the dark smudges beneath his eyes gave the lie to that assumption.

She'd seen her share of faces like that since the War. He looked like a man who'd walked through hell and lived to tell about it. The experience had aged him fast.

Long yellow hair brushed his shoulders. He pulled his weathered hat off and held it and his reins just below his waist and to the side. The hat covered the butt of his pistol, but not the long barrel that reached almost to his knee. He wore the gun on his right hip. A closer look told her that he was rigged for a crossdraw with his left hand.

On the Missouri-Kansas border, she'd learned to observe those things. Chaney had taught her, talked to her about them. Since most men were right-handed, a left-handed gunman had a clear advantage. Any opponent who made the mistake of thinking that his enemy had to drop his hat and reins before he could draw would end up with a bullet between the eyes while he was reaching for his own pistol.

As she stared, the stranger let his arm swing down to his side. He'd realized that she knew his trick and decided it wasn't concealing anything any longer.

She crossed her arms in front of her chest and eyed him coldly.

He looked away, then dropped his chin with the hint of a coaxing smile. "I guess I spooked you, ma'am. I'm sure sorry."

The smile drew her brows together in a frown. It looked familiar somehow. Or perhaps it was only that his reason for smiling was strange to her. No one smiled at her to coax her into anything. She returned it a bit uncertainly.

"That's all right," she heard herself saying. "You didn't really scare me. I just didn't expect anyone to be here."

She clamped her lips together and frowned again. What was she doing explaining perfectly reasonable behavior to a stranger?

He nodded. His pale blue stare raked her up and down before settling on her face. In fact it was making her a little uncomfortable. Behind her she heard footsteps. A small knot of tension relaxed inside her. She let out her breath in a small sigh and turned. Before she could speak, Luther Tibbets barreled past her.

"You'd better have a damn good reason for ridin' in here, stranger," he growled. Hastily, the foreman stepped in front of her, pushing his way forward, forcing the stranger to back away from her.

The man rocked back on his heels and indicated with a toss of his head the lane and the road beyond. "I'm looking for work," he said. "I rode over from Rich Hill. And beyond. Name's Noah Rollins."

He looked at Beth Anne significantly almost as if he expected her to know the name. She searched her memory. It didn't sound familiar. Nor, now that she thought about it, did he look all *that* familiar. His face was as thin as the rest of him. His cheekbones thrust through the weathered skin. A pale blond stubble showed on his chin, but the rest of his jaw was nearly beardless. His hair was probably the same butter color when it wasn't plastered to his scalp by sweat.

Luther gestured toward the ancient gray mare that stood with her head sagging and one hip cocked. "That don't mean nothing to me. Climb back on that crowbait and head on back to beyond. There's no work around here."

Noah Rollins recovered his balance. His eyes narrowed. A muscle in his jaw clenched. "I reckon I'll wait around to talk to the boss."

Luther blinked and then frowned horrendously. He stabbed a thumb toward his chest. "I talk for the boss. He don't got time to waste on drifters. Now get on out of here."

Putting his hat back on, the stranger shot Beth Anne an icy look—one part appeal, two parts accusation. It hit her hard. Nevertheless, he hooked his foot in the stirrup and grabbed the saddlehorn.

Something stirred deep within her. "Luther."

The foreman swung around. "Now, Miz Taggart, you go on up to the house. Mary Nell knocked off half an hour ago. You've done more than your share today. I'll take care of this."

She shook her head. Motioning the foreman to follow, she led the way into the stable. When they were nearly halfway down the shedrow, well out of earshot, she spoke. "Luther, we need extra hands."

He shook his head. "Not some goddamn—pardon me, ma'am—drifter that happens by."

"He looks hungry." She glanced over her shoulder. Noah Rollins had stepped away from his horse. He lounged with his thumbs hooked in his gunbelt. He was squinting intently into the dimness. She knew he couldn't see her eyes. He probably couldn't even make out the expression on her face.

Luther thrust out his jaw belligerently. "Now, Miz Taggart—"

She'd made him angry. His shoulders were stiff and his voice steely. The muscles in her own shoulders tensed. She dropped her gaze. A nervous fluttering began in her belly. She could feel her determination oozing away and hated herself for her lack of backbone. She was such a timid, rabbity person. She wouldn't fight for anything.

The foreman folded his arms across his chest. "It just ain't practical, Bethie."

She knew what was coming. He always called her Bethie when he was putting her back in her place as the child he'd helped to rear.

"There ain't no way we can hire everybody that comes by looking for a handout. Most of 'em won't work enough to make no difference. Some of 'em will steal anything that's not nailed down. You can't—"

He broke off. Over her shoulder he spoke, "Chaney, you tell her. She wants me to hire that drifter."

She hadn't heard his approach. She didn't have a chance to turn before Chaney dropped his arm over her shoulders. He was hot, and he smelled of leather, dust, and horse, but she couldn't keep from leaning against him. Everything seemed right with Chaney beside her.

"The fella that came in on the gray?" His deep voice rumbled out of his chest.

She relaxed. Her head drifted to Chaney's shoulder in spite of the fact that Luther was standing right there. Even though her husband would probably side with his foreman, she'd feel better about the refusal if it came from him.

"The damn drifter come right up to her," Luther growled.

"He's a hungry young man with an old tired horse," she said firmly. "He didn't ask for a handout. He's looking for work. And we could use the hand. He's young and he's got good manners. He apologized for scaring me by riding in too close. I think we should take another look at him."

Her reasons sounded silly even to herself. She didn't have much hope. She could hear Chaney's heartbeat, strong beneath her ear. Every so often it would hesitate, then give a little extra jump. She loved the sound of it. She could feel her heartbeat trying to match it and her body heat rising a notch. If they'd been alone—

He must have felt it too. He sucked in a deep breath. His heart gave the extra beat and stepped up its rhythm. She tipped back her head to meet his smile.

"Well, I've never heard of a saddle tramp with good manners," he said. "I sure want to meet this fella."

With Luther leading the way, shaking his head and muttering, the three of them stepped out into the sunlight. Beth Anne would have pulled away from Chaney's side, but his arm slid down around her waist, keeping her tight against him.

Chaney stared a long time at the stranger. His face revealed nothing—neither approval nor disapproval.

To Noah Rollins's credit he didn't flinch or fidget. In fact, he stared as hard at Chaney as Chaney did at him. They reminded Beth Anne of a couple of stud horses sizing each other up. Another minute and they'd start to paw the ground. She could feel a nervous giggle rising in her throat. Was this how a filly felt?

"My wife thinks I should hire you," Chaney said at last.

"She's a gracious lady," came the reply. "I came in too

close and scared her as she was coming out of the barn."
Noah's pale blue eyes were chill and hard. He certainly
didn't have his hat in his hand now.

"This is a horse farm." Chaney tilted his head to one
side to scan the gray mare, so old that she was nearly solid
white, including knees, hocks, and ankles. "Are you any
good with horses?"

Noah Rollins followed his stare. He gave his horse's neck
an affectionate pat. "Babe's moving on toward fifteen, for
sure. But I promise you I can ride anything, and I've worked
with horses all the way to Kentucky and back."

"I don't raise racers," Chaney informed him coolly.
"We're training remounts for the U.S. Army."

"I can do that for you."

Chaney hesitated. The two men stared into each other's
eyes. Beth held her breath. She could feel the tension in
his shoulders. His grip was almost painful around her waist.

Then he relaxed. "Take a bunk in the longhouse down
by the stream. Luther'll show you where. Tomorrow morning, you meet me here. I'll see what you know."

Rollins nodded. "Fair enough." He lifted his hat and
swept it across his chest. When he bowed, strands of lank
blond hair fell forward to brush his cheeks. "Mrs. Taggart.
I do thank you."

She smiled. "See that you do a good job. My husband
will get after me if you don't."

Mary Nell Tibbets stood on tiptoe to pull aside the ging-
ham curtain to get a better view out of the kitchen window.
"Is that a new man?" She watched Noah turn the mare
into the corral and saunter down toward the stream. "Oh,
Lordy. It is. And he's young."

Beth Anne hung her hat and coat on the pegs beside
the door and pulled her braid around her shoulder. As

usual, the wind had left it a snarly mess as well as blown dust and bits of chaff into it. She took up the glass of cool water her friend had poured for her and dropped into a chair beside the table. "He's new all right. And I suppose he's young. He's kind of underfed right now. His name's Noah Rollins. He came looking for work."

Mary Nell leaned farther out. Her voice was a little breathless. "He looks real tall. And would you get a load of that yellow hair? Hair that color always makes me think of Galahad."

Beth Anne had to stop herself from getting up and coming to the window to see too. Even though she'd met the man, she hadn't really looked at him as if he were handsome.

She mustn't encourage Mary Nell to be silly. Luther's daughter was man-crazy. She had a different perspective on nearly everything in pants.

"Is he handsome?" Mary Nell asked.

"He had nice regular features." Beth Anne had to remind herself that she was too mature for such discussions. Besides, they weren't proper for her. She was married. She wasn't interested in Noah Rollins. So his hair was long and yellow. It was sweaty and dirty too.

For no reason at all the name "Josey" flitted through her mind. She drained the glass and rose to draw herself another from the ironstone crock.

Mary Nell looked over her shoulder with a mischievous grin. " 'Bout time we got a young man around here. Everybody on this farm is *so old.*" Her voice turned into a whine as if the pain were unendurable. "You do realize, don't you, that Chaney's the youngest man around here and he's married to you?"

Beth Anne had never thought about that particular fact, if fact it was. She frowned. Surely Mary Nell was mistaken.

Still, "Everybody's not *so old*," she objected. "They've just been working here a long time."

"Forever. They were old when we got here and we've been here nearly ten years." She made the time sound like centuries. She spun away from the window and selected a peach from the wooden bowl in the middle of the table. "I'm never going to find anyone to marry if I don't get to go to that finishing school in St. Louis next year."

Beth Anne had to acknowledge the truth of Mary Nell's predicament. Most of the hands were in their forties, quite a bit older than Chaney. Luther and Gunderson, the man who doctored the hands and the horses, were easily in their fifties. Since the girls almost never went into the little town of Rich Hill except to catch the train to Kansas City, Mary Nell hadn't had much opportunity to meet a young man.

"You'll get to go," Beth Anne promised. "If your dad shows signs of backing out, I'll get Chaney to talk to him."

Mary Nell returned to the window. Dusk was falling. Noah Rollins had disappeared. She took a bite out of the ripe fruit and wiped the juice off her chin. "I'm glad he's here. At last I'll have someone to practice on."

Beth Anne choked on her water. When she could get her breath, she caught her friend by the shoulders. "Don't you dare," she warned. "You don't know who this man is. He's just someone who came up looking for work. He might be perfectly fine, or he could have all sorts of disgusting habits. He could have a wife and children somewhere. He could be wanted for murder."

Mary Nell refused to be properly chastened. "I didn't mean I was going to throw myself at him. I just meant I'd like to talk to someone whose age isn't more than double mine about something other than horses."

"Don't start something you can't finish," Beth Anne warned.

"I won't. I promise. I don't intend to give up St. Louis for anyone."

Beth Anne had to be satisfied with that statement as footsteps thudded up on the back porch. The kitchen door swung open and Amos Hardy, the cook, backed in, carrying the two baskets that contained their supper.

"Evenin', girls," he rasped. Hardy was a small, thin man with a voice ruined from a wound incurred in the War. He wore a bandanna around his throat to hide the deep indentation where a rifle stock had crushed his larynx but somehow hadn't ruptured his jugular nor broken his neck.

Ordinarily, Beth Anne and Mary Nell cooked for Chaney and Luther; but when the girls had taken to working the horses, Chaney had decided that Hardy would cook for them all in the cookshack where he cooked for the hands.

One glance at the kitchen table, and he began to scold. "How come you didn't git the table set? How come you all just standin' around talkin'? I ain't no waiter in some fancy hotel, y' know. I brung yours up first just like I been told. Them men down there are gonna tear the place down if I gotta stop and get out ever'thing and set it all up."

He continued fretting while he took the food out of the baskets. Calves' liver, seasoned with bacon and onions, boiled potatoes, cooked tomatoes, and a pot of hot coffee.

Grinning, Mary Nell spread the tablecloth and Beth Anne laid four plates, knives, forks, and coffee cups and saucers in a minute. Mary Nell took the platters and bowls from the old man. Beth Anne took the coffeepot and kissed him on his grizzled cheek. "We're sorry, Hardy. We talked too long."

He growled and batted at her shoulder, but the kiss did the trick. His griping stopped in midsentence. He thrust his hands in the pockets of his overalls and stomped out the door.

Behind him the girls grinned at each other.

"I'll call Chaney," Beth Anne said. "You pour the coffee."

"You're gonna be sorry over this deal this afternoon." Luther was scowling and puffing on the cigar Chaney offered him.

Chaney shrugged. A little cautiously he straightened out his right leg where the sorrel had brushed him against the fence. The knee was bruised. It would swell during the night and he'd have to work that out tomorrow.

His foreman caught the movement. "You're gonna be sorry about that fool sorrel too."

Chaney scowled. "I was talking to Beth Anne and didn't watch what I was doing."

"You can't trust him," Luther continued. "His get'll be just like him. You mark my words."

"He's just spirited," Chaney insisted doggedly. He was determined to work the kinks out of the stallion. He couldn't afford to have made a mistake on the horse. A stud was an investment that was a long time proving itself. His plans would be set back several years if this horse was the wrong choice.

"He's strong and fast, with great conformation," he went on, as much to convince himself as Luther. "Half the studs in the country can't be ridden."

"That's probably why we got so many bad horses."

Chaney glanced longingly at the kitchen door. One of his pleasures was Beth Anne's cooking. Even as a little girl she'd been a good cook.

At first they'd lived in boardinghouses, but when he rented a small cottage, much to his surprise, she'd taken over the cooking with neither question nor discussion. She could make biscuits and pancakes. Her watermelon pickles were delicious. Her candied sweet potatoes would make a strong man bust out crying.

He purely hated having her working those jughead horses, but she'd volunteered because at this time of the year, he needed every hand he could get.

Returning to the subject of the new hand, he said, "I didn't know who that fellow was, but surely to God he can clean out the stalls and the corrals if nothing else. That'll free up somebody to work."

"I don't like him."

Chaney sighed. "I don't like him either. He's carrying around a nasty load. But I need him."

Luther grunted and limped to the window, staring out into the thickening dusk.

Chaney flexed his knee. His first impulse had been to order Noah Rollins off the place, but from what he'd overheard and seen, Beth Anne wanted to hire him. He knew she was put out at him over the Josey thing, so he'd seized the opportunity to make it up to her.

He closed his eyes. Just a few more days and he could let himself ease up. God willing, they'd ship the horses without a hitch, the money would come through, and his wife would be pregnant without a care or a worry in the world. Twenty-one and pregnant with their first child.

He knew Beth Anne. She'd be so happy, looking forward to the baby that she'd forget everything else. Afterward, running after it and the others to follow would keep her so busy that she'd sleep like a log for the rest of her life.

He was counting on it. The thought of her with his baby in her arms, his children around her skirts, made his breath catch in his throat. His smile was especially warm when she appeared in the doorway to call them in for supper. Her nightmare—and his—would be over at the same time.

God willing.

* * *

Beth Anne sat before her dressing table to brush her hair. She held a lock out from her temple and scowled at it. It was fine and straight and red. In her considered opinion, those were the three worst things that any person could have wrong with her hair. On any day she had to brush it, braid it, and anchor it with about a dozen pins to keep it from coming undone.

Today, she'd begun to unpin it as soon as she'd finished supper. The next step had been to unbraid it. Now she had to take more time to brush the dust and trash out of it. All this came when the last twenty-four hours had left her so tired she could barely lift her arms.

With a sigh she swiveled around on the stool and let her head fall back. Then in a practiced snap, she flipped the entire mass of hair straight up and over her head. With legs spread and head bent, she gathered the flying strands and smoothed them until they hung between her thighs, their ends almost touching the floor.

She picked up her hairbrush, a richly chased piece with a sterling silver back that Chaney had given her for a Christmas gift. Without further thought she began the nightly ritual. Brush. Brush. Brush. Side. Side. Side. Over. Under. Over. Her body swayed in rhythm.

She could hear Chaney whistling off-key in the bathroom. She paused to imagine him standing in front of the mirror above the washstand, two mahogany-backed brushes in his hands. A couple of neat swipes back from his forehead, two more over his ears to smooth the sides, and he was through. The wavy black strands, liberally laced with gray, would lie in perfectly aligned waves.

Through the veil of hair, she made a face in his direction.

She lifted her brush to begin again. The small white scar showed in the palm of her hand. She turned her hand

over. The scar was on the back too. At sometime in her
past, something had passed all the way through the middle
of her hand. No doubt the two wounds had happened at
the same time she'd received the scar at her hairline.

A bullet? It didn't look round, but she didn't know what
bullet scars looked like. Had she, sometime before she was
ten years old, flung up her hand to protect herself and
been shot? Or stabbed? Who would have been so cruel as
to try to kill a child?

She examined the scars on her hand as she had so many
times before. And just as before, her head began to throb.
She could feel tension prickling in her scalp. The tendons
in the back of her neck knotted. She groaned. If she didn't
stop thinking about this, she was going to have a full-blown
headache in a few minutes. But she couldn't control her
thoughts.

Josey. She whispered the word. "Josey?"

Hastily, she resumed her brushing with more vigor than
necessary as if she could brush it all out of her consciousness. But her heart stepped up its rhythm. Her body tensed.
Angry with herself, she brushed harder. Her thoughts
whirled. Shadows crept in from the corners of her mind.
Her heart began to pound. A sick feeling rose in her
stomach.

She didn't hear the door to the bathroom open. When
Chaney's cool hand touched the back of her neck, she
jumped and almost toppled off the stool.

"Hey. Whoa. Easy there." He chuckled as he caught her
arm and steadied her.

His laugh was the last straw. "Damn it, Chaney Taggart."
She jerked her arm out of his grasp and snapped her hair
back over her head. "Damn it." Leaping to her feet, she
flung the brush onto the dressing table.

His teasing smile vanished. His mouth tightened and
his eyes narrowed. He hated to hear her cuss. He was

putting on his father-face to deliver a lecture, but she forestalled him by catching up the brush and brandishing it under his nose.

"Why don't you wear a bell or something? You scared me to death."

Hands up, he backed away. "Steady, girl, steady."

"D— Stop it! Just stop it! I am not a horse!" To her disgust, she could feel the tears starting, burning in her eyes, trickling down her cheeks. How dared he joke when she was going crazy?

His smile came back, but now it was tender, understanding. She couldn't bear it. How could he be so wonderful and yet not understand her at all? "Did I say that?" he said. "No. I never said you were."

"No!" She had lost her temper completely. Her overheated emotions boiled over. "No. You never said I was. You just ride me and work me and give me a pat on the neck once in a while, but you never give me credit for being a human being."

He was sober now. He ran his hand around the back of his neck. His expression turned guarded. "What's this all about? You know I give you full credit. You're my partner. I couldn't run this place without you. Didn't I hire the man you wanted today?"

She wouldn't be put off. Nothing he could say would be right until he told her what she wanted to know. "Probably because you knew I was mad at you. The only time I ever get any attention paid me is when I get mad and raise a ruckus."

He came toward her and tried to take her in his arms. His voice was low and soothing. "Now, Beth Anne—"

But she wouldn't have it. "Get away. Get away. Get away! Don't come near me until you can give me some answers. I can't stand not knowing about ten years of my life anymore."

He scowled. "Sure you're not still upset about that dream?"

Finally. She flung her arms wide and rolled her eyes toward the ceiling. "Yes. Yes. I am. I'm upset about it. And them! The d— the nightmares. All of them. I've been upset for years. Ever since they started happening."

He opened his mouth, but before he could say anything, she cut across his argument. She was crying in earnest now, crying as hard as she'd ever cried after a nightmare. "I know what you're going to say. But they're not getting better. They're getting worse."

"Beth Anne—"

She had to tilt her head back to keep the tears from drowning her. She could taste them. They were choking her. "You don't know. You don't know. They aren't happening to you. They're happening to me and they keep getting worse and you keep telling me just to forget about them. You keep saying they'll go away. But they're not. They're not!"

He squared his shoulders. It was his military stance, his I-know-what's-best-for-you stance. His father-face was firmly in place. "Beth Anne—"

Frustrated almost beyond endurance, she flung herself at him. Her eyes and throat burned. Tears trickled down her cheeks. Her fists knotted in the front of his nightshirt. "I'm coming up on my twenty-first birthday, Chaney Taggart. We're going to start a family. What kind of mother am I going to be if I don't know my past? What am I going to answer when my little girl asks me who her grandfather and grandmother were?"

He swung his long arms around her and tried to pull her against his chest. "Stop it. Stop crying, honey. Please stop crying."

"Someone tried to kill me, didn't they? Tell me. Tell me."

"Honey, I don't know what to tell you."

She was trembling and hiccuping. She knew she should get control of herself. Instead of relaxing against him, she shoved the palms of her hands right in his face.

He caught one wrist and then other and pulled her to his chest.

She shook her head. Her hair flew everywhere. Strands stuck to her cheeks and caught on her lips. They crackled with electricity, as if she stood in the eye of some kind of storm. They clung to his broadcloth nightshirt. She tried to push him away, but he only hugged her tighter.

He gathered her wrists together in one hand. He used the other to cup her head and try to smooth the hair back from her face. His fingers slid between the strands. "Beth Anne," he crooned. "Beth Anne. Hush. Don't do this to yourself."

He drew her in inexorably, supporting her with his body, rubbing her back. She wouldn't be soothed. She was almost choking on her unhappiness. The lump in her throat hurt every time she swallowed, but she was getting herself under control. It was like the nightmare, except this time she was awake. Still she couldn't remember any of it. Except the one word. "Josey."

"So you're still thinking about Josey?" Chaney murmured. She could hear the sadness in his voice. She loved Chaney so much. When she made him unhappy, she made herself unhappy too.

"Yes."

He pushed her back at arm's length and bent his head. "Will you believe me if I tell you I don't know anyone named Josey?"

For a full minute, she stared into his dark eyes—the eyes that held her secrets? In the room was the same stillness of the farm before a storm. Her hair floated down strand by strand until it lay on her shoulders. *"Did* you ever know anyone named Josey?"

"No."

Even though he didn't hesitate, she wasn't sure that she had asked the right question. She tried again. "Did you ever *hear*—" Her voice wobbled. She gulped back tears. "—of anyone named Josey?"

He looked away. Hands on his hips, he took a deep breath. When he looked back at her, his eyes were infinitely sad. He laid two fingers across her lips. "Don't. Don't say another word. Don't ask another question. Tomorrow will be better. You're exhausted. You're so tired you couldn't get your hair brushed, let alone braided. Isn't that right?"

She closed her eyes. Instantly, the whole room dipped and swayed. She felt as if she were going to pass out on her feet. Chaney's arms closed around her shoulders and under her knees. With sure strength he lifted her. She settled her head against his chest where his heart thrummed in its own dear, peculiar, lolloping rhythm.

She didn't want to go to sleep with her questions unanswered. But suddenly, she couldn't help herself.

He carried her to the bed and slipped her into it. He slid her feet neatly under the covers, turned her on her side, arranged her hands, her hair, her head on the pillow, and then pulled the covers up around her shoulders. He did it without wasting a single motion.

And why shouldn't he do it right? she thought drowsily. He'd been doing it for eleven years. Eleven years ago, she'd waked up to find him beside her. Since then, she'd been tucked into bed by Chaney Taggart every single night.

Her limbs were heavy, her mind drifting. Her body jerked once as the muscles and tendons gave up their work. With her last thought she felt Chaney's hand on her hip, caressing her.

"Go to sleep," he whispered. "Go to sleep. You've had a busy day, little girl. A real busy day."

That was the problem, she realized. She was still Chaney's little girl. He was still protecting her from everything. Until he stopped thinking of her as a child, she wouldn't ever really be his wife.

If she was going to be a mother, she had to be a wife.

She had to defy him. Had to. Had to let him know that this wasn't the end. Just before she slid into the darkness, she willed herself to one last act. Her lips moved. Her breath slipped between them. "Josey?"

Chapter Three

Chaney never paused in his rhythmic stroking of Beth Anne's back. He sat on the side of the bed, her rounded bottom pressed warmly against his hip. One hand massaged the tight knots of muscle along her spine. The other gently caressed her hip. He could tell by her very stillness that she wasn't asleep. He knew she had whispered the name deliberately. And he knew why she'd done it.

His mouth curled in self-mockery as he let his gaze drift round their bedroom—the bedroom she'd made comfortable for him just as she'd made the rest of the house a home long before she'd moved into his bed.

Beth Anne had never been an easy person to manage. In fact, he couldn't say that he'd ever managed her at all. This warm room with its woven rugs covering the hardwood floors and carefully waxed and polished furniture was her idea. All the clothing in the wardrobe and drawers smelled of fresh air and sunshine and "potpourri," a woman's touch he'd never even heard of.

The very quilt on the bed had been a project she and
Mary Nell had taken on one long winter. They'd pieced
and quilted one apiece with more enthusiasm than skill,
as their uneven stitches testified. Her steely determination
had amazed him at the same time it made him a little
uncomfortable as he compared her production to his own
during his feckless youth. He had to admit he came up
lacking.

Even as a child of ten with her memory gone, her stubborn streak had driven him crazy. Many a time she'd defied
him. At such a time he'd wondered at himself. Why did
he keep her with him? Why not find a good family to take
care of her? Why not put her in an orphanage?

He shuddered. He knew why. Guilt had been only a
small part of his reasoning. Admiration for her incredible
bravery had come first. With it came the sense that such
bravery should be honored. And rewarded. He could not
imagine what she as a child must have endured in the
shadowy darkness filling her mind. How lost she must have
felt as she found herself in the care of a stranger, her
memory gone.

The wounds on her hands and head had healed. Their
scars had faded long before she'd really looked at him
with any sense. Then she hadn't remembered anything.
For more than a year the young face had been a stony
mask, but the eyes had been pools of despair stirred at
times by terror.

Then he'd watched fascinated as she'd gather herself
together with tight-lipped determination. Even though he
was more than twice her age, he'd found himself giving
way. If she thought she was right, thunder and lightning
wouldn't turn her. Like a string of bells, she'd jingled,
jangled, and sometimes clanged in his ears, demanding
that he treat her as if her opinions mattered.

Before he quite realized what had happened to him,

she'd organized his life. As if determined to make herself important to him, she started keeping his clothing, cooking his food, seeing to his comforts. He became the object of her attention, her care and affection, her smiles and tenderness. At first she was convenient, then necessary, then indispensable. He'd come to love her. Then, to his emotional and physical discomfort, long before his conscience told him his longings were decent, he'd fallen in love with her.

Slowly, her breathing deepened under his hands. Her slender body relaxed completely in sleep. Since he'd first gotten her, the nightmares had racked her. Only within the last two years had she started to remember them. Before that, touching her had been his way of calming her.

He leaned down to kiss her cheek, letting his lips remain there while he inhaled her warm fragrance. His Beth Anne of sun and sky, of "potpourri" and milled rose soap. He could feel his body stir at the same time that tears prickled at the backs of his eyes.

Then he straightened and lifted his hands away.

His smile was wry. Tinged with misery. He hadn't heard the last of Josey. The subject was going to come up in the morning. What was he going to say?

Quietly, he left the bedroom for the solitude of his office. There he dropped wearily into his chair and closed his eyes.

Oh, yes, he knew who Josey was. Josey McNeil. Short for Joseph or Josiah or maybe Josephus. A youth a few years older than Beth Anne. Her brother. And her father, Oliver. Confederate sympathizer. And most damning of all—distant kin of William Clarke Quantrill.

Oliver McNeil. With his white beard and long, wind-tossed hair and a cast in one eye. Looking like a Confederate incarnation of "Old Osawatomie" Brown, he'd been just as determined as his fanatical antislavery counterpart to lead his son to his death. He'd dropped down on one knee on the porch of his house. White-oak railing and one thick pillar shielding him, he'd pumped cartridges into his rifle and squeezed off the rounds with rhythmical and deadly precision.

Chaney closed his eyes in a vain attempt to keep from seeing the youngsters on the wagon seat, leaping over the household goods and springing to the ground, dashing toward their father.

Josey had gone first and Beth Anne at ten had followed him, leaping down, screaming her brother's name. Chaney had spurred his horse to intercept them both. Josey had stumbled and fallen to his knees.

Chaney had had troopers on his right and left. Josey had fumbled to bring up his rifle. Before Chaney could order the troopers to hold their fire, one had shot the boy. Josey had spun sideways and crashed to the ground.

Chaney had yelled wordlessly as the younger child stepped over the body. He didn't know it was a girl. Couldn't have stopped himself if he tried. Quick as thought, she'd swung her own singleshot to her shoulder and squeezed the trigger.

His reflexes had been the equal of hers. Her rifle had been empty, but he'd already pulled off a shot from his service revolver. She fell over backwards, her rifle flying—

He'd swung off his horse to drop to his knees between the bloody bodies.

Abruptly, Chaney jerked open the drawer of his desk and pulled out a bottle. It was almost full of good whiskey. He kept it for medicinal purposes only. And tonight he was in desperate need of medicine. He set his teeth in the cork, pulled it, and took a draft neat. He scarcely felt the burn. He drank again. And again.

Finally, it caught him by the throat and set him to coughing.

"God!" He shook his head and whistled through his teeth. "Oh, God!"

He opened another drawer, the last one on the right side. His face contorted as he pulled out his service revolver. The very same one. He stared at the thing. Everyone it had wounded or killed, he regretted. Everyone. He'd never seen the faces of some. Some he remembered all too clearly. Tonight they weighed heavily.

Deliberately, he turned the muzzle toward his face, breaking a hard and fast rule, even though he knew it wasn't loaded. Light slid down the oiled barrel. Clear-headed and clear-eyed, he stared into the small black hole. If he died this minute, he wouldn't have to tell Beth Anne who Josey was. But he wasn't a coward. Aiming it away from himself, he squeezed the trigger. The gun clicked.

So much for suicide. He'd face his problems tomorrow. Somehow he'd find a way to keep from telling her what had happened. And then the night of her twenty-first birthday, God willing, he'd make her pregnant.

The thought brought a warm flush to his face, and the muscles rippled in his limbs and belly.

She'd love their child always, even if she couldn't love the child's father. He took another drink.

Glumly, he laid the pistol back in the drawer. Cradling the bottle between his thighs, he leaned back and stared into the blue heart of the lamp flame.

Seated with his back against a tree, Noah Rollins rolled a cigarette. He set it between his lips at the same time he struck a match on the tree trunk.

The light was still on in the big house. He didn't dare hope the people in it were worrying about him. No, Beth

Anne hadn't recognized him. Hell, he knew he'd changed, but he'd recognized her right off. Just like he'd recognized Taggart's name.

No, they weren't worried. But if he had anything to do with it, they would be before long.

The sun was up high enough to glance off the marshal's shield Barney Mallott wore on his calico shirt pocket. He glanced down appreciatively, then glanced around to see if any of his men were looking. Satisfied that they weren't paying him any mind, he raised his hand to scratch the grizzled stubble on his cheek and neck. With his cuff, he polished the badge of his authority.

This symbolized his first real job. It had taken some politicking to get to wear it. The town of Rich Hill wasn't anything but a whistle-stop on the railroad line from Shreveport, Louisiana, to Kansas City, Missouri. But he'd come to realize it was the most he could hope for. He had to make something of himself there or nowhere.

He'd had to talk fast to convince the citizens, most of them former Jayhawks, that they needed a former Yankee. Even if he'd gone over the hill just before the war was over, to some he was still mighty unpopular.

Of course, his job practically guaranteed that he would be. He wasn't just the marshal. He was the tax assessor and collector. And his first act was going to be to make them some money off that railroad. After all, it ran through the town. The town ought to share in its profits.

So he'd told his plan to the town council—all three of them, the Drorsens, father and son, and their cousin Ned Ransom.

They'd nodded their heads and grinned slyly at each other. So long as the taxes didn't come out of their pockets, they were all for them. Barney had heard about towns doing stuff like this south of here. While he was tax collector, for every head of cattle that anybody shipped from the loading pen at Rich Hill, they would have to pay twenty-five cents tax. He got to keep two and a half cents of it.

Of course, that wasn't going to amount to a hill of beans because there weren't any cattle ranches around here. But for every head of horses—specifically those army remounts that Chaney Taggart was shipping—the tax was going to be a dollar.

Everybody knew what the army paid. Ten dollars for raw stock. Thirteen for saddle-broke. And Barney was going to pick up one dollar of that.

Barney got an ache in his gut every time he looked at that pretty horse farm sitting out there in the southeast corner of Bates County. He purely admired that sweet-faced little wife of Chaney's too. How come that know-it-all smartypants lieutenant got all the luck? Picking out that sweet piece of land with the best house in the county on it had been bad enough, but who'd have thought the scrawny little kid that came with it would have turned out like she did?

Brooding on the unfairness of fate, Barney again rubbed his shirtsleeve against the silver star with its points touching a circle that had the word "Marshal" on it. It glinted. Out of the corner of his eye, he caught Eustace Fisher watching him.

Hastily, he stuck his fingers inside his shirt and scratched his chest. Then he wallowed the plug of tobacco from one side of his mouth to the other and spat between the two horses.

Undeterred, Eustace kneed his horse up alongside Barney's. "The lieutenant ain't gonna like what you're fixin' to do."

Barney rolled his beefy shoulders. "War's over. He ain't

lieutenant no more. He can howl if he wants, but I got the law on my side."

Eustace said nothing. They clopped along in silence for several minutes. Then he let his horse fall back. His voice came from behind, well out of reach of Barney's long arm. "Just 'cause you and them dad-blasted Drorsens put this deal together, it don't make it law."

Barney swung around glaring, but Eustace was well out of reach and the rest of his deputies were bunched up behind him. He didn't want to argue in front of them. He contented himself with, "Shut your damn mouth or I'll climb outta this saddle and shut it for you!"

Eustace merely grinned.

Barney swung back around and gigged his horse into a lope.

Eustace looked over his shoulder. "Better get ready for some rough weather, boys. Lieutenant Taggart ain't gonna roll over and play dead for this."

On the brow of the hill, Barney halted his horse. The whole of White Oak Farms lay before them, stretched out both east and west with the bend of the Marais des Cygnes River at its back.

Barney felt his temper rising at the sight. Fine farmhouse, big barn and stables, corrals, the road winding down to it, lined with oak trees. It could have been his. It should have been his. But the lieutenant had grabbed it first.

Damn Chaney Taggart to hell! He swiped his hand through the half-inch stubble that covered his jaw.

Damn it all! He'd get his share now, one way or another.

Beth Anne knew exactly when Chaney had crawled into bed. She hadn't known the time, only that his big body was chilled. His bare feet and legs were so cold, she'd drawn her own up to her chest to conserve her own heat.

When he'd rolled over, the whiskey on his breath disgusted her.

A few minutes later he'd started to snore. Chaney only snored after he drank. She'd elbowed him, but he'd been out.

Chaney had no head for whiskey. When she had first come to know him, he had gotten drunk on several occasions. In each case she'd taken care of him the next day. She'd brought him coffee and cold cloths to wipe the sweat off his face. He'd moaned and groaned and swallowed hard. Once he'd barely made the chamber pot.

When she became more certain of herself, she'd told him that whiskey was the instrument of the devil. The temperance lecture about the body as a temple of the soul and the defilement of that temple leading to others of the Seven Deadly Sins had poured out of her mouth. She hadn't stopped to think where those words had come from. But she'd said them with authority, after which she'd exhorted him not to get drunk ever again.

He'd rolled over in the sweaty sheets and looked her right in the eye as if he hated her. But he'd never gotten drunk again. At least not that drunk. Now he hardly drank at all.

But he had last night.

Now, from her seat on the top rail of the corral, she watched walk across the yard. He was walking slow, she noted with perverse delight.

Dark circles under his eyes and a hollow, drawn look about his cheeks and mouth were clearly discernible in the morning sunlight. Three deep grooves between his eyebrows were also a sure indication that he had a pounding headache. She had to bite the inside of her cheek to keep from grinning.

Good enough for him.

Shielding his eyes from the blinding sunlight, he looked

up at her. He couldn't know that she felt just as bad in her own way as he did. She'd bawled like a baby last night. She'd cried so much she'd had to use witch hazel on her eyes to reduce the puffiness. They still burned.

Her sleep hadn't really rested her. She was still tired. Mostly, she was so ashamed of her behavior that she wanted to crawl back under the covers and hide. Nevertheless, she'd be hanged before she'd let him know. Eventually, she was going to find out who Josey was.

Meeting her husband's glare, she mustered the sweetest expression she was capable of. "Does your head ache badly?"

"No!" He dropped his hand and spun away, but his head wouldn't allow him to execute that maneuver with his usual lithe grace. He set his foot wrong, his ankle turned, and he staggered sideways.

She clapped her hand to her mouth too late to stop the nervous giggle.

He heard it. His shoulders hunched. Without a backward glance, he righted himself and stalked off.

She'd won that part of the fight hands down.

"You sure you'll be safe riding this horse?"

She jumped at the unexpected question, then negotiated a turn on the top rail. Noah Rollins stood beneath her. *How long had he been standing there?* she wondered. Probably, he'd just walked up. Chaney hadn't said a word.

"Tibbets picked out this horse," the new hand went on doubtfully. He had a tight hold on the short rope attached to the sorrel's bridle.

Beth Anne smiled brightly. She had worked yesterday with the gelding—a tall, powerful animal with a docile disposition. "Oh, sure. Everybody on the farm rides when the contracts are about to come due. The horses need all the training they can get."

She started to climb down. Rollins stepped forward. His

right arm encircled her waist and brought her down effort-lessly. The motion ended with her pressed against his side. Her feet barely touched the ground.

She gasped and tilted her head back, more than a little surprised. He met her eyes, his own hard, calculating. He looked as if he were angry with her. Why? She could feel his heat, feel his muscles. When she tried to step away, she could swear his arm tightened. Then he let her go.

She stepped back hastily. No one except Chaney had ever put his arm around her waist and held her against him. She'd never been that close to another man before. She'd never felt another man's chest rise against her breast. Her belly had never been pressed against another man's hard hip. She sucked in her breath hard. She could hear the nervousness in her laugh.

"I guess I'd better get aboard. Time's wasting."

She ducked around to the left side of the horse with the intention of mounting quickly, but Noah Rollins was right behind her. Still keeping the horse snubbed, he held the stirrup and then thrust his hand under her arm to give her an added boost. His fingers brushed her breast.

She could feel the color surging into her cheeks. She refused to look down at him. Instead, she pulled the gelding's reins tight. "Let 'im go."

Rollins stepped back and she turned the sorrel out into the center of the corral.

Chaney's hand clenched over the two-by-four. The sight of Noah Rollins handling Beth Anne drove the headache right out of his consciousness. He'd fire the son-of-a-bitch on the spot.

He took one step, then eased back. No sense giving her another stick to beat him with. He ran his hand over his face. The grooves on either side of his mouth felt inches deep. His hair was gray. His knees were going. In the morning he had to move slowly to work the kinks out of them.

Rollins must have taken a bath last night. His long hair was butter yellow in the morning sun. His freshly shaved face was unshadowed and unlined. No worries, no weighty responsibilities, no guilt had disturbed his sleep or sent him after the whiskey bottle.

Chaney swung around and leaned against the stall. In the dimness of the stable, he took stock of himself. Rage boiled in him, a sick feeling rose in his gut. The headache came rolling back in a throbbing wave. A strange emotion was wracking him. He'd never felt it before.

He finally realized he was jealous.

It took him five full minutes to master himself. Then he set out to find the foreman. Noah Rollins wouldn't look so young and handsome if he cleaned stalls all day.

Luther saw the riders coming. He passed the word to the hands to get ready for anything and hurried over to the corral where Chaney was again trying to take the edge off the sorrel stallion.

"Got to be trouble," the foreman prophesied. "Barney Mallott's leadin' a good-sized troop. Now, you know he wouldn't set his fat rear in the saddle 'cept to cause some."

Chaney lowered his head for an instant. They were about all he needed to make a real hell of a day. He didn't know what they were all about, but he would bet even money that they were going to cost him. He sighed. "Open the gate, Luther. I'll ride out to meet them."

"Let 'em come on in, Lieutenant," the foreman objected. "We got 'em outnumbered. With us to back your play, they won't try anything."

"I won't ride out that far. You all keep back, but in plain

sight. Let them see you're watching them. It'll get on their nerves, Sergeant."

"Yes, sir." The foreman grinned at the familiar strategy.

"But be ready to duck for cover." Chaney tugged at his hat, pulling it tighter on his brow.

"Yes, sir." From force of habit, Luther snapped a salute.

Chaney grinned as he guided the testy stallion through the open gate. The horse pranced and champed at the bit. Rivulets of sweat ran down its neck. It sidled down the lane, iron-shod hooves tearing up the sod, mane tossing, tail erect. Only Chaney's strength held its bad temper in check.

Barney Mallott's teeth bared in a grimace in his unshaven face. A badge glinted on his chest, and he had his old Navy Colt strapped to his hip. Four other men strung out behind him. Chaney didn't recognize any of them until at the very tail end of the line Eustace Fisher hove into view.

Chaney risked a glance over his shoulder. Where was Beth Anne? She should be in the house instead of outside in the stables or corral.

Thank God for Luther Tibbets. His old sergeant had deployed the troops in menacing squads beside the horse trough and in the shadow of the stable door. One quick step or a dive and they would be undercover. Luther himself took his stand beside the hitching post. For an added show, he cradled the varmint rifle in the crook of his arm.

The new man Noah Rollins leaned against the corner of the tackroom. The wind lifted his coattails, revealing his long-barreled pistol strapped to his hip.

A puff of wind blew dust across the road. The sorrel tossed its head and tugged at the bit. Foam dripped from its jaw.

"...asy, son," Chaney muttered. "Easy."

The horse must have been feeling its rider's tension, for it ducked its head and kicked out behind.

"Settle down, son. Settle down." Beneath the blighted oak, Chaney halted the animal. He leaned forward to pat the glistening neck. For the fourth or fifth time, he wished he'd taken the time to change to a solid mount. This one was a tornado rearing to rip. He pulled the sorrel's head up. "What can I do for you, Barney?"

"Just came to bring you the news, Lieutenant." Barney's jaw clamped tightly over the word. He blinked and shook his head slightly.

Chaney would have bet even money the man hadn't meant to call him by his former rank. He waited on military alert, studying the force assembled before him.

When Chaney didn't move, Barney fidgeted in the saddle. He knew what was going on but was helpless to fight his own feelings. His nervous glance beyond Chaney's shoulder took in the dozen White Oaks men arrayed against him. They were staring at him. He looked long at the varmint rifle on the old sergeant's arm. "Er—we— that is, the town council—er—"

His nerve was failing him. He wiped his hand across his mouth. "The town—"

"Spit it out, Private!" Chaney's barked command spiked the deputies to attention. One actually jerked back on his mount's reins.

Eustace Fisher guffawed.

Barney's face reddened. "Now, Lieutenant. You'd just better show me a little respect. I might be willing to cut you some slack."

The stallion tossed its head. Chaney tightened his grip on the reins. "Why would I need you to cut me some slack?"

Barney nodded his head toward the stables. "You got them army remounts about ready to ship?"

Chaney looked back over his shoulder. What he saw froze his blood. Both Beth Anne and Mary Nell had appeared in the door of the stable. His men had their backs to them. All but Rollins.

Even as Chaney would have signaled, Rollins straightened off the wall of the tackroom and strode across the yard. Without touching the two women, he herded them back into the darkness. Chaney swung back to Barney.

"Mighty pretty woman, your wife." Barney's mouth was a little slack. Moisture glistened on his pendulous lower lip. "Mighty pretty."

"Say what you came to say."

Barney hooked his thumb under his badge and pulled it off his chest. It was an obvious effort to flaunt his authority. "You think you're better'n the rest of us Jayhawks—"

"I was never a Jayhawk," Chaney interrupted. "Never."

"You was there, Chaney Taggart," Barney reminded him. "You was there. That's how you got this place and that little—"

Chaney leaned forward. His voice dropped to a whisper meant for Barney's ears only. "Say one more word on that subject and you won't ride out of here."

Barney gulped. He let the badge fall back on his chest. The other men stirred and grumbled, all except Eustace, who grinned and winked as if he and Chaney were great friends. Barney took a deep breath. "You planning on shipping a herd of remounts from Rich Hill sometime soon?"

Even though Barney's voice rose at the end as if he asked a question, Chaney didn't bother to answer. They both knew the answer.

"Well, I'm here to tell you the citizens are entitled to some 'revenoo' off that railroad."

Chaney's expression never altered. He supposed he

should have been expecting something like this. A quarter a head wouldn't be unreasonable. He was prepared to go to thirty-five cents.

"We got a new school to build," Barney whined. Now that he actually had to state the amount, he fidgeted more and more. He crossed his arms and recrossed them over the saddlebow.

"How much?"

Barney swallowed. "A dollar a head."

Chaney stared at him for a full twenty seconds. The other men held their breath. Barney drew back, his hand slipping to the butt of his gun. Then Chaney laughed. "You're out of your mind."

"It's the law," Barney argued desperately. "We need that school for the chillerns."

"How much do you get?" Chaney snapped.

Barney jerked back on the reins. His horse backed into the others, setting the whole contingent to milling. "Damn you! I don't get hardly nothing."

" 'Bout twenty cents on the dollar," Eustace called. "Ain't that about the size of it, Barn?"

"Shut your trap!"

The air crackled with tension. The sorrel stallion couldn't keep still. Its hooves churned up the road. It neighed and bowed its neck trying to work the bit between its teeth. Chaney rode it like a centaur. "You men have delivered your message. Now get off White Oak. Turn around and ride back where you came from."

But Barney wasn't through. "We'll be waiting for you, Taggart. You can bet on it. Me and my men'll be standing there at the loading chute a-counting. You won't load a head on that train without you pay for it."

The sorrel half rose on its hind legs. It shook its head. The blond mane flew.

Chaney eased the horse down. Across the lane, he faced

the party. "You can take this message back to the Drorsens for me. I'll drive my horses all the way to Fort Leavenworth before I'll pay that kind of money. If I want to be robbed on the railroad, I'll wait for Jesse James to do it."

Barney stared at the imposing figure. He could feel his stomach turning over. He could feel his bladder aching. *Goddamn.* Was he going to piss all over himself? His courage had long evaporated. Even unarmed, the lieutenant was hell on wheels.

Chaney's big horse reared again, but he never looked down, never even leaned forward in the saddle. Just kept staring with those awful black eyes.

Barney took a deep breath. He realized he could smell himself. Smell his own fear as sour sweat trickled down his ribs. He cast an anxious glance around him. His men, the damned cowards, were already riding away. Only Eustace was staying to grin at him. His told-you-so expression sent a bolt of rage through Barney Mallott.

His hand closed over the butt of his pistol.

"Don't do it, Private!"

Barney looked back at his former commander. "You don't got no right to give orders no more. I could shoot the both of you down right now."

"Maybe one of us," Chaney agreed. "But you'd never make it back to town."

Barney fell to cussing. "Tibbets was in it, same as me. Same as you, Eustace. All of us Jayhawkers. We all did it. All of us. Order No. 11!"

Even as he said the infamous words, Barney could feel the chill.

Chaney reined the stallion around and clapped spurs to its sides.

"Hey!"

Barney's mount couldn't move fast enough. The sorrel hit the ewe-necked bay at the shoulder. The stallion's mouth was open, its yellow teeth champed inches from Barney's face. He threw himself backward even as he felt his horse's legs buckle. Mount and rider staggered, then fell heavily tangled together in a melee of arms and legs, steel-shod hooves, and numbing shock.

The sorrel stallion with Chaney Taggart on its back cleared them both with a scream like a freight train.

Chapter Four

Beth Anne had just about finished giving Noah Rollins a piece of her mind when the sorrel stallion's scream froze her in the middle of a sentence. The hair rose on the back of her neck. With a frightened glance at Mary Nell, she pushed her way between them and plunged out into the blinding sunlight.

"Wait! Don't go out there!" Noah cried, but she didn't wait. Nor did she see Mary Nell catch his arm and dig in her heels when he would have caught Beth Anne.

Instead, Beth Anne ran to catch up to Luther and the other men of White Oak as they thudded down the lane. In a few seconds her eyes adjusted to the light, allowing her to see the horse and rider down in the roadway as well as her husband astride a stamping, rearing fury of a sorrel stallion. To her frightened eyes, the furious animal seemed a far worse threat than the downed man.

Barney Mallott rolled over onto his hands and knees.

Spitting out a mouthful of dirt, he got one foot under him and hoisted himself up with his gun drawn.

Beth Anne yelled a wordless warning.

Luther Tibbets was way ahead of her. Clapping the varmint rifle to his shoulder, he stepped to one side and squeezed the trigger. The shot spanged dust from the roadway a yard in front of the marshal.

The sorrel reared and sunfished. Chaney bailed out of the saddle before the maddened animal went over on its back still fighting and screaming.

Beth Anne screamed too.

Barney twisted around, searching for the shooter. His pistol swept the oncoming men, who dived for the roadside at the same time they drew their sidearms.

Only Luther stood his ground. With the calm of a seasoned campaigner, he jacked the hot shell out of the varmint rifle and thumbed a fresh round in. All the time, the sight never wavered from dead center on the marshal's chest.

"Drop it, Barney," he called.

Beth Anne just had time to see Chaney climb to his feet before Noah Rollins caught up to her. No one had ever manhandled her like he did now. As if she were a child, he grabbed her around the waist and swung her around.

"Let go, damn you."

But he wrapped his arms around her and held her tightly, putting himself between her and the scene. She had to crane her neck to see over the top of his broad shoulder.

Meanwhile, Barney Mallott scowled furiously as he raised his hands. As an ex-soldier, he understood his situation at a glance. He was unhorsed, outnumbered, and surrounded. His frustration came out in a hoarse growl. "This don't make no difference a-tall."

"How about if my finger slips on the trigger?" Luther

suggested in his mildest voice. "Now, that'd make a damn sight of difference, wouldn't it?"

"I'm the law."

The stallion scrambled to its feet and stood with head hanging, breathing hard, the fight knocked out of it for the moment.

Chaney left the horse to come to stand at Luther's shoulder. "You're wearing the badge, Barney. But you know what you really are. And you know what you're doing and why you're doing it."

Mallott started to protest, but the rancher cut him off. "The citizens of this county don't know, but they'll soon find out when it hits them in their pockets. Then they aren't going to put up with it. Using the law to steal is mighty bad business."

The marshal lowered his arms and shuffled his feet while his horse climbed to its feet, shook itself, and limped away, reins trailing. Stubborn as a bull, he tucked his chin into his chest, so he wouldn't have to meet Chaney's eyes. "It's been done before. And just like before, I've got the law on my side." His voice turned belligerent. "If I say you gotta pay, then you damn sure gotta pay. The war's over and—"

Chaney interrupted him before he could get himself worked up enough to be dangerous. "You've said your piece, Mallott. I don't need any lectures about the war. As you say, it's over. Now get the hell off my property and don't ever set foot on it again."

"You think you're somethin' special—" But the words dried up in his mouth as Chaney's men gathered behind him.

"Let me go," Beth Anne said to Noah, "or I swear I'll have Chaney fire you."

Rollins pulled his arms away and stepped back. She

straightened her clothing and pushed past him to Chaney's side.

Mallott had caught his horse and was cursing as he guided his toe into the stirrup while the animal sidled and turned. His face was red as fire and his language grew fouler.

"Will you get back to the house?" Chaney snarled out of the side of his mouth.

"I've heard it all before," Beth Anne replied.

"I'm not worried about your ears. You're in the way. I can't fight when you're liable to draw a bullet," he rejoined. "And you haven't heard nearly all the meanness that Barney Mallott can spout."

But she held her ground just behind Chaney's shoulder. Together the White Oak men and women watched Barney finally have to fling himself belly down across the saddle to mount.

"You ain't a one of you better'n me," Barney yelled as, by dint of strength, he managed to throw a leg over the bow and find the stirrups. "You all know what you did. Hey! Lieutenant, sir, does that little gal know what you did to get this place? Have you ever read her Order No. 11?"

On hearing that question, Chaney drew his gun. "That'll be enough, Mallott. One more word and you're a dead man."

The sight of the weapon let the air out of the marshal's rage. Beth Anne had never seen such a change. His mouth snapped shut. The color drained from his face. He jerked his battered hat tight down over his forehead, reined his horse around, and raked his spurs over the animal's flanks.

The cloud of dust raised by its galloping hooves continued until the road curved round the bend.

Luther Tibbets clapped Chaney on the back. "Good job, old son. You kept it holstered a hell of a lot longer than I would have."

Slowly, Chaney slid the pistol back into its place. He put his arm across Beth Anne's shoulder and turned to his men. Pressed against his ribs, she could feel his heart beating like a triphammer, all sign of its comfortable bobble gone. The cavalry officer who'd rescued her half her life ago was back again.

She had never felt so safe.

Together they led the way back up the lane.

Noah pulled Mary Nell into an empty stall at the end of the shedrow. "Why'd you try and stop me? You might have got your friend killed."

Mary Nell's eyes narrowed. She pushed his hand away from her arm and doubled up her fist. "You grab me again, Buster Brown, and you'll get 'why.' Right in the mouth."

Noah folded his arms. "Why'd you do it?"

"Because it wasn't any of your business."

"What d'you mean, business? She went charging out there into a gunfight. She could've— Ow!" He broke off when Mary Nell knocked her fist against his breastbone. Pretending to be hurt, he rubbed the spot.

She made her lower lip quiver contemptuously. "It was her husband who was in that gunfight that didn't happen. He might have needed her help."

"She's a girl!"

"She's his wife!" Mary Nell swept her hand in a wide arc. "She'd just about die if anything happened to Chaney Taggart. She was in the right."

Noah frowned. "Women hadn't ought to stick their noses in men's business."

Mary Nell threw up her hands. "Stubborn. Stupid. Believe that if you want to, but don't get in her way again. Someone's got to save you men from yourselves. I don't have time to stand here and tell you all the things we do to protect you big-shouldered galoots and pull your bacon out of the fire.''

She turned on her heel and marched to the end of the shedrow. Just before she stepped out into the light, she turned around. "I'll give you the word 'cause I think you need to hear it. If you tried to get between her and her lieutenant, Beth Anne Taggart would just about stomp a mudhole in you and track it dry. So don't get in her way.''

For several seconds Noah Rollins stood in the stable staring at the rectangle of light Mary Nell had stormed through. A bemused smile quirked the corners of his mouth as he rubbed the spot on his breastbone where she'd socked him.

Chaney knew he should wash his hands and face, grab a long cool drink of water, and get back to the horses. Instead, he dropped down in his chair and hung his head. Now that the immediate danger had passed, he found himself shaking with reaction.

Never had he felt older than he did now. Worse than old, he felt foolish. He'd lost his temper and charged into Barney Mallott. And he'd bitten off more than he could chew. He'd tried a dangerous stunt on a half-wild horse. He'd have been shot as he bailed out of the saddle if Luther Tibbets hadn't backed his play.

Barney Mallott might be stupid as an ox, but, provoked, he'd kill in the blink of an eye. He'd have pleaded the performance of his duty and gotten away with the whole thing.

Chaney shuddered as he raked his hands through his hair. On the other hand, if Barney had uttered another word, he'd have been a dead man. Chaney had promised himself after the war that he'd never draw his gun to kill anything but a varmint. Men who knew him knew his reputation.

But when Barney had threatened to tell Beth Anne—

He pressed his thumb and third finger tightly against his eyelids as if that could block out the hateful visions that exploded from his memory.

Every man in the four counties that formed the western border of Missouri knew about Order No. 11. And every one of them lied about his part in it.

Four days after Quantrill burned Lawrence, Kansas, Brigadier General Thomas Ewing, the commander of the District of the Border, had given the order for the removal of all Southern sympathizers and their families from Cass, Jackson, Bates, and Vernon Counties. Issued on August 25, 1863, it was to be carried out within fifteen days. No one had time to object. No one had time to appeal. No one had time even to think.

And Lieutenant Chaney Taggart, fresh from Tennessee, had ridden off to obey, not really knowing what his order entailed. He'd expected to encounter some resistance, but he'd been pretty sure that in the end everyone would obey without violence. He hadn't even thought about bloodshed.

What he hadn't counted on was the attitudes of the veterans of his own troop as well as of the strangers that followed them like vultures. He found he couldn't control his men, who were, of course, Union soldiers. His own orders to keep their sidearms holstered and their sabers in their sheaths had been ignored. In the case of Private Barney Mallott, they'd been flagrantly disobeyed. Larceny was in Barney's mind.

Revenge was the order of the day.

Order No. 11 became a license to murder and to steal not just the homes and land but the personal property as well.

He'd led his troops into yards where the families had been packed ready to pull out. The Jayhawkers from Kansas who'd been following along behind him would swoop in behind him and his men. Though he ordered his men to drive them off, his own soldiers merely crossed their arms over their saddlehorns and watched.

At gunpoint, the Jayhawkers dragged the families off the wagons. Men, women, and children were left standing on the hot, dusty roads as everything they'd loaded so carefully, everything they owned, was hauled off to Kansas by their own teams of horses and oxen.

Late in the evening of September 5, he'd met with real resistance. That night had changed his life forever.

As if fingers were trailing up his spine, Chaney realized he was no longer alone. He jerked upright in his chair.

Beth Anne had entered. Considerate of him as ever, she stood at the door, waiting to see if he was awake.

Guilt had driven him back into the past. Now that same guilt made him start and swing around in alarm. Just as hastily, he looked away for fear she could read every shameful secret in his eyes.

Instead, she held out a tall glass of water. He licked his dry lips and accepted it. She watched him while he drank it greedily. When he'd finished, she set the glass aside.

"I've never been so frightened." Tears shone in her eyes. "I couldn't get to you fast enough. Every blessed man at White Oaks came between me and you."

He shook his head. "Honey, that's what they're supposed to do. I wouldn't have you hurt for anything in the world."

Suddenly, she dropped to her knees between his legs. With a sob she threw her arms around him.

"Chaney. Chaney. Chaney. I love you so much." She

pressed her face against his chest. Her tears wet his shirt. Her palms slid up and down his back and over his shoulders, satisfying herself that he was all right.

"Beth Anne. Honey, don't take on like this." He kissed the top of her head. His eyes stung as tears of happiness mixed with his despair. He knew how much she loved him. Her love surrounded him from morning till night. No one in his entire life had cared about him the way Beth Anne did. The hell of his life was knowing how undeserving he was of her love.

"But you could have died," she cried, her tears dampening his shirt. "That damned horse could have thrown you and stomped you to death. Or Barney could have shot you. He's so stupid and mean. He'd have played like he was sorry for it, but he wouldn't have been at all. And you'd have been d-dead." Her voice rose. She burrowed deeper into his arms.

"Beth Anne." He held her tighter. "Shh, honey. Shh. I'm all right."

She tipped her head back to look up into his eyes. "Why did you do such a crazy thing?"

He stared down at her tear-streaked face. "I didn't have a choice."

She moaned deep in her throat. Real pain. He closed his eyes and held her close. His vitals felt as if knives were slicing into them. He'd always done his level best to keep her from being hurt.

As if she understood what he was feeling, she pulled back in his arms. Using the tips of the fingers of both hands, she brushed the tears away. "You always have a choice, Chaney. Shouldn't I be your first choice?"

He swallowed hard. She was right. She was his first choice. And the family they were going to have. He nodded.

She rose, pulling him up with her, winding herself around him. Her arms went around his chest and over his shoulders. Her hand clasped the back of his head, her fingers splayed to pull him down to her.

She fitted her face to him, kissing him with her mouth wide open, sucking his tongue. Heat lightning tore into him as he wrapped his arms around her, but she wasn't having any of it. Instead, when she was through kissing him, she tilted her head back.

"You're all that I have in the world, Chaney Taggart. You can't put yourself in such danger. You have to take care of yourself for me."

He stared into her eyes. What he read there humbled him. He gave a little shiver. "I know."

That evening he gathered his men. Their ages reflected in their faces struck him forcibly. They were the best of the best with horses. No horse that came from White Oak Farms was untrustworthy. No horse but was in the peak of physical condition and trained to give good service to his rider.

More important, most of them like Luther had been with him for nearly a dozen years. They'd ridden with him through the war years and followed his fortunes to White Oak. They all knew his secrets. He trusted them implicitly.

Only Noah Rollins, lounging in the deep shadow, was an unknown quantity.

With Luther at attention at a right angle, like a good top sergeant presenting his troop, Chaney addressed them. "Much obliged for standing behind me, men. It looked for a minute there like things were going to get hot. We probably got off lucky, considering Barney was used to going off half-cocked. Another second and we'd have had to shoot him.''

A chuckle went through the rank.

With Beth Anne's passionate plea fresh in his mind, Chaney felt he needed to say something more. He squared his shoulders. ''I can't tell you how much I appreciate it,'' he went on. ''Beth Anne—er—reminded me— Well, actually, she read me a lesson on how I had to be careful. So I'm thanking you for backing my play for her.''

They lost the grins. Everyone loved Beth Anne. If she was upset, then they had to make it right. They stirred uneasily.

Finally, Rusty Huff wallowed his plug of tobacco to the other side of his jaw and spat into the dust. ''Hell, Lieutenant, you don't need to thank us. Just tell us what you want us to do about Barney.''

''We could still shoot him,'' Hardy grumbled. The cook nodded his grizzled head. ''First excitement we've got around here in a coon's age. And it wuz done over way too soon.''

Chaney shook his head. ''I think the thing for us to do is let it go by. He can't touch us unless we ship the herd.''

''A dollar a head's mighty steep,'' Luther observed.

Chaney crossed his arms over his chest. ''Rich Hill isn't the only stop on the railroad line.''

The men digested this, then smiled. Rusty punched the man beside him. ''What'd I tell you?''

Chaney looked them over. No man could ask for better than they. ''That's all I have to say. Hardy, break out the medicine bottle and give everybody a snort.''

A cheer went up.

''Just one apiece, mind you. Get a good night's sleep. This next week, I'll work you so hard you'll squeal, but we'll have the string finished up. We don't want to keep Fort Leavenworth waiting.''

As the men followed Hardy to the cookshack, Chaney caught Noah's arm. "Rollins, I want you out on patrol from now on."

Noah thrust his hands into his back pockets and looked down at the ground. "I didn't sign on to be a gunhand."

"I'm not asking you to shoot anybody. I'm telling you to patrol. If Mallott or someone like him brings another squad in on us, we need to have a couple of minutes to get the women into the house."

He knew he'd said the right thing as the stubborn expression lightened on Noah's face. At the same time he felt a stab of jealousy. He shouldn't have been upset that this man was interested in his wife. Hell! A man would have to be blind and a brute not to be. But someone so young, so good-looking as Rollins set his teeth on edge. Women liked good looks. If Beth Anne ever took to comparing looks, he'd lose in spades. "Can I count on you?"

Noah shrugged. He shifted his weight from one hip to the other. "Can I refuse the order, Captain?"

"Not captain. Not lieutenant either. That's a long time ago. Mr. Taggart will do."

"All right, Mis-ter Taggart. Can I refuse the order?"

Chaney didn't allow his irritation to show. He merely waited.

The silence sank like lead between them. Then Noah shifted his weight again. "Guess I'd better go catch up my horse."

"Guess you'd better. You don't have to ride around the entire place. Barney's not interested in rustling. But he's a crack shot with a rifle. He could sneak in and pick someone off just to let us know he means business."

Noah's lip curled. "Just so long as the someone he picks isn't me."

"If you're doing your job, you should be all right."

"And if I'm not, you figure you've taken care of your wife's hired man without getting yourself all dirty."

Chaney felt his blood sizzle. His heartbeat stepped up. He clenched his fists but kept them at his sides. Over Rollins's shoulder, he could see the other men milling around the cookshack with tin cups in their hands. They were laughing and talking. Hardy stood among them, a benevolent smile on his face, a three-quarters-gone bottle of whiskey in his hand.

Chaney's gaze locked with the young man's. "Go catch up your horse. Either take a ride down the river road, or ride on out."

Rollins ran his fingers through his long hair and pulled his hat down tight on his head. "You're sure a smart man, Mis-ter Taggart. If I kill Mallott, you win. If Mallott kills me, you win."

Beth Anne galloped the chestnut gelding over the obstacle course Chaney had built to simulate a battlefield. She swerved him round a barricade of fenceposts and urged him to jump the extended tongue of an overturned wagon. Bridle-wise, he avoided the boxes and barrels at her guiding, didn't shy at the waving strips of cloth on the end of a fishing pole, and leaped into a stream without hesitation.

"Good boy."

She wheeled him out of the course and touched him lightly with her spurs. The chestnut was tall and rangy. He stretched out his neck and split the wind for home. His long stride ate up the pasture. In a matter of minutes, she was slowing him at the corral gate.

Luther came out to open it for her. He wrapped his hand around the chestnut's reins just below his chin and led the horse to one of the corral posts.

Beth Anne slipped off his back and patted his neck

approvingly. "He's good," she told the foreman. "He went over that course from all four directions without a stumble. I turned him every which way."

"Some boy's going to owe his life to you," Luther told her.

She sighed as she stepped away, for Luther to unsaddle her mount. "I'd rather not think about somebody being in danger of being shot."

Luther grunted as he pulled the saddle off and hung it over the top rail.

Beth Anne hesitated. The events of the morning still troubled her. Something in particular stood out in her mind. "Luther, why did Barney Mallott turn white when Chaney drew his pistol?"

The foreman measured her over the chestnut's back. Then he shrugged his shoulders. "Because Chaney pretty much hung up his gun after the war. Nowadays he don't draw it hardly at all. So everybody knows if he draws it, he means to shoot it."

"Oh."

She waited, but Luther didn't volunteer any more information.

At last she had to ask. "Would Chaney have shot him?"

"Oh, you bet."

She didn't doubt it. Nor did she doubt that Luther would have shot Barney just as quickly, if he hadn't backed off when he did. "He's the marshal."

"He's a Jayhawker through and through. And one of the worst. No telling how much looting and murdering he's done."

"How could Chaney know a man like that?" She stared hard at Luther, trying to catch some fleeting expression that might give her more. "He does know him?"

Luther slipped the bit out of the chestnut's mouth and slipped a feedbag over his nose. "Barney and Chaney knew each other during the war, Bethie." He held up his hand. "And that's as much as I'm going to say. Why don't you head on up to the house and take it easy for the rest of the day?"

She scowled at him. Getting information out of Luther was like getting a stone to talk. He frustrated her so much some days that she wanted to stomp and scream. She really was tired. The chestnut was her third horse that day, but she didn't want to give Luther the satisfaction of telling her what to do.

"It's too early in the afternoon. I'll take out the sorrel. He balked at the stream yesterday. He needs to be run through it until he's got it figured out."

Muttering something about noses and faces, Luther saddled the other horse. As she mounted a little stiffly, Beth Anne realized that her satisfaction might hurt her before the day was over.

On the other hand, she had some pieces of information to mull over. Barney Mallott knew her husband. And her husband, the kindest, dearest man in the world, had a reputation that made men afraid of him.

The sorrel had gone into the water fine three times in a row. Then on the fourth he'd balked right at the water's edge. Already shifting her weight forward to bring him up when he hit the bottom, she slid over his neck and went into the stream.

When the cold water splashed in his face, the sorrel whinnied and wheeled away.

His action jerked the reins from Beth Anne's hand. She had all she could do to keep upright as her mount loped up the muddy bank. Wet to the waist, her boots filled with water, she cursed vividly as she waded after him.

"Damned jughead!"

Stirrups flopping, the sorrel kept going until he stepped on a rein and brought himself to a halt.

Beth Anne started after him, but when she started to climb the bank, she found she couldn't make it. It was a slippery mire, all its vegetation churned under by the many horses that had galloped in and out for days now.

The slick leather soles of her boots slipped out from under her. She fell to her knees. Damn. Damn. Damn. "Whoa, boy," she called in her calmest voice. "Easy, boy. Whoa, there."

The sorrel flicked an ear in her direction, decided to move away, then caught the other rein under a hoof. It brought him up short. He shook his head but couldn't pull the trailing leather free.

Beth Anne tried to climb again. This time, she made it halfway up before she slipped back flat on her face. She closed her eyes as her chin hit the mud.

Oh, Lord. She was going to have to ride in looking like a pig. She'd never hear the end of it. Damn fool animal.

She glared in his direction. He'd found a clump of grass and started to graze. Now was her chance to catch him up. If she didn't get him, she'd probably have to walk back and she'd be humiliated for years.

If she could only get up the bank. Knowing she couldn't be any wetter or muddier, she began to crawl.

"Need any help?"

She closed her eyes. Thank heaven, someone had come up. At least he could catch the horse. She threw a look over her shoulder.

Noah Rollins sat calmly on his gray mare on the other side of the stream.

She could feel an embarrassed blush rising in her cheeks. Why did she have to look a muddy mess in front of the only young man on the farm?

Then she wondered why she cared. After all, she was

Chaney Taggart's wife and anyone could have an accident. Since she couldn't be any filthier, she rolled over on one hip and managed a bedraggled smile.

"If you'll catch that jughead sorrel for me, I'll be much obliged. The only place the cavalry can use him is the New Mexican desert. He'll never go into a stream of his own accord."

Noah chuckled. "Some are like that."

He clicked his tongue. Obediently, his mare picked her way down to the water. Without hesitation she walked right in. Noah guided her up beside Beth Anne.

"Here." He leaned from the saddle and held down a hand.

She reached up and took it. "Much obliged."

Instead of merely pulling her to her feet as she had expected, he kept on lifting.

"Wait. You'll get yourself all dirty."

"Put your foot in the stirrup." He shifted his boot out.

"This isn't necessary," she protested. "I'm covered in mud."

"Come on."

Rather than fight him, she slipped her foot in and grasped the pommel with her free hand.

The mare adjusted herself to the uneven load and skillfully picked her way up the bank.

Under the trees on level ground, Beth Anne became aware that Noah Rollins's knee and thigh were against the back of her legs. His knee was bony, his thigh was hard. The arm he'd somehow wrapped around her waist was hard too and warm. His heartbeat beneath the bony ribs was steady as a triphammer.

Instinctively, she waited for it to miss a beat and then race ahead to catch up the way Chaney's did. Her embarrassment deepened. He was a wandering cowboy who'd lent her a hand when she needed it. She shouldn't even be aware that she was pressed against his side.

Instead, she was reacting to him, as if this incident were something special. Worse, she was comparing him to her husband.

Worst was that she wasn't sure whether Chaney had won or lost in the comparison.

"You can let me down now."

"Can I?" He guided the mare away from the sorrel.

A chill skittered up her spine. What did he think he was doing? "Stop right here and let me down."

He moved on downstream until they were out of sight of the trail where the men rode the horses down to the water. All embarrassment vanished in a trickle of fear. She faced the real possibility that all Chaney's care about the men he hired had been justified and that she had nobody to blame but herself if this man hurt her.

She doubled up her fist. "Let me down this second, Noah Rollins."

He pulled his arm away. She leaped backward. Her boot heels sank into the sod. She staggered and fell to one knee.

He slipped off his horse on the other side and came round.

Thoroughly frightened, she scrambled to her feet and backed away, holding out her hands to ward him off.

He reached for her. "You shouldn't be out here."

She prayed he was going to deliver the standard male lecture. "I'm working. This is White Oak land. No one ever comes here except White Oak men. You'd better get back on your horse and go on about your business."

He caught her by the arms, giving her a teeth-rattling shake. "This is my business. You're my business if you're in danger."

"You're trying to frighten me," she accused. His long fingers tightened around her arms. There was more to this than just patrolling the land. "Chaney will fire you for frightening me like this."

"If I frighten you, that's good." His face was only inches from hers. He had a small white scar near the corner of his left eye. Something in her memory—

"He might fire me," Noah Rollins declared, "if you tell him a bunch of lies."

"I wouldn't be lying."

He laughed scornfully. "What are you going to tell him? That I rescued you from the mud and put you down where the ground was dry."

"That you carried me away from my horse, when I told you to put me down. That you manhandled me."

"I didn't hurt you. But if I'd've been Barney Mallott or somebody like that, I sure could've." He gave her another little shake, but she'd said the proper words. They made him realize how hard he was holding her. He dropped his hands. He looked around significantly. The fields were empty.

She followed his gaze. He was right. If he were Barney Mallott, she could be screaming her lungs out right now and no one would hear her. She closed her eyes for a brief instant to collect her thoughts. Then she lifted her chin. "You'd be here to rescue me. It's what Chaney ordered you to do. It's what you did."

He grinned. "So I did."

She nodded. "So now I'll just go back and catch that sorrel and ride back to the house. I'm getting cold."

He caught her arm as she went by. "Wait."

A wave of anger swept through her. She wasn't going to stand for this one more minute. Her reaction was calculated. She swung her fist at him with all her might. Her knuckles struck the side of his jaw and rocked his head back on his shoulders.

"Don't you manhandle me," she snarled.

He let go of her and staggered back. His eyes blazed.

She didn't wait to hear what he might say to her. She lunged away from him and raced back toward the horse.

Chapter Five

She could hear the mare's hoofbeats loping along behind her. Unreasonable anger tinged with fear made her redouble her efforts. She ducked into the trees, hoping their low-hanging branches would slow him down until she could reach her horse.

Her heavy divided skirt flapped around her legs. Her squishy boots felt like lead, but up ahead she saw the sorrel. As she dashed toward him, he threw up his head. His eyes rolled white. He shied sideways.

She heard the mare behind her. She didn't dare slow to a sedate pace even though she knew better than to run at a horse.

As she burst into the clearing, the sorrel wheeled but blundered against a tree. The reins trailed along the ground.

Beth Anne flung herself bodily on them, rolled over, and came up. Rather than waste time searching for the stirrup, she flung herself at the saddleback. She hit belly down, hard enough to knock the breath from her body, but she caught the horn in one hand and the bow in the other. While the sorrel blundered away, she threw her leg across his rump, then wriggled her body over the bow.

Once mounted, she gathered the reins and wheeled him back.

Noah had halted his mare some twenty feet away. Across the space they glared at each other. She noted with satisfaction the swelling lump on his jaw.

Then he broke into a grin and tipped his battered felt hat. "I got to hand it to you, Miz Taggart. That was quite a mount."

She should hightail it for home. She was sure the water-shy sorrel could run away from the elderly mare, but pride made her straighten in the saddle. White Oak was her farm. Nobody was going to make her run away on her own land. Besides, she wanted the last word.

"Chaney's made sure I can take care of myself. You were barking up the wrong tree if you thought you could carry me around like a rag doll."

"I never thought of you as a rag doll," he said mildly. He raised his hands to shoulder height. "Listen, I didn't mean to scare you. You handled yourself pretty well for a girl."

She nodded. "I'm not a girl. I'm a woman. I'm Chaney Taggart's wife. And you were lucky I didn't have a gun."

He shook his head. "If you'd threatened me, I'd never have believed it. I'd have taken it away from you."

She clenched her jaw so tight her teeth ached. If she'd had a gun at that moment, she'd have creased him. "I wouldn't have threatened."

"No?" He looked as if he didn't believe her.

"No." A crease would have been too easy on him.

He shrugged. "I figured you were an old man's darlin'. I didn't think he'd let you—"

"Close your mouth, Mr. Rollins. Don't say another word, or I'll have that 'old man' fire you."

He closed it. Silence fell like lead between them. She didn't like the way he studied her. At last he asked, "Why don't you?"

"Because Chaney needs every hand he can get. It's not just a matter of training the horses and driving them into town. It's a matter of finding some place where we can load them and not pay a dollar a head."

"And the marshal don't like your husband a bit. I'll be damned." Noah crossed his arms over the saddlehorn and shook his head as if he couldn't believe himself. He smiled, a tiny mirthless curl of one side of his mouth.

She shivered. Now that whatever wild hair had gotten into Noah Rollins seemed to be over, she remembered she was cold and muddy. She wriggled her toes in her boots and gathered the reins. "Mr. Rollins, I'm ordering you right now to ride on your patrol route. I'll forget all about this if you'll do your job and keep your own counsel. Or I can tell Chaney what happened just before he kills you."

A muscle jumped in his cheek. She could imagine him clenching his jaw, and good enough for him. She hoped he broke a tooth.

He pulled his hat down tighter over his brow and lifted the reins. He made a clicking noise out of the side of his mouth. The mare started forward.

Just when she thought he was going to ride past her, he halted. His face twisted as if he'd had a pain. "Why'd you do it?"

"What? Why'd I do what?"

"Marry that old man? Marry Chaney Taggart?" He fairly spat out her husband's name.

She blinked. For her there was only one answer. "Because I love him."

"After what he did?" Noah Rollins cursed. Then he whipped the reins over the mare's withers and headed down toward the creek.

Beth Anne stared after him. She wanted to call him back and ask him what Chaney had done. She wanted to ask him who he was, a stranger, to ride in one day and know Chaney's name. A shudder ran up her spine.

A few days ago everything had seemed perfect and wonderful. Now nothing seemed quite right. As if she'd called a ghost from its grave, she'd remembered a name that made her nearly ill every time it slipped into her mind. Noah Rollins had drifted in from nowhere with a hate against her husband, and she'd been fool enough to get him hired. Chaney had been threatened by Barney Mallott, the marshal of Rich Hill, their hometown. The government contract was in jeopardy if they couldn't get the horses to Kansas City by the delivery date.

The shiver that rattled her teeth had little to do with her wet, muddy state. Her common sense couldn't totally convince her that all this couldn't have been triggered by her memory.

Josey. "Josey!"

She spurred the sorrel. *Damned crowbait! Throw her in the water, would he?* He stretched out into a tearing run toward the stable.

Luther saw her coming and swung the corral gate open for her. She brought the animal in faster than she usually did. Then she had to yank him back so hard, his hind legs cut a perfect eleven in the dirt.

Her head was swimming. She closed her eyes as his sides heaved and he blew a roller through his nose. The hard ride had punished him and her.

She welcomed the distraction.

Her thoughts were frighteningly complicated.

* * *

She put on kettles of water to boil and stripped to the skin. Pulling on her robe, she sat down in Chaney's rocking chair and wrapped her arms around her knees. She told herself she was shaking from being cold and wet.

She needed a hot bath. She needed a cup of coffee. She needed— *Oh God! What was happening to her!* She needed to remember.

If Noah Rollins had known Chaney before, he must have known her as well. *Josey.* He couldn't be Josey. He was Noah. Then who was Josey?

One of the kettles began to sing. She fetched it and emptied it into the tub, then went back for the other. She poured it in with a kettle of cold water and sat down in the tub. The water was shallow and barely warm, but it was better than nothing.

Determined to wash it all away, she dipped the washrag. "Beth Anne."

She closed her eyes. *Not now.* "I'm in here, Mary Nell."

Her best friend in all the world, the girl with whom she should be able to share any secret, stuck her head around the edge of the door. "Daddy said something was wrong."

She swallowed hard. She had to say this exactly right. "Something *is* wrong." She made her voice strong and irritated. "That sorrel is going to get some trooper killed at the water's edge. He balked and I went over his head."

"Oh, no." Mary Nell smothered a giggle, but not before Beth Anne heard it.

"Oh, yes, dear friend." Beth Anne's acted irritation turned real. "I'll let you take him out tomorrow and see how well *you* do."

Mary Nell pulled her hand down. "I'm sorry. It's only funny if it didn't happen to you." She came to the bathtub. "How about if I wash your hair for you?"

Beth Anne waved her away. "I didn't get completely dunked, just from the waist down. It would take too long to dry. Thanks anyway."

Suddenly, Mary Nell gasped. "Oh, Beth Anne, look at those terrible bruises on your arms."

She looked down at herself, then clapped her hands over the places. The imprints of Noah Rollins fingers were clear on her skin. If Chaney saw this—or heard—

Mary Nell was staring at her—dawning incredulity in her face. "Did you really fall from a horse?"

Beth Anne tried for a dismissive laugh. It failed miserably. "Of course I did. Look at my boots and skirt. I was drenched from the waist down. Those must have happened when I fell."

Mary Nell tilted her head to one side. "Not unless the horse had fingers. It doesn't take a doctor to know what makes bruises like that."

She went down on her knees beside the tub. "Oh, Beth Anne, what happened to you? You can tell me."

More than anything, Beth Anne wished Mary Nell would just go away and forget about this. Reaching for the towel, she climbed out of the tub on the other side. "I don't have anything to tell that I'm ashamed of."

Mary Nell rose. "Of course not. I never thought you did. But someone manhandled you—" She stopped. Her mouth opened wide. She raised both hands to cover it. "Noah Rollins." Her eyes narrowed. Her fists clenched. She looked as angry as Beth Anne had ever seen her. "Noah Rollins! Just wait till I tell Daddy."

Beth Anne barely caught her in time. "You'll do no such thing."

Mary Nell looked at her with a mixture of questions and accusations.

Beth Anne took her friend's hands. "He came along. And he—er—did—"

"That's all! I'm going to Chaney."

"—and I socked him on the jaw."

"Good for you." Mary Nell's blood was up. Her eyes snapped with anticipation. "Tomorrow you'll fire him."

"No."

Mary Nell stared at her. Something like horror began to dawn in her eyes.

"No. I was furious and insulted and I told him so. I socked him and I ran and got back on the horse."

"But—but you ran your horse into a lather getting back here. Daddy told me. Noah scared you. He manhandled you."

"But not before I warned him." She took Mary Nell's hands and sat with her on the edge of the bed. For just a second she closed her eyes and took a deep breath. What she had to say was very important.

She had to make herself clear. She'd hired Noah Rollins. Now she should be the one to control him. Noah Rollins had become part of her entrance into adulthood.

Mary Nell wasn't giving her much chance to think. "You've got to be crazy. A man—a big man—practically a stranger puts his hands on you—"

"He helped me out of the creek."

"—takes advantage of a situation while you're nearly drowning, then holds on to you so hard he makes bruises on your arms." She reached out a hand to touch Beth Anne's shoulder beneath the robe. "Those are ugly. He could have hurt you real bad."

"I know." Beth Anne took a deep breath. "Listen, Mary Nell. You know the situation here at White Oak. We can't afford to lose a single hand. Especially one that's young and strong and healthy. You've complained and complained about how every man on the place is over forty."

"We don't need a man in his twenties who'll beat you up."

"He didn't beat me up. He wanted to talk to me. He found out that he was going about it all wrong. I wouldn't listen to him when he was manhandling me. But I didn't run home screaming to Chaney."

"You should have."

"I shouldn't." Her throat was so tight she felt as if she were shouting. Yet she had to keep her voice low. "If I'd done that, I might have gotten Chaney killed."

That statement froze Mary Nell. Her eyes opened wider as recognition dawned. "Oh. I see what you mean. If Chaney had ordered him off the place or tried to beat him up—"

"Noah Rollins might have won."

Mary Nell pressed her hands to her cheeks. Her expression faded from angry defiance to concern. Perhaps for the first time in her life, she caught a glimpse of the future when her father and Chaney were old men and she and Beth Anne would have to run White Oak.

For herself, Beth Anne felt like a turncoat to her marriage. She should have perfect confidence in her husband, yet she couldn't have him take any more risks than he was already taking. He was the dearest thing in the world to her. Her voice when she went on was low, but no longer intense.

"Chaney's nearly thirty-six years old. He's getting gray hairs. He's—" She broke off, unwilling to tell her friend about Chaney's irregular heartbeat.

Mary Nell let her hands fall to her sides. Her expression became genuinely alarmed.

Beth Anne hastened on. "Oh, he's strong and healthy and—and—he's wonderful. He's all I've ever known or wanted. I love him every way it's possible to love a man. Nothing's going to happen to him. Not Chaney Taggart. It'll be years and years before he sits in a rocker on the front porch."

Mary Nell let out a relieved breath. "I still think Noah Rollins should go."

"Noah Rollins is nothing. I can keep out of his way. Maybe someday he'll be a man like Chaney, but I'm not interested enough even to make a bet on it. All I want is for White Oak to get these damned horses to the army and go back to being h-happy again."

She could feel the tears starting in her eyes. The month had been awful, the week had been awful, the day had been the most awful of all.

"Chancy mustn't know anything about this," she finished.

Mary Nell's tender heart melted. She pulled her friend into her arms and patted her back. "Of course he won't. I understand. Don't cry, Beth Anne. Chaney'll know something's wrong if you cry."

But Beth Anne didn't stop. Once started, the tears kept falling. And she hated them. She vowed at that moment, while they streamed down her cheeks, that she was going to get to the point where she never cried again.

Ever since she'd remembered Josey, she seemed to cry more and more. This couldn't go on. No wonder Chaney thought of her as a child. If he thought she wouldn't lose her mind, he'd probably tell her who Josey was.

While she struggled to get control of herself, Mary Nell held her and patted her and spoke soothing meaningless words.

Finally, Beth Anne pulled away. "I'll just tell him I got soap in my eyes."

Mary Nell shook her head. "You would have had to rub them with the bar. And your nose too. Don't tell him anything. He won't be in for an hour or more. Just lie down on the bed and have a nice rest. When you wake up, you'll feel better and your face will look normal again and dry."

Grateful to have satisfied someone, Beth Anne let Mary Nell lead her to the bed and pull the covers over her. "What about the bathwater?"

"I'll take care of it."

"I should go help Hardy with supper."

"Go to sleep."

At twilight Noah Rollins leaned against the corral while he rolled a cigarette. The horses moved restlessly, not yet settled down for the night.

Nevertheless, Mary Nell took special care to step lightly. Only when she was directly behind him did she speak. "You're nothing but a polecat."

He took his time to finish his smoke and tuck the makings back into his shirt pocket before he turned around. "Why, good evening, Miss Tibbets. Did you come looking for me just to tell me that?"

"I came looking for you to tell you that if you so much as lay a finger on my friend again, I'll shoot you."

Noah fished a match from his pocket and struck it on the top rail. When he'd blown a stream of blue smoke into the air, he grinned at her. "You're the second woman today who's threatened to shoot me."

"That takes care of every woman on the ranch. Not exactly the sort of thing you'd want the boss to know."

He pushed his hat back on his head. A lock of hair flopped over his forehead. He took another drag off the cigarette. "Well, I guess you're pretty excited about telling him."

"Me?" She tossed her head. "You don't know me very well or you'd know I wasn't a snitch. I don't tell tales. I keep my mouth shut and lie in wait somewheres. Then when you're least expecting me—ambush!" She slammed the last word at him in the hopes that he'd flinch or draw back or frown or something. He didn't do anything.

His infuriating grin might have been plastered on his mouth.

"Well, at least I know what's coming."

He still wasn't scared enough, but she hadn't thought beyond the threat to ambush him. Obviously, he wasn't taking her seriously. "That's right," she said. "When you least expect it, you'll—er—get ambushed."

He took another pull at the cigarette and dropped it on the ground where the tiny red glow disappeared beneath the sole of his boot. "Are you going to shoot for the heart or just wound me?"

She gasped. She couldn't understand the man. How could he be so calm? "I—er—I guess that would depend on you."

He straightened lazily and tucked his thumbs into his belt. "You mean if I promise you here and now I'd try to be good?"

She knew a moment's relief. "That would be swell."

"But I might be lying." His voice had a quaver to it.

He was laughing at her. He was standing there with his back to the light and laughing at her. She couldn't stand to be laughed at, not when this was so serious.

Damn you, Noah Rollins. She hit him in the chest with her fist.

He moved so fast she couldn't catch her breath. One big, callused hand wrapped around her wrist and whipped her arm down to his side. His arm snaked around her waist and dragged her in against him.

"So you're going to shoot me." His voice still sounded as if he were laughing.

He was laughing, and she was terrified. She couldn't move. She hadn't expected this. She sucked in her breath to scream.

"I wouldn't scream if I were you." His voice was low. It rumbled out of his chest, setting up a vibration against her.

She held her breath. "Why not?"

"Your papa might come and try to beat the tar out of me. And then I'd have to shoot him."

She went cold all over. Beth Anne's fear for Chaney flashed through her mind. Suddenly, she was afraid for her poppa. She swung her left arm at his head. His hat went flying into the corral, but she hadn't hurt him. She hit at him again but missed completely.

He ducked his head. His mouth came down on hers.

Then she did try to scream—too late. She might have been a kitten in a haystack for all the sound she made.

He let go of her right arm and put both arms around her body, pressing her tighter and tighter against him. He was warm and smelled of leather and horses.

She couldn't get free. She had to stand like a statue and wait for him to get through, then she'd show him what for. She'd show him—

His lips moved against hers. He wasn't pressing down as hard. The tip of his tongue touched the crease between her lips. She wouldn't open her mouth for him. No, sir, she wouldn't—

She couldn't help herself. Against her better judgment, against the stern refusals of her will, her lips parted. Like a bandit he slipped inside. He was stealing from her. And she couldn't stop him.

Still kissing her, he wrapped his arms tight around her and straightened. When her toes left the ground, she couldn't help herself. She wrapped her arms around him too.

He pulled his tongue out of her mouth and was kissing her cheek and her lips again. She supposed she could turn her head away and scream now, but she didn't. Her lips moved.

Well, damn me too.

She kissed him back. She didn't have any more will than a kid presented with an candy stick and told not to lick it.

He set her down. He seemed to know she was so breathless and dizzy she couldn't find her footing because he held her. She didn't want him to let her go.

The moment stretched out between them. They were standing like two lovers on a Valentine card staring at each other.

Thank heavens, the night was nearly pitch-black now.

One of the horses moved against another. The second animal shied and snorted.

Noah Rollins stepped back. "Maybe you'd better go in."

She didn't want to. Her whole body burned where he'd pressed up against her. She was embarrassed. That was it. He'd embarrassed her. And shamed her. She was burning with shame.

"Just don't you touch me again."

He raked his fingers through his lank hair and looked around for his hat. "No, ma'am. I sure wouldn't dare."

"And don't you laugh at me again."

"No, ma'am."

"And don't—"

He interrupted her. "Miss Tibbets, I think you'd better go in."

She spun on her heel and started back toward the house. She imagined she could feel his eyes on her. She had started off slowly, determined to walk like a lady. A chill skittered down her spine—like a goose walking across her grave.

Again her will failed her. She broke into a run.

* * *

"Got a minute, boss?"

"Sure thing." Chaney finished clearing a stone from the tender center of his horse's hoof and straightened. He gave the animal a pat and headed for the horse trough.

Noah Rollins followed him and waited while Chaney worked the pump handle and washed his hands. "I don't think its a good idea for the women to ride far from the corral."

His boss's eyes narrowed. "I take it you've seen something."

Noah nodded. "Across the river someone's set up a post. I reckon he's been using a spyglass. I've seen the light reflected off it more than once."

"Barney was always pigheaded when there's something in it for him." A muscle in Chaney's jaw flickered. He stared at the rippling water as if he might find an answer in its depths. "I hate to do it, but I guess I'm going to have ride into town and see how the wind blows."

"Tomorrow?"

"First thing."

Beth Anne sat her horse like a statue, her mouth set, the reins firmly in her left hand while Chaney swore at her. Of course, he didn't use the language she'd overheard him use when a horse stepped on his foot or the time when a hand had beaten a timid mare who'd shied and thrown him.

Nevertheless, what came out this morning was enough to set her stomach to jumping and little nervous chills running down her spine.

"I'm going with you," she said for the fifth time. She'd

said it as he sat up on the side of the bed. She'd said it as they dressed. She'd said it when they finished their coffee. She'd said it when she mounted.

His face was flushed and his black eyes snapped. He jerked off his hat and swiped his arm across his forehead.

"We're wasting time," she reminded him in a voice much cooler than the way she was feeling.

He opened his mouth, then closed it like a wolf trap. Without another word, he swung aboard the sorrel stallion. When the animal ducked its head and arched its back, he hauled its head up so viciously that the horse stopped in mid buck and stood quietly.

"We'll take care of things," Luther assured them. "There's not more'n but half a dozen left to smooth some rough edges off. Just be careful, Lieutenant."

Chaney growled something unintelligible.

Beth Anne had been exchanging grins and knowing looks with Mary Nell from the minute the pair had come down to the stable. Now she waved to her friend and clicked her tongue to a sorrel gelding with a lope like a rocking chair.

She had already turned into the road toward Rich Hill when her husband galloped up behind her. In uneasy silence they rode, but she could feel him seething as he kept the sorrel's nose even with her stirrup. She could feel the trembling in her belly ease as she congratulated herself on making her point. Still, she made up her mind to scold Chaney when they got home. They should have been riding along enjoying themselves.

Once they were trotting down Rich Hill's dusty main street, Chaney trotted on ahead, head up, back straight, hand resting on his thigh, the perfect cavalry officer riding forth to parley with the enemy.

In front of the bank, he climbed down and hitched the sorrel. He scowled again as Beth Anne steered her horse in beside him. "I'm going in here," he announced unnecessarily.

"I'll go too."

"No danger that Barney's going to be lying in wait in here."

"You never know."

He took her arm as she climbed up on the sidewalk and ushered her in.

When Eleazar Drorsen heard the door open, he raised his head, an affable smile on his face. Quickly it faded before the cold-steel expression on Chaney's face. "Mr. Taggart, well, this is sure a surprise. I—I guess I mean we didn't expect—I mean—um—glad to see you. What can I do for you?"

Two customers were standing in front of the teller's window, but they looked at Chaney and then quickly stepped aside. Beth Anne recognized one as the farrier who shod the White Oak horses. He ducked his head instead of returning her smile.

Behind the teller Nettie Drorsen looked up from the desk where she posted figures in the ledger. Throwing a frightened glance at her husband, she rose, clasping her hands in front of her.

Chaney crossed the floor, his boot heels thwacking on the oiled boards. "What's your stand on this tax?"

Drorsen's florid complexion turned even redder.

Beth Anne hoped apoplexy didn't run in his family. On the other hand, if he fell over in a fit, they might have a chance of getting this tax changed.

"I don't really have time to talk about this right now." Rich Hill's city council president rubbed his hands together. "If you want, I guess we could call a meeting for—oh, say—end of the week."

Chaney stooped slightly so that his eyes were level with

Drorsen's through the teller's window. "I want answers now, and I don't have time to wait."

"Mr. Taggart, you got no call to come in here and shout at my husband." Nettie's voice rose in pitch and volume as she fluttered out from behind her desk.

Chaney didn't so much as glance in Nettie's direction, Beth Anne was pleased to see. Instead, he slammed his fist on the counter. Every person in the bank jumped and the flimsy cage shook. "You know what this is all about, Drorsen. Are you going to hold me up like this?"

Perspiration had popped out on Drorsen's face. He patted it with a crumpled handkerchief. "The city council voted, Mr. Taggart."

"You and your brother and Barney Mallott are the city council."

"The—er—school. You know. The school for the children."

The door opened. Stan Carruthers, the owner of the general store, strode in. He wore his apron, and a pencil was still stuck behind one ear. Clearly, he hadn't come to make a deposit, but to watch what was going to happen.

He frowned when he saw Beth Anne. Her smile of greeting faded. Slowly she looked into the faces of the occupants. In that minute she knew Chaney was wasting his time. They were all in it. Probably they hadn't been to begin with, but now they all knew.

One of the customers had the grace to look shamefaced. The other had folded his arms and was scowling, his lower lip pooched out.

"We've got needs in this community," Carruthers called. "You've had it your way long enough, Taggart."

Chaney wheeled. "What in hell do you mean, 'my way,' Stan? I'm just like the rest of you, trying to make a living."

One of the customers sidled toward the door.

"Nobody's stopping you from doing that," Drorsen hurried to say.

Surrounded, Chaney stepped back to face the room. "Charging a dollar a head for loading horses will sure just about do it."

"Now, Mr. Taggart, you've got a government contract."

"And men to pay. How much of their paychecks do you suppose they spend in Rich Hill?"

Beth Anne saw the storekeeper start. His eyes widened. The belligerence faded from his face. She doubted he'd given those paychecks a thought when he'd sided with Barney Mallott.

Chaney must have seen him too because he turned back to Drorsen. "How much are you charging for cattle?"

"Well—"

"Why, Mr. Taggart," Nettie interrupted her husband, her voice like a piece of metal dragged over a tin roof. "You know hardly anybody loads cattle around here. Your horses are the only things that—"

"Shut up, Nettie."

"Eleazar Drorsen, don't you tell me to shut up."

The door swung open again, catching Carruthers in the middle of the back. Barney Mallott brushed him aside and burst into the center of the room. "What's a-goin' on here?"

For a moment no one answered. Chaney stepped to the grilled window and laid his arm along its ledge. His right hand rested on the butt of his gun. "Just come in to make a withdrawal, Mallott."

Barney glared.

The timid customer eeled out the door. The other one cleared his throat and stepped back against the wall.

"I'll take all the money in my personal account and the White Oak account too." Chaney's voice didn't have a scrap of emotion.

"Mr. Taggart!" Nettie looked aghast at her husband. Then she turned. "Beth Anne, you can't let him do that."

"Why not? It's our money."

"Now, Mr. Taggart." From apoplectic red to pale as a corpse, Drorsen's face changed in seconds. "I don't think you need to do that."

Chaney rapped the ledge with his knuckles. "What do you think you're on the city council for, Eleazar? You're supposed to protect the interests of the businessmen who make deposits in your bank."

"Well, the children—"

"You voted the way Barney Mallott told you to. How much money does he have on deposit?"

Barney reddened. "That's none of yore damn business."

Drorsen clutched the cashbox. His knuckles showed white.

"I'll take it all. I can always bank over in Nevada when I go after my supplies—"

Carruthers, the storekeeper, grunted as if he'd been punched in the gut.

"—and get my horses shod." With this statement he threw a look at the farrier who'd been standing with his arms folded in disapproval.

The man's eyebrows rose almost to his hat brim, and he turned his horrified gaze at Barney. In fact, they all did.

The marshal coughed and shuffled his feet. "You better not cause any trouble," he warned. "You ain't got any business to come in here and throw yore weight around."

"Mr. Taggart." Drorsen looked as if he might burst into tears.

"It's my money." Chaney hooked his thumb over his gunbelt. "I don't want a crooked town marshal protecting it."

"Who you callin' crooked?"

Drorsen's voice cracked in desperation. "I don't think we have that amount in cash."

"Cash!" Barney barked. "What're you doing?"

"I'm conducting my private business." Chaney rapped his knuckles on the ledge again. "If you don't have cash money, I'll take gold."

Nettie Drorsen gave a high-pitched shriek and swooned into the arms of the disgruntled farrier.

Chapter Six

The gelding and the stallion stretched out in earth-covering gallops. The dust from their hooves covered Beth Anne and Chaney, but they didn't dare rest the horses.

Chaney had handed Drorsen two saddlebags with instructions to divide the gold coins and silver equally between them and stuff the cash in on top.

Barney had scuttled out when Drorsen started announcing the amounts. Nettie had regained consciousness and embarrassed herself by begging Beth Anne to please—please—please ask Chaney to reconsider.

Beth Anne's only answer was a shrug and a shake of her head. She hadn't known what she'd expected when she'd ridden into town with Chaney. Somehow she'd imagined she'd be a soothing influence on the proceedings. Surely, no one would try to attack him with her there.

Now she had a prickling feeling in the middle of her back as she remembered Barney's hate-filled stare.

The best she could say she'd done was provide a packhorse. She couldn't imagine how Chaney would have gotten out of town with the gold on the sorrel.

At that moment the big horse stumbled and broke stride. Chaney pulled him back to a walk. The stallion's lungs were pumping like a bellows. Lather ran down his forelegs in streams.

Her gelding was tired too, but the seventy-five pounds less he carried—the difference between her weight and Chaney's—had kept him fresher. They'd galloped and trotted for miles now.

"Let's change horses," she suggested. To suit her suggestion, she dismounted and went to her horse's head.

Chaney looked as if he wanted to object. But the sorrel was too nearly done to lift his head, much less buck. Chaney looked back over his shoulder. "No sign of Barney yet. But he'll be coming. We can count on that and he won't come alone."

"Surely, honest citizens won't come after a man because he's taken his own money out of the bank."

Chaney looked at her a little pityingly. "They'll come. I doubt if Drorsen's got enough left to cover their own deposits."

Up until that minute Beth Anne had thought that the only thing banks did with money was hold it for people. Now was not the time to ask questions, but she was determined to find out what banks really did with people's money.

Chaney shifted in the saddle, then swung down reluctantly. He ran his hand over the sorrel's lathered neck. "We can't make it. He's given all he's got. Damn! I thought he had more bottom than that."

For herself, Beth Anne couldn't fault the sorrel. He'd carried more than 350 pounds for nearly five miles. She could see his body trembling with his heartbeats. She patted her gelding gratefully.

"Where shall we hide?"

Chaney shook his head. *"We* aren't hiding anywhere. I'm turning off the road and into that wash over there."

She started to protest, but he tossed her his reins. "Tie these around your horn. I'll take the saddlebags with me. Don't lead the horses after me. Turn them around and around here in the middle of the road, then ride on as fast as you can. When your horse gets tired, switch over to mine. Keep switching back and forth."

Cold fear clutched her heart. A great empty nausea roiled in her stomach. She had to be strong, had to say the right thing. The only thing that came out was, "Chaney, I hate to leave you."

He reached across to unstrap her saddlebag. "I hate to send you on ahead." His eyes glittered through the dust that grayed his face. He slid the saddlebag over his shoulder. "You do realize that you're the bait."

She hadn't thought about it like that. This was more reponsibility than she'd ever expected. She clenched her fist. "They'll never catch me."

He grinned. "That's what I'm counting on." He settled both saddlebags over his shoulders.

She could feel the tears starting. Desperately she reached out for him. Her fist closed around his shirt. She pulled their bodies together. "Oh, Chaney."

"Don't cry, honey." He kissed her with his mouth open. His tongue filled her mouth. She could feel the hot spurt of desire in response.

Oh, God! "Chaney."

"You've got to go." His voice was shaking too. He caressed her cheek.

"Yes."

Leading the stallion to cover his bootprints, he crossed to a seam of crumbled slate that lined the bottom of the drainage ditch beside the road.

She followed with the gelding.

"Now. Climb up. I'll hide out in that wash. Come back for me after dark. Not before. Tell Luther."

"Chaney!"

"Ride, Beth Anne. Don't let us lose everything we've worked for." He stepped off the gray rock that crackled under his feet and onto the grass. There he was careful to put his boots to the side of the tufts rather than in the center.

Despite the danger, a thrill went through her. He'd said *us. Don't let* us *lose everything.*

She didn't wait for him to make the wash. He had set her a task, a dangerous one. He expected his wife to do it. She was Taggart's wife. She'd do it the way Taggart would.

Glancing over her shoulder, she tried to mark the spot. The wash was just before a slight rise in the land. A pair of oak trees stood some distance to the right.

She heeled the gelding in the ribs and he started off with a will. The sorrel had no choice but to follow.

At the top of the slight rise she looked back. Chaney had disappeared from view. She looked around. From the top of the rise, she could see another wash—and more oak trees. How was she going to find this place in the dark? The Missouri prairie stretched for miles with almost no landmarks. She was going to have to—

A cloud of dust drifted across the horizon back to her north.

Barney Mallott.

She didn't dare spare the horses or herself. She slapped her reins over the gelding's withers. "Let's go, boy. Hyah-up!"

One mile. Two. Three. The gelding began to flag. She looked behind her. The dust was no closer but no farther either. She couldn't stop even for a minute.

The sorrel was proving to be the stronger horse after all. Relieved of Chaney's weight and the weight of the gold, he'd begun to gain strength. His head was up now.

She pulled her mount to a halt and swung down. To her surprise, her legs wouldn't hold her. Until they stopped quivering, she had to hang on to the gelding's horn. When she started to mount the stallion, he laid back his ears and bared his teeth at her.

"Damn you!" Jack o' Diamonds, was he? She was too exhausted to put up with this foolishness. "Hold still, Jackass." She lost her temper. A smart blow of her glove across his nose convinced him to behave.

When she tried to mount, she had to make two tries before she could heave herself into the saddle. Her clothing was dusty and her cheeks were streaked with black runnels from her tears.

She looked behind her, wondering if she'd taken too long. The dust seemed closer. The men were on fresh horses, and Barney Mallott wouldn't care if he rode his mount to death. He wanted White Oak gold.

She looked ahead. Maybe four miles. It was a long run for two tired horses. She could feel the sorrel's black heart beating like a blacksmith's hammer. She patted his neck. He tossed his head and champed at the bit. So much for gentleness.

She leaned far along his neck. "Run! You son-of-a-bitch!"

Screamed in his ear, the words galvanized him. He leaped forward, dragging the gelding with him. She clung to his back, pulling leather for all she was worth, all pride in her horsemanship fading with the need to stay on while the stallion's speed ate up the ground.

* * *

In the end she nearly ran them both to death before she saw the tree-lined lane at White Oak. In sight of the farm, she let the gelding's reins drop. The boys could round him up later. He staggered to a halt and stood with sides heaving.

The sorrel must have smelled the farm. His head and tail came up. His stride lengthened. With mane and tail whipping like battle flags, he galloped into the stable yard.

"Bethie!" Luther came running.

"Beth Anne!" Mary Nell wheeled her mount to the edge of the corral and skinned over the fence.

"It's Miz Taggart!" Hardy and Rusty saw her from the back course and all but fell off their mounts.

She tried to get down, but this time neither her arms nor her legs would hold her. She dropped in an embarrassing heap in the dust. The sorrel jerked the reins out of her hand and trotted over to the horse trough. He plunged his head halfway into the water and came up snorting.

Luther knelt beside her.

"Don't let him drink too much," she rasped. Her throat hurt from the dust. She couldn't blame the sorrel. If she could get her legs under her, she'd probably throw herself in head first.

"Where's Chaney?"

"He's—he's back along the road." Her voice faded completely.

"Bring her some water!" Luther yelled as the hands came pounding down the shedrow. "And get that sorrel out of the trough before he founders."

Hardy cut out for the cookshack while Rusty pulled the reluctant animal away.

Mary Nell knelt on her other side and took her hand. "What happened?"

Beth Anne looked at her best friend. "Got to get in the

house. Barney Mallott's right behind me. Can't let him know Chaney and I aren't at the house."

Luther's chin set. "I'll call 'em in."

"Help me stand." Beth Anne reached out for Mary Nell's shoulder. With the help of her friend, she managed to stand. How could she be so stiff! She rode every day. Yet every muscle from the waist down protested. Leaning on her friend, she limped toward the house.

Behind them the bells began to jangle as Luther whirled them. Nine brass bells mounted on a wheel with a handle set up a terrific din.

As they rang, Beth Anne scanned the horizon to the south. The dust cloud was drawing closer.

"Where's Chaney?" Luther caught up to them as the noise of the bells died.

"In a wash about four miles back. He closed our accounts with Drorsen's bank. They didn't have enough cash. We had to take half of it in gold. Barney's coming after us to get it."

"That son-of-a—er—so-and-so."

Beth Anne had to lean on the porch rail to climb the steps. "He's out to rob us. He's not even pretending he's the law anymore."

Once inside the kitchen, she collapsed in a chair. Mary Nell brought her a glass of water and a wet cloth to wipe her face. Over the rim of the glass, she stared at Luther. "Chaney wants us to come back for him after dark. We'll have to sneak, though. And we'll have to drive Barney off. If he takes the slightest notion that Chaney's not here, he'll be out to find him."

She buried her face in the washcloth. She had to think, but she was so tired. She could see the complications. Not for the first time she wished she and Chaney had changed places. He would know what to do. He'd been a lieutenant with the U.S. Cavalry. She should have stayed with the gold. All she would have had to do was wait.

"You get some rest." Luther laid a comforting hand on her shoulder. "Nothing for you to do until dark. We'll take care of it."

When he was gone, Beth Anne looked helplessly at Mary Nell. "We need at least two men to go with me to get him," she quavered. "And an extra horse for him and a packhorse for the gold."

"You don't have to go," Mary Nell suggested. "You can tell Daddy where you left him."

Beth Anne could feel the tears starting again, but she tipped her head back and swallowed them. She couldn't let Luther see them. He still thought of her as a little girl. "That's just it. I can't describe where I left him. It's like every other place along the road."

"Give us some idea," Luther begged, but Beth Anne shook her head. "A wash, a rise—"

Shots interrupted her. She pushed herself to her feet.

"Barney's made it." Luther bolted from the kitchen.

Beth Anne exchanged a level glance with her friend, three years younger. She couldn't ask—

"Shouldn't we be doing something?" Mary Nell prompted.

"I know what I want to do."

"Then let's get to doing it."

While Mary Nell danced up and down with eagerness, Beth Anne took Chaney's keys and opened the gunbox. Without hesitation she passed her friend a Sharps and took one and a box of shells for herself.

"Get to the front of the house. We won't shoot unless we have to. We don't want them to think something's wrong."

"Oh, right." Mary Nell's tone was sarcastic. "Everybody's turned out—with guns—but nothing's wrong."

Beth Anne uttered a little prayer for Chaney as she crouched on one knee beneath the window.

Barney Mallott at the head of a knot of men was turning into the lane.

"Look at them," Mary Nell bit her lip. "There must be eight or nine."

A fearsome yell accompanied by the thunder of hoof-beats startled both girls.

Noah Rollins streaked by. He rode bent low over his mare's neck, his rifle in his right hand.

Mary Nell started up with a gasp. "He'll get himself killed."

Beth Anne shook her head. It was going to be all right. "He might be just what we needed. If I were Barney Mallott and the drifters and barflies he's managed to round up, I'd hate to see *that* riding toward me."

Mary Nell sighed. "I can't help but worry."

Beth Anne stared at her. She wanted to ask why, but she knew her friend would tell her in good time.

With Noah leading the charge, the four White Oak men set out at a run on foot as the first line of intruders came out from behind the trees. Luther and Gunderson came galloping after Noah, making a combined cavalry and infantry charge of seven.

A few of Barney's men had dismounted at the head of the lane. Barney rode back and forth behind them, yelling at them. At the sight of Noah charging toward him and a united front coming down the lane, he wheeled his horse and spurred away.

Seeing his defection, his men stumbled and fumbled to mount their own horses. One lost his stirrup and reins and had to chase his terrified beast up the dusty road.

A cheer went up. The foe had retired from the field without a shot fired.

Beth Anne hurried out onto the porch in time to see

her men coming back. Luther was clapping Noah on the back and Rusty was hanging on to his stirrup.

Mary Nell leaped down the steps and ran to meet them.

Noah's grin was spread across his face. His hat had blown off in the mad run and his shock of yellow hair fell over his forehead. He looked about sixteen.

A warning buzz began in Beth Anne's brain. She recognized him looking like this. She'd seen him before.

Josey?

Barney Mallott shook with fury and frustration, cussing the cowards who'd run instead of fighting.

"We're gonna camp right here," he yelled, stomping up and down in the rutted road. "We're gonna wait till plumb dark and ride in and shoot the place up and—"

"We ain't got no food nor water," the farrier's helper growled. "You didn't tell us we was gonna spend the goddamn night."

Barney fell to cussing again. When he'd calmed down, he remembered. "There's a stream 'bout a mile and a half back. We'll stop by it. You can drown your fool self if you wanta."

On tired horses, their butts sore and their throats craving whiskey, the posse loped away.

Two of the White Oak men, one of whom had been a scout for the Union Army, volunteered to trail the marshal's party.

"No need to wait for dark," Luther told Beth Anne. "We'll start out as soon as Saul comes back."

She looked at him gratefully. In spite of Mary Nell's urgings, she hadn't been able to rest. All she could think about was Chaney. He was thirsty. He was hungry. He was in danger. She prowled the house like a crazy lobo—on the one hand longing to find her mate, on the other guarding her den against intruders.

She found excuses to go out onto the front porch. The empty lane tied her stomach in knots. The waiting was making her ill. Chaney was clever, but if they found out where she'd left him— They had to leave now—immediately. Her nerves strung tighter and tighter.

Within an hour Saul returned with the location of Barney's camp. "They've got a couple of bottles they're passing around." He spat contemptuously at such lack of discipline. "Another hour or two and we can probably ride right through 'em."

She pulled her hat down tight over her ears. "We'll go right now."

Neither Luther nor Noah, who had been called in because of his obvious skill in a fight, dared to question her.

Quietly, they mounted. Luther led the saddled mount for Chaney and the packhorse. With Noah leading the way, they headed out across country.

Beth Anne was sweating and quietly hysterical by the time they turned into the roadway nearly a mile beyond Barney's camp. Never had the Missouri countryside been so flat, so without markings of any kind. Which tree was which? She was terrified that she might not be able to find Chaney.

At last when she was sure they were going to have to turn back and search more closely, they rode over another rise like twenty others.

Her eyes scanned the monotonous landscape. Nothing! Nothing and everything looked familiar.

Then he rose from the wash, a black silhouette against the dark landscape. He waved.

Tears of thanksgiving choked her throat and streamed

down her cheeks. She flung herself off the horse and ran
toward her husband. Six feet from him, she launched herself into his arms.

"I want to thank you." Beth Anne found Noah Rollins
rolling a smoke beside the horse trough after Hardy's late,
late supper.

A nighthawk chased insects across the full moon. Its
image floated in the black water.

"You don't have to thank me." Noah pinched the ends
of the twist together and struck a match. "In fact, I wish
you'd just forget about the whole thing."

"I'm sure you do." She was smart enough to know that
he didn't like her, but since he wouldn't tell her why, he
could just be mad. She was paying her debts. "But thank
you anyway. Thanks to you, Barney Mallott and his men
didn't get close enough to the house to find that Chaney
wasn't here. We got him back safe and whole."

"Doing my job."

She wrapped her arms across her body. The silence grew
between them. She turned to hurry back to the house.

"I guess I owe it to you," he said to the darkness. "Does
your guilty conscience feel eased?"

She bridled instantly. "I don't have a guilty conscience."

"You should."

"Just so we understand each other, Mr. Rollins, I love
my husband very much."

"Ah-huh!"

"He's taken care of me ever since I was a little girl."

"And that makes it all right?" Noah took a drag off the
cigarette and regarded it somberly as he blew the smoke
out of his lungs.

She was certain Noah knew something from her past.

He was too angry to just be a Rebel sympathizer who hated anything Yankee. "Why shouldn't it?"

"Right. You're just a number in a long line of gals who've climbed into bed with the scum that—"

"Stop right there. Chaney is not scum and I did not climb into bed with him. I married him."

He took a final drag and flipped the cigarette into the water. It hissed and went out.

"What's more," Beth Anne continued, "he hired you. You rode in looking for work, half-starved, on a horse that should have been put out to pasture at least a year ago."

"And you think I should say how grateful I am."

"Yes, I do." She hesitated. "But you don't have to say it. I can see you didn't have any advantages as a child." She started to hurry back toward the house.

When she heard him thudding after her, she whirled. Her hand slapped the butt of the gun strapped to her hip. "Don't! Don't you dare lay a hand on me. I won't be manhandled."

He skidded to a halt and raised his hands. "I'm not going to touch you. I'm just going to remind you that we both had advantages as a children."

"I did?" A chill of presentiment ran down her spine. "I had advantages as a child? How do you know that? Did you know me as a child?"

He was a silhouette in the darkness. His hat tipped back on his head with the moon over his shoulder.

"Tell me." She reached for him, but he backed away. "Tell me."

"Ask your husband," he said before he strode back to the bunkhouse.

Beth Anne had everything she could do to keep from running after him. He knew her. Noah Rollins knew her past. She didn't have to guess about it anymore. He'd told her.

She should run after him and make him tell her. She
should go straight to Chaney. Together—

Chaney was the problem. He didn't want her to remember. He'd tried to keep her from remembering Josey. What
if she ran after Noah Rollins and shouted the name *Josey*?

Would he answer? She sucked in a deep breath, but he'd
already closed the door to the bunkhouse.

"We still have a few raw horses," Chaney acknowledged
at the war council the next morning, "but we've got to
move now. Now they've really got reasons to come after
us. The word gets around that we've got our life savings
out here and we won't be able to keep the Jayhawks out."

"What are we going to do?" Beth Anne had slept poorly
the night before. She'd heard the clock strike one and then
two. Finally, she'd drifted off, but dreams kept niggling at
the corners of her mind—dreams hidden in boiling black
clouds with flashes of light like gunshots in the dark.

She didn't want to dream those dreams. Consequently,
she kept waking up. Her eyes were still blurred with sleep.
Mary Nell had tried to comfort her at breakfast, but she'd
brushed her friend's efforts aside. She was going to work
this out one way or another by herself.

She must have dozed, for suddenly her body jerked
involuntarily. She blinked at her husband.

He directed a sober stare to her. "We're going to drive
the horses out of Bates County."

The men exchanged glances. Luther heaved a sigh. "It's
a long pull up to Harrison, Lieutenant."

Chaney snapped his fingers. His face spread in a grin
that made him look young. Like the young lieutenant of
her first memories. "We're not going north to Harrison.
That's the way Barney will expect us to go. We're going
to take 'em south to Nevada."

Beth Anne looked from one face to another. Slow smiles spread across their mouths. It could work. Hell, if the lieutenant planned it, it would work. And they wouldn't lose a single man.

"We may have to pay a little more than we were expecting," Chaney went on, "but it sure won't be a dollar a head."

She could imagine Barney's frustrated cussing as the train chugged through Rich Hill with the White Oak horses loaded on the Missouri Pacific and bound for Kansas City and the White Oak men sitting up front smoking and playing cards.

She looked from one to the other. "When do we leave?"

"You can't go!"

"It's my place to!"

"You'd just get in the way." He'd tried that argument before. She'd looked at him the way she'd looked at him when she was fourteen and he'd tried to send her to the St. Louis finishing school instead of letting her follow him to his next post.

She'd done it about the same time too—in the evening. Sometimes before supper like now, sometimes at bedtime. Except now she was inside the bedroom where she had plenty of good reasons to think she was going to get her way.

Of course, she thought she ought to go. Chaney wrung his hands in frustration. She'd gone into Rich Hill against his better judgment—and look how that had turned out.

"You might need me again for a decoy."

He caught hold of her shoulders. "I'll regret that so long as I live."

Instead of backing off in anger as he'd expected, she smiled and put her arms around his neck. "I won't. I was scared and exhausted and filthy and worried to death about you. You trusted me. I'll never ever forget that. And I managed to bring it all off." She kissed him on his mouth with more than usual force. "I did it. You're safe. Our money's safe and our gold."

He tried to unwind her arms from around his neck. Too late! She pressed against him, hooking one leg over his hip and opening herself to him. "Beth Anne. Stop this. You aren't going."

She kissed him again, smiling, wriggling against him. "Try and stop me, Chaney Taggart. What have you got to use that can stop me?"

"You are not going to get your way about this, little girl." He lowered his voice to a menacing growl—the kind of voice that used to scare her until she'd discovered he didn't have any intention of doing anything terrible to her. "You are not."

Smiling, shaking her head, her whole body telling him how he was wasting his time, she brought her palms up to his cheeks and threaded her hands through his hair. Her fingertips traced tiny circles over the back of his skull, her thumbs rubbed his temples. Chills of pleasure prickled his skin. At the same time, she closed her teeth lightly on his lower lip and sucked at it.

He closed his eyes. Heaven help him! He couldn't refuse her a single, solitary thing when she treated him like this.

Pleasure heated his body. Even with several layers of clothing still separating them, in his mind he'd already slid into her. She'd already closed around him, hot and wet, dripping with wanting him. He grasped her thigh and pulled her tighter, stretching her, lifting her onto her toes.

Stupid men he'd overheard during his army days had boasted about how many women they'd had even though they had wives and families at home. The same woman over and over again meant a man just went through the motions.

A different one every night was what a real man wanted, they said.

Either they were damned liars or he pitied them their ignorance. Beth Anne's passion excited him from first kiss to last gasp. Because she was totally honest about her desires and because she loved him.

She pressed her heel into the small of his back. He'd never taught her to do that. She just loved to do it, loved to climb all over him. Most times he felt like a tree with a wild thing skinning it. His loins throbbed. His heart thundered like a triphammer.

She slung the other leg around his waist and pushed herself up. Her breasts were underneath his chin as he swayed backward from his hips.

"We've got too many clothes on," she complained between wild kisses. "Why don't you stop me when I start this? I hate to get down and get undressed."

He pivoted and carried her toward their bed. Against her neck he mocked her with a mournful tone. "Why do you think I can stop you when you can't stop yourself? I'm just a thing. You don't have any consideration for this old man's—"

She pulled his hair.

"Ow!"

He turned around again and fell backward on the bed with her on top of him. "Someday you're going to kill me. My crazy old ticker will just stop in midstroke and—"

While he complained, she made short work of the buttons on his pants, pushed aside his thin cotton underwear, and dragged him out into the light of day.

A gusty sigh burst from her as she closed her mouth over him.

"Lord, honey, someday you're going to—"

He couldn't help himself. His whole body convulsed. His hips lifted off the bed, stabbing upward into her throat.

She clutched his buttocks and hung on as he let himself go the way he could only with her.

Only with her. Only with Beth Anne. "Beth Anne, Beth Anne, Beth Anne."

He felt weightless and drained. His feet rested flat on the floor. His belly sagged between his hipbones. His chest barely rose and fell.

The bedsprings creaked as she rose. He heard the rustle of her clothing, heard her breathing a little deeper than usual. She lifted one foot and then the other to pull off his boots. He barely managed to lift his hips enough for her to pull off his pants.

"Lazy, lazy," she scolded.

He could hear the laughter in her voice. Behind a yawn, he promised, "I'll be back in the fight in a few minutes."

She climbed back on top of him and lay down, her breasts against his chest. From long practice she draped herself comfortably and pulled the covers over them both. The light was fading. "We'll just take a quick nap before supper."

"Sure we will." He chuckled softly. His palms were already moving under the covers. She might have worn part of him slick, but he still had a trick or two left to please her, no matter how good she was.

She awoke in the grip of the worst nightmare she'd had in years. Shots and yells and the galloping of horses hooves. A man crouched behind the porch railing, his white hair and beard whipped around his face.

She had to get to him. Dark figures galloped between

them. He fired a rifle at the men on horseback circling back and forth.

He was defending his house. Her house. She had to get to him. Get him away from there. She sprang from the wagon. Her ankle turned and sent her sprawling. Someone jumped down beside her.

She screamed as a great force seemed to knock him sideways. As if he curled into a ball as he fell, he hit and rolled into the darkness.

The bearded man rose, firing, firing, jacking the shells out of a Spencer repeater, plugging shells into the chamber.

The riders were coming back. She scrambled to her feet screaming.

"Beth Anne! Beth Anne!"

She opened her eyes. The scene disappeared. Chaney lifted her into his arms. She hid her face against his nightshirt. She felt as if pieces of herself were cracking inside her. Sharp pains tore at her lungs and belly. She didn't want to cry, but the pain was too intense. She couldn't stop herself.

She didn't want to remember. She didn't want to. "No," she whispered. "No, no, no."

The dream disappeared like morning mist before the sun.

She didn't want to remember anything so horrible. As she'd done for the last three years, she sought refuge in her husband's body. Chaney was right not to let her remember.

Mary Nell Tibbets caught Noah Rollins by surprise before he could get his horse saddled and start his morning patrol around the perimeter.

"You listen to me," she fairly hissed. "You pack your

gear and clear out right now." Hands on hips, head thrown back to look into his blue eyes, she delivered her order.

He tilted his head to one side. A corner of his mouth quirked up in a grin that irritated her so that she had to grit her teeth to keep from slapping him. "I calculate Miz Taggart sent you."

"She did not! She doesn't need anybody to run her errands for her. If she'd wanted you fired, she'd have fired you. I'm the one who wants you gone."

He pushed his hat back so his hair flopped over his forehead. That hair was another thing that irritated her. Why didn't he comb it, for heaven's sake? "Now, why would you want me gone, Miss Tibbets?"

She didn't want to tell him that when her best friend had come in to breakfast that morning, she'd looked as if she'd cried all night long. She'd looked this way almost every day since Noah's coming.

The tired shake of her head had wrung Mary Nell's heart and when Beth Anne had said, "Good morning," the sound that rasped out of her throat was painful to hear.

"Because you've outstayed your welcome."

His mouth twisted some more until it was almost like a smirk. Ooh! but he made her mad. "Nobody said anything about my welcome when I went charging after that marshal and his gang to protect your poppa."

He was right. She could feel her righteous anger deserting her. Beth Anne had had a bad night. Mary Nell knew Noah Rollins had had some sort of dust-up with Beth Anne a few days ago. But that didn't necessarily mean he was the cause of her bad dreams. To be honest, now that Mary Nell thought about it, Beth Anne had had bad dreams before Noah appeared.

Still, she'd gone to thank him and had come back looking upset and bothered. While Mary Nell was rethinking her reasons, Noah spoke again.

"Did Miz Taggart lose a night's sleep?"

Mary Nell pounced on the question like a duck on a June bug. "So you did say something to her."

"No, ma'am. She said something to me. Matter of fact, she thanked me. I told her she didn't owe me any thanks."

"And what else?"

"I think you should ask her. If she wants you to know, she'll tell you." The smirk disappeared from his face. "Just like what you say to me and I say to you doesn't go any farther."

His voice was softer than she'd ever heard it. It rolled over her ruffled feelings like molasses. She didn't want to get all soft, but he wasn't helping her to stay mad. "I don't care who you tell."

He nodded. "Mary Nell, you're a real good friend to Miz Taggart."

She knew how a cat felt when someone's palm stroked it.

"Believe me, I don't have any intention of hurting her. And as a matter of fact, I like it here at White Oak real well." He took a step toward her.

Somehow her fists weren't digging into her hips anymore. They'd come unclenched and she had them up in front of her. What's more, her fingertips were tingling. Noah Rollins's chest was inches from them. She could almost feel the heat from his body.

He took another step. His own hands came up.

She made a little mewing sound as their palms touched. His fingers laced among her own. His hand was so much bigger than hers, so much warmer.

She had to tilt her head back even farther. He bent over and lowered her mouth to his. His lips brushed hers, brushed the corner of her mouth, brushed across her cheek as she turned her head away, nibbled at her earlobe.

She sighed.

He stepped back. "I'd purely hate to leave here, Mary Nell Tibbets."

"I—I—Why?"

He pushed his hat back on his head. "Because I think you're what I've been looking for my whole life long."

Chapter Seven

"Mr. Taggart! Oh, Mr. Taggart!"

Eleazar Drorsen had gotten down from his buggy and stood hat in hand beside the hitching post.

Chaney opened the door. He'd been watching for Drorsen, but he hadn't expected the man to come alone. A delegation including his family and several cronies all prepared to beg first, then act nasty, was more his style.

The buggy's slow progress up the lane had been unremarkable, but Chaney was still suspicious. His gaze swept the lane and the surrounding pastures.

At the window Beth Anne stared too. Neither one of them believed that the president of the Rich Hill bank had come alone.

The small man put his foot on the first step, but Chaney's black stare flicked across him. He stepped back from it as if he'd put his fancy polished shoe into a campfire. Red mottling appeared above his starched collar and stained his cheeks.

He cleared his throat. His voice squeaked before he got it under control. "Mr. Taggart, I've come out to discuss our problems face to face."

"*Our* problems, Drorsen? I thought we'd settled those."

"Oh, no. Lord, no. You misunderstood—that is—Marshal Mallott—"

Chaney's voice cut like a knife. "I understood he rounded up a posse and chased me and my wife all the way back to White Oak."

"Um—no." Drorsen cleared his throat. His tone became more saccharine by the minute. "That's what you misunderstood. Barney was just doing his job."

Chaney snorted in disbelief.

"I told him you were carrying a large sum of money. He was trying to give you an escort."

"Why'd he shoot at the house?"

"He was just doing his— What?"

"Why'd he shoot at us?"

Drorsen's face turned bright red. "I—er—"

"Why'd they camp down the road a piece and try to sneak back during the night?"

Drorsen looked apoplectic. He ran his finger around the edge of the starched collar and swallowed hard. "Listen, Mr. Taggart, this was all a mistake from the beginning—"

"And you boys made it." Convinced that Drorsen didn't have the will to bushwhack him, Chaney stepped out on the porch.

He'd warned Beth Anne not to follow him. Still, he had a prickling feeling along his spine. She was in enough danger beside the window.

He risked a glance over his shoulder. There she was, down on one knee, head and shoulders in plain sight. He could also see the black tip of the rifle barrel at her side.

He shuddered. He didn't want her even to think about shooting Eleazar.

"—the bank will be your friend."

"This discussion is a waste of your time, Drorsen." Chaney shook his head. "I've made my decision. When you started carrying on about building a school when the one we've got isn't but eight years old and only half full—"

"We've got to look to the future." Drorsen continued to argue even though he looked about to burst into tears.

Chaney nodded. "That's what I always say."

Drorsen turned his hat in his hand, his fingers chasing each other around the brim. "Please, Mr. Taggart. You just can't take your money out of the bank. It'll have to close. The town—"

"Maybe Barney Mallott and your brother on the town council can help you come up with a way to keep it open."

"But, Mr. Taggart—"

"Good-bye, Mr. Drorsen."

The banker looked as if he would die. Sweat popped out on his forehead. With a shaking hand, he pulled a handkerchief out of the crown of his derby. A big white handkerchief that he shook out ceremoniously.

Chaney's eyes widened. "Damn you, Drorsen!" Then he dropped flat on the porch.

The thunder of the rifle couldn't cover the spang of the bullet striking the front door. The thick etched glass held, but a round hole appeared as if by magic on the petal of one of the lilies. The lace curtain behind it bucked backward.

Beth Anne cringed in horror as the glass in a picture high on the wall shattered and fell to the floor.

"Chaney!"

"Stay down." He opened the door and crawled through it.

Drorsen sprang into his buggy and whipped his horse.

As it wheeled around and clattered down the lane, Chaney reached for Beth Anne's rifle.

He opened the door in time to see the bulky figure of Barney Mallott leap from behind one of the oaks in the lane and fling himself into the buggy.

"I thought Drorsen was taking too long to get up here. That skunk hid in the back and rolled out."

Chaney clapped the rifle to his shoulder. As the buggy turned into the road, he put a neat hole all the way through the bonnet.

Eleazar Drorsen popped his head around the edge of the rocking canvas. He was too far away for Chaney to read his expression, but Chaney made himself a bet that the banker had wet his britches.

He jacked the shell out of the rifle and slipped another one in. He should have shot them both. But he couldn't count on the results of a jury trial in Bates County.

"Chaney," Beth Anne spoke behind him.

He turned back to her. "We'll leave tomorrow, honey."

She was standing with her hands clasped in front of her breasts, unconsciously assuming an attitude of prayer. Her unspoken question hung between them in the air.

Smiling grimly, he put his arm around her shoulders and turned her back into the house. "You're coming with me and so is Mary Nell. Those people have lost what decency and sense they ever had. We can't leave anyone here that they might be able to use as a hostage."

At least she hadn't let Chaney see how badly she was shaking. As she'd leaned the barrel against the glass, the past and present seemed to blur together. She'd had a sharp feeling that she'd done this before.

But when?

Josey.

The episode at the bank had made her realize that Chaney would probably operate better if he didn't have to worry about her. Yet she'd felt the rightness of her going with him. When she'd ridden on without him, he hadn't doubted her. She could almost see Chaney's attitude changing toward her. She'd wager that if she hadn't had the blasted nightmare last night, he wouldn't have had any doubts about her going.

No, he hadn't hesitated to place his life in her hands. He never doubted that she could ride on to the farm and bring help back for him.

She didn't think she could have shot Eleazar, who was a rabbity little man married to a sweet woman without an ounce of brains. Still, those thoughts hadn't been in her mind when she crouched there. Her hand had curled around the breech of the rifle with an easy familiarity that surprised her.

She wondered if she could have snugged that rifle into her shoulder and fired.

Josey?

When the White Oak herd, two hundred remounts destined for the Army of the West, forded the Marais des Cygnes River, the sorrel stallion took it into his head to roll in the shallows.

Beth Anne screamed in alarm, even as Chaney managed to bail out of the saddle. Cussing a blue streak, wet to the waist, he splashed around the animal, pulling on the reins, and finally delivering a terrific kick on the horse's rump.

Scrambling up, the stallion kicked backward. His hind legs narrowly missed Chaney's face.

Spread out behind the herd, the drovers couldn't help. When Chaney finally got to the horse's head, the animal tried to bite him as he mounted.

Beth Anne was a nervous wreck just watching the strug-
gle. Finally, she rode up the opposite bank and turned her
back on the whole thing. Silently, she vowed the horse
would be gone within the month. If she couldn't get a
price for him in Kansas City, she'd sell him to the first
trader that came by.

If nobody would buy him—a distinct possibility given
the animal's temper—she could always shoot him some
dark night. Anything to get rid of him.

Chaney might be the stubbornest man alive, but he
wasn't going to get his way in this. The animal was too
dangerous ever to ride. He was an outlaw, and she was
pretty certain his colts would show the same traits.

When Chaney rode up beside her, she put her hand
out. "Please take him back to the stable."

"Damned if I will." Her husband shot her a look that
would have made her cringe if she hadn't known that he
was disgusted to his soul with the animal and taking his
bad temper out on her because she'd been there to witness
the fight.

"You could catch up with us in an hour."

He pretended not to hear.

The herd began to string out of the water. Two hundred
geldings and mares trooped up the bank, churning it into
a quagmire. The trick now was to get them bunched to
drive the dozen miles south to Nevada in Vernon County
to catch the Missouri Pacific.

Giving the stallion a light rein, Chaney let him do the
work he was born to do.

Much as Beth Anne hated to give the sorrel any credit,
he did have the right instincts for herding. Of course, only
the mares interested him. He wasted a lot of time and
energy herding them, circling them, and trying to cut them
out from geldings.

When Chaney forced him to bunch them all, he

champed at the bit. Obviously, he hated the man on his back.

"I've never seen anything like this." Mary Nell rode up beside Beth Anne. "They're turning what ought to be a simple drive into a fight to the death."

"I know." Beth Anne made a helpless gesture toward the herd.

"Sure makes me appreciate old Babe here." Noah Rollins pulled up on Mary Nell's left. He patted the gray mare, who flicked an ear back.

Both girls nodded in agreement as the sorrel snaked after a tall mare, nipping her flank. When she turned back into the herd, he bared his teeth at a chestnut gelding that followed too close to her.

Instead of moving along at a sedate pace, every horse was skittish. The slightest stirring of a leaf, a rabbit starting up from behind a bunch of grass, a whorl of dust, all and everything sent the normally calm horses shying and wheeling. The drovers had to work twice as hard dashing after the strays and bringing them back.

Every time Chaney reined him in, the sorrel stamped and whinnied and reared. The constant battle raised dust, shortened tempers, exhausted them both.

At last Luther threw a loop over a placid roan gelding with a white blaze down its face. As the herd moved on, he dragged spare tack from the wagon, saddled the animal, and led it up.

"Lieutenant. Get the hell off that horse!"

Chaney blinked.

Beth Anne came up on his other side. "Please, Chaney."

He looked dully at her as if he'd forgotten where he was. Wearily, he climbed down. Noah Rollins dropped a loop around the sorrel's lathered neck and led the horse to the back of the herd. Luther pulled Chaney's tack off and tossed it in the back of the supply wagon.

The drovers bunched the herd together again. Chaney sat slumped in the saddle as it moved past him.

Beth Anne considered going over and commiserating, but Mary Nell shook her head. "Let him figure it out."

Mickey O'Doole's brown beard streaked with gray hung halfway down his chest, nearly covering his tarnished sheriff's star. His enormous fat belly rested on the saddlehorn. His huge hand gripped a double-barrel shotgun. The sheriff of Vernon County, along with half a dozen hard-faced deputies and a grinning Barney Mallott, waited for Chaney's herd at the county line.

O'Doole did not grin.

The minute Chaney saw him, he knew the game was up. The man's reputation extended back to shady dealings before the war. It had been blackened beyond redemption with the issuance of Order No. 11.

When O'Doole had carried out his version of the order, not a single Southern sympathizer no matter how poor or innocuous made it out of Vernon County with more than the clothes on his back.

For himself, O'Doole had seized one of the best pieces of land with a fine house on it along with its furnishings including the jewelry and silver of the owner's wife. The rest of the loot he'd divided among his most loyal supporters.

Ten years later, the remaining citizens had no choice but to keep electing a crooked sheriff who turned a blind eye to the most blatant graft. In a word, O'Doole owned the whole county, lock, stock, and barrel.

Chaney had known the risk, but his plan had been to hold the horses outside Nevada until a couple of hours before the Missouri Pacific rolled in. At least a dozen cattle cars were always available on the siding in the yards. His animals could be loaded and switched onto the train with a minimum of fuss. If a telegraph should happen to tap out a message up the line to Rich Hill, it would be too late for anyone to do anything about it.

Unfortunately, Barney had beat him to O'Doole. The deputies had their long guns out of their scabbards and across their saddlebows.

"Reckon you ain't heard about our town council's new law," O'Doole began without preamble.

Chaney slipped his hand onto his pistol butt. "Since you can't wait to tell me, spit it out."

"We done passed an order that quarantines every animal brought into this county for six weeks."

"Six weeks, huh?" Chaney didn't flinch. He was conscious of Noah Rollins on his left. Beth Anne and Mary Nell were right behind him.

"Gotta be safe," O'Doole continued. "Can't have hoof-and-mouth or some such thing gettin' started in the county."

"Hoof-and-mouth from horses?"

O'Doole squinted into the sun and sighed. "Can't be too careful."

"Yeah. Milk production could go way down," Chaney observed dryly.

O'Doole rocked his heavy weight back and forth in the saddle. The leather creaked and his horse shifted with him.

Chaney wondered at the weight the animal carried. He doubted that O'Doole went anywhere except at a walk. Certainly a gallop or even a trot would have been impossible.

Barney chimed in. "You can ship 'em out of Rich Hill, Lieutenant, or you can hold 'em back at your damn farm that you stole until your contract runs out."

Anger streaked through Chaney. His pulse stepped up

its beat. He flexed his fingers over the pistol. One shot! O'Doole. A second shot to take out Barney. It would all be over. He doubted the deputies would fight if their bosses were down. Their kind didn't practice loyalty if the paycheck looked in peril.

"You want to see that hellcat wife of yours dead, you draw that gun," Barney sneered. He jerked his head toward the man on his right. "Slim's got her in his sights—and he don't care that she's a woman. He just likes to shoot. He's got a bet with hisself that he can plug anything that moves dead center at a hundred yards."

Chaney's hand did not relax. His expression didn't change. "You're a dead man, Mallott."

Barney laughed again. "Or a rich one. I think I'm gonna be rich. You work that there farm and I get my share. I think that's the way it's gonna be from now on."

"Does O'Doole get his cut?"

A sudden frown deepened the creases in the sheriff's fat forehead. "A cut? You didn't say nothin' about a cut. How about my cut, Barney?"

Barney stiffened in the saddle. His fulsome grin disappeared, replaced by a glare that willed Chaney's death on the spot.

Chaney gave no sign of the elation he felt. With five words he'd shattered the uneasy alliance between Barney and Mickey. He felt the deadly calm before the battle settle over him. His hand was steady, his senses acute. Now was the time. The seeds of discord were sprouting. He could draw his gun and shoot them both.

He could hear his men gathering behind him. He didn't need to glance over his shoulder to know they'd lined up ready to charge when he gave the order. Pride and confidence warmed him. O'Doole's deputies straightened in the saddle. Their hands tightened on their weapons.

Like a buzzard's shadow, cold commmon sense replaced

the fighting heat. His men weren't young anymore—
they'd lost their fighting edge, just as he had.

He had too much to lose—this wasn't a matter of life
and death. He wasn't even likely to lose the farm. This was
a matter of principle. Of pride, if the truth were known.
One of the deadly sins.

He wasn't going to allow them to blackmail him, but he
wasn't under orders here. He hadn't sworn an oath to
fight an enemy. He couldn't lead these good, loyal men
into a fight where some of them would get killed.

"Which one you want me to plug, Lieutenant?" Luther
called. "I'm a damn good shot."

"Let 'em live a day or two longer, Luther." Chaney
raised his arm. "We'll take the herd back to White Oak."

Leaving the lawmen gaping, he turned his back on them
and gave his orders.

Barney Mallott sent two of his best men galloping around
by the road to spy on White Oak. "Camp a couple of miles
north," he told them. "Keep yore eyes and ears open. If
he takes that herd out again, Sylvester, you foller him. And,
Hollis, you come back and get us real quick."

"Sure thing, Marshal." Sylvester Limburg nodded affa-
bly. "We'll take turns. Won't nobody get by us."

Hollis rubbed his bristly chin. "Where you gonna be,
Marshal?"

Barney grinned in Eustace Fisher's direction. "That's
the beauty part of it. We're gonna camp here for a spell.
Let 'em think they've got some time. Before first light,
we'll move in on 'em."

He waited, but nobody said anything.

"Just like an army, boys. We're gonna stage a surprise
attack."

Still no one said anything.

He scowled. Well, damn their eyes. They'd see how his plan would work. He'd never got to command during the war, but he'd always known he could. He gestured to Sylvester and Hollis. "You boys get on down the road. When you hear the shootin' at White Oak, come runnin'."

Beth Anne could feel tears stinging her eyes. Chaney's men, her men, were so courageous. When she and Mary Nell turned their horses, Rusty Huff and Doc Gunderson closed in behind them. They were offering their broad backs to be shot by those Vernon County deputies.

They were the very best. Every one of them was like a father to her. She looked over at Mary Nell, but her friend wasn't looking in her direction. An expression of concern mixed with longing and maybe something more softened her mouth.

Beth Anne followed Mary Nell's gaze. Her friend was looking at Noah Rollins, who had galloped his gray mare ahead of the herd to the rise. Now he crested it and halted. Dismounting, he dropped down in Babe's shadow, jacked up his knees, braced his elbows on them, and steadied his rifle against his shoulder.

From there he could draw a bead past the herd and the White Oak riders to the deputies.

"He's covering us," Mary Nell said in a voice that vibrated with emotion. "He's covering our retreat. Oh, Beth Anne—"

"I know. They're all so brave. I can't stand the thought that somebody might get shot. Your father. My husband. Our friends. For a damned herd of horses."

"You're right," Mary Nell agreed softly. "It's not worth it."

"But try to get them to see reason."

Look out! You devil! No! No!

She aimed her singleshot at the galloping horseman and squeezed the trigger. Her target wore a uniform with a broad yellow stripe down his leg. He reeled in the saddle, caught himself by the horn, and rode on.

Josey! Josey! Devil! Poppa! Devil! Poppa! She reached into the pocket of her skirt for another cartridge.

An old man with a long white beard stepped out onto the porch of White Oak. It was White Oak. For the first time the dream seemed familiar. The images of violence were recognizable instead of distorted. She could see his face.

Poppa.

More horsemen flashed by. He was shooting at them. He had a repeater—just like the Henry.

More shots. They came from all directions. She was trying to climb onto the wagon seat. Josey was behind her.

Suddenly, he caught her around the waist and gave her a great shove. She lost her grip and fell sprawling in the dirt.

"Stay down!"

No!

Josey knelt beside her, firing his rifle. One shot. Two. How many had he fired already? Now he was up and running across the yard. The horsemen came galloping by, wheeling their animals. The horses' hooves tore up the yard, the flowers. A big horse with white stockings. White to the knees.

Poppa was waving, waving to Josey, shouting. "Get back!"

She scrambled to her feet to run after Josey. Toward Poppa.

"Get back!" Poppa was coming down the steps.

She took two steps. Horsemen galloped between Josey and her. A massive figure, a silhouette, pulled his horse to a stop. It whinnied and grunted as he reined it toward her. She raised her empty rifle. The huge black figure advanced. The horse's white forelegs rose in front of her eyes as it reared.

She threw up her rifle to protect her head.

A scream tore out of her throat. A terrific blow struck her rifle down. Odd. There was no pain. She didn't feel any pain. Her body buckled. She was collapsing like a jointed doll.

Blood—hot and terrifying gushed down her wrists, down her forehead. Then she knew. She'd been shot.

She screamed.

And then the pain hit.

She sat up in bed wringing wet with perspiration. Desperately she stared into the darkness. *Josey! Poppa!*

Where was Chaney?

"Chaney?"

She pulled her knees up to her chest and wrapped her arms around them. She was alone in the bedroom. She was alone with her abject terror and her hideous memories. At last she did remember. And she wished she hadn't. She began to rock back and forth. A moan escaped her lips. It came out of her chest, out of her heart. She couldn't seem to stop it.

With her right thumb she found the scar in her left palm. She didn't need to feel for the scar in her left. Instead, she ran her fingertips over the scar on her forehead.

A soldier had shot her. He'd tried to kill her. He'd believed he had killed her. She was sure of that.

Poppa—her father. She hadn't seen what happened to

him. Nor to Josey. Josey—her brother. Noah Rollins. Who was Noah Rollins?

He seemed more familiar than ever. At least she thought he did. She hadn't seen Josey's face. Who was Noah Rollins?

Chills that had nothing to do with the temperature of the room set her shivering. She gathered the quilt around her shoulders and huddled beneath it, rubbing the scars in her palms.

Josey. Poppa. Who was she? Was she really Beth Anne? "Beth Anne—Taggart." No, she hadn't been born Beth Anne Taggart. Taggart was Chaney's name. Even though she'd carried the name most of her life.

Where had Chaney gotten the name Beth Anne?

"Chaney."

He didn't answer. He hadn't slept in twenty-four hours. He was in the tackroom. Except it wasn't a tackroom. It hadn't been one since the first month they'd come to White Oak.

He and Luther, Hardy, and Doc Gunderson had built a big tackroom apart from the stable. It had been like a military tackroom with proper frames for the saddles, pegs for the bridles, boxes and cabinets for the dozens of items needed to care for good horses, treat sick horses, groom and dress fine horses, breed and raise exceptional horses.

They'd moved all their equipment into it and over the years they'd added more and more.

Chaney had turned the old tackroom into his records room, his office, his library, his study. It had a desk, file boxes, chairs, and a cot on which he seldom lay. In this room he could take an occasional rest while waiting for mares to foal.

Tonight he was planning.

Oh, how she wished he were here to drive the horrors away. She needed him. She'd never before had such a dream when he wasn't there to awaken her. For all of the life she could remember when she started screaming, he would waken her and hold her. Since they'd married, he'd made love to her until she settled back to sleep.

Tonight her solitude had allowed the dream to come to its end, and she had learned the identities of the sharers of the dream.

Josey and her poppa. Were they dead? Or alive somewhere? She'd been shot herself. She hadn't seen what happened to them. Did they think she was dead?

Grief and a sense of abandonment added their weight to her overcharged senses.

She rolled over in the bed, pulling the covers tight around her, clenching her fists under her chin, drawing her knees against her chest.

What had they been like, those two shadowy figures? Poppa and Josey? She probed her memory. Nothing.

Why couldn't she remember any more of her life? When something so vivid had come back to her, why didn't she remember everything?

She concentrated, trying to imagine White Oak as it had been fifteen years ago. She tried to imagine herself as a child, before that night. Before Chaney found her.

Chaney. She'd awakened in Chaney's arms. Nothing had been changed by the dream. The whole world was still Chaney Taggart.

She remembered the young man he'd been. He'd saved her. She'd loved him almost from the beginning. And from the beginning of their life together, he'd loved her. No, she'd never lacked for love.

Maybe now that she'd dreamed the dream to the end, she could put it all behind her. Maybe she wouldn't dream it again. That thought comforted her.

Gradually, she began to settle down. Her heartbeat slowed. Her breathing returned to normal. She could feel herself drifting away.

She began to warm beneath the quilts. Chaney loved her. She loved him. When the horses were delivered, she'd tell him what she'd remembered. He would help her find out what had happened. Together they'd find the truth.

The next morning Luther, Hardy, and Beth Anne crowded into the small tackroom. Noah Rollins leaned against the door.

Chaney hadn't shaved in forty-eight hours. His face was gaunt. He'd had too little sleep, too much coffee, too little food. Beth Anne was thoroughly disgusted with him for letting himself get in this condition, but he hadn't come into the house for her to scold.

On the desk he'd unrolled hand-drawn land plats anchored with bricks that kept them from curling up again. On the wall behind him was a map of Missouri.

"Looks like you're plannin' a war, Lieutenant." Luther grinned.

"That's about the size of it, Sergeant." Chaney smiled back. Despite his dilapidated condition, he looked young.

Beth Anne couldn't help but see the perfect understanding that passed between them. The commander was about to give an order and the war-wise sergeant, his friend who'd ridden with him through hell and high water, was about to back him again.

As he rose and straightened his shoulders, she caught a glimpse of the Chaney she hadn't seen in years.

Her husband indicated the map on the wall. "We're going to drive that herd to the Army depot at Fort Leavenworth, Kansas."

Neither Luther nor Hardy seemed surprised, but Noah Rollins pushed away from the wall. "I guess you've thought this through, boss."

Chaney's mouth twisted. He rubbed the back of his hand

against his grizzled jaw. His eyes took on a steely glint. "I surely have, Mr. Rollins. I haven't thought about anything else for the last two days. I know where we can go to do it and how we can go about it."

He waited, but Noah said nothing more. Before he went on, he looked at Beth Anne. She could feel the heat jump between them. He wanted some sign from her.

She grinned, a blush started in her cheeks. A sense of pride welled in her. She was proud of him and pleased that he wanted her approval. But she couldn't say what she wanted in front of the men. Instead, she said, "Thank heavens you've got it worked out. Now maybe you'll come back to bed."

Luther chuckled and slapped his thigh. Hardy choked and ducked his head. Noah Rollins showed no sign that he'd heard.

Chaney nodded. His own grin spread from ear to ear. "Just for one night. We're leaving first thing in the morning."

"All of us?" Beth Anne asked quickly.

"You've got to come too," Chaney said regretfully. "It's a hundred miles the way I've worked it out. I figure two days, three at most, to Kansas City, a half a day to cross the line into Kansas." He looked at Hardy. "Have we got enough supplies?"

Hardy scratched his head. "I'll make do."

Chaney nodded. "Enough ammunition?"

Luther shrugged. "More than enough to take out Barney Mallott."

Noah Rollins had pulled the makings from his pocket and rolled a cigarette. Now he stuck the end in his mouth and struck a match on the door facing.

Chaney met his gaze through a cloud of blue smoke. "Are you with us?"

Noah took another drag and pretended to study the

cobwebs stretched in the corners of the rafters. "You want me to scout ahead?"

"Behind."

"Sounds interesting. What do I get if I don't get killed?"

"What do you want?"

Surprisingly, Noah looked at Luther. "I'll think of something."

Chapter Eight

At four o'clock the next morning, Beth Anne held on to her husband for dear life. She was trembling, her teeth chattering with excitement and chill.

"Don't you be afraid," he cautioned. "With any luck we'll be gone twenty-four hours before anyone knows it."

She shook her head. "Barney Mallott will know before then. He's going to come after us."

"Let him come." He tightened his jaw. She could see the muscle jump in the lamplight. He dropped a kiss on her forehead, then pressed his cheek against it.

Even with his arms tight around her, she couldn't stop shivering. She wasn't cold. Instead, every nerve in her body seemed to be vibrating. She didn't fool herself that this was an adventure. It was serious and it wasn't going to be easy.

He stepped back. "Drink your coffee. Eat a handful of Hardy's flapjacks. And stick on Luther's tail like a burr."

"And where will you be?"

"Noah and I are going on a little hunting expedition."

"Oh, no! Chaney."

He pulled his hat down tight on his head. She realized it wasn't the one he usually wore. Instead it was his old campaign hat with the tarnished gold cord and acorns on the brim. "Don't worry, honey," he said with a grin. "We're just going to reconnoiter. Know our enemy up close."

She searched his face, then drew back her fist and punched him in the arm. "You're enjoying this."

His eyes crinkled at the corners. "I'd be lying if I said I wasn't."

"They're gonna be gone, Barney." Eustace Fisher's voice was hoarse after sleeping on the damp ground.

The marshal chuckled. "They're still there. Hollis would've been back with the word if they'd moved. Anyway it don't matter if they are. If Chaney Taggart's taken his horses off to find another railroad, we'll take that little gal of his. For her own protection, don't y'know? He can pay us for takin' care of her."

At the head of his men, he rode down the lane as the first pink of dawn streaked the horizon.

"She was with him yesterday," Eustace said to no one in particular. "Her and that friend of hers, Luther Tibbet's little girl."

Barney growled something unintelligible as he swung down from his horse. He motioned for them to dismount and follow him up the front steps of White Oak.

"Now!" he yelled.

With a snarl he kicked the front door in. Etched glass shattered as it crashed against wall.

He blundered into the parlor, followed by his men. When they stopped moving around, only silence greeted them.

"Told you so," Eustace remarked.

Barney exploded. "How in hell did they get by Hollis and Sylvester? Goddamn!" He fumbled till he found a lamp, lighted it, and turned round and round. Nothing. He could have cried. Instead, he screamed. "Search the goddam place from top to bottom! Find that money!"

Fuming, his hands twitching, his mouth working, he strode from room to room, striking matches, finding lamps, wreaking havoc.

Like men possessed, they kicked tables and chairs across the rooms, pulled out all the drawers, turned over the armoires and cedar chests, tore up the rugs.

As fine furniture was scarred and splintered, the marshal kicked at it some more. This should have been his. They'd robbed him of it. They wouldn't have any of it now that he could have his way.

The sun was fairly up when at last the crew stood panting in the living room, and Barney had to face the bitter truth. The gold and the cash money from the White Oak bank weren't there.

Chaney Taggart had been too smart for him. He'd taken it with him and his women too. Barney clenched his fists and kicked at a marble-top table. The polished stone broke away from the mahogany base and crashed to the floor.

Almost insane with fury, he caught up the lamp and thudded into the bedroom.

Sheets, pillows, handmade quilts, and down mattresses had been jerked from the bed and slung into a pile in the middle of the floor. Heading straight for it, he raised the coal-oil lamp above his head.

"I think you've had about enough fun for one night, Barn."

He swung around. "Hell and damnation. I'm just beginning."

Eustace Fisher stood in the doorway, his gun drawn but

still aimed at the floor. "Nope. You're finished here. Just blow it out and let's go."

Eustace wouldn't shoot him. The old soldier wasn't man enough to shoot. Mallott considered dropping the lamp anyway, calling Eustace's bluff.

Eustace grinned. His unshaven cheeks and snaggled teeth stained brown from tobacco made him look tough as any border outlaw. "Go ahead. Nobody'll ever know how you got caught in your own fire. Must've splattered that coal-oil all over you."

"You got no stake in this," the marshal argued.

"You got no reason to be here," Eustace countered. He raised the barrel of the gun a few inches. Another couple and he'd have the marshal in his sights.

Mallott shivered at the light in the steady eyes. Carefully, he eased back off the bedding and set the lamp on the floor beside the washstand.

Eustace spun the pistol once and let it slip back into his holster. "That's a good move, Barney. That way neither one of us does something he might regret later. You might thank me for saving your life. You know you'd never live past the end of the week if you burned this house down."

Still, Barney hesitated. The truth was hard to swallow, but he knew Eustace was right. He kicked futilely at the pile of bedding.

"That's enough, Barney." Eustace jerked his head toward the door. "Now let's get the hell out of here."

With Luther leading the way, the herd headed due west to the railroad tracks. Beth Anne stuck to his tail like a burr. Mary Nell rode beside her. The moon was a pale crescent on the horizon with the morning star in its tip.

"Until we get north of Rich Hill, we won't trespass on anybody's land," Chaney had ordered. "Once out of Bates

County, there's plenty of empty country. We shouldn't damage anything."

As they rode, she was aware of the noise they were making. Two hundred horses plus a dozen riders and two wagons loaded with supplies and equipment sounded like an army moving through the quiet countryside.

Twice she heard a dog bay. Once a light went on in a farmhouse. People couldn't help but know something was passing through.

"Sleeping like babies," Noah whispered.

"No reason not to." Chaney's tone was ironic. "They've got the law on their side."

Despite the darkness, they could make out the silhouettes of two horses tethered to the fenceline. Two mounds formed by bedrolls and sleeping men lay beneath a tree, their feet to a fire that still glowed faintly.

"Ready?"

"Ready."

Chaney made a movement with his hand. Together the men crept forward. Chaney went down on one knee beside the nearest bedroll and prodded it with his gun. Noah crouched beside the other.

The man stirred and grunted.

"Time to get up, fellas," Chaney commanded in his lieutenant's voice.

"What the hell—?" The second man sat bolt upright in his blankets. "Hollis! Wake up!"

Noah jabbed the muzzle of his .44 against the man's cheek. "Don't say another word. Just listen and do what we say."

"Wha's matter, Sylvester?" his companion murmured sleepily.

Chaney nudged his ribs. "Reveille, Hollis. Time to ride."

With no fuss at all, the two were soon mounted on their horses, their hands tied behind them. Noah and Chaney led them at a wild gallop east. For miles they kept the horses at a breakneck pace.

Finally, as dawn was breaking, they halted.

At Chaney's orders, the men were untied and climbed down. "Give me your boots."

"Aw, hell," the one called Sylvester groaned. "You ain't gonna put us afoot without boots."

" 'Fraid so." Chaney motioned with his gun. "You have a choice. No boots or a hole in your foot. I've seen the results of both. I recommend barefoot. It takes just as long to walk back, but you know you won't bleed to death."

While Sylvester was cussing and complaining, his companion took off his boots and handed them up.

"Thank you, sir. Take it easy. Twenty-four hours is all we need."

"I'll sure take my time," Hollis said. "Damn Barney Mallott anyway. He done just about wrecked the whole damn town."

Sylvester continued to cuss—including Hollis in his diatribe.

Noah Rollins heeled the gray mare in close. "You want me to knock his teeth out, Lieutenant?"

"Only if he doesn't hand you his boots on three. One—"

Sylvester dropped like a stone and began to tug.

Chaney and Noah rode for more than a mile before they halted the horses to rest and blow. Chaney took each boot and flung it as far as he could throw it in a different direction.

"We'll tie the horses back at the campsite. With any luck, whoever Barney sends to relieve this pair will spend an hour or two looking for them before he even reports them missing."

Noah shifted in the saddle. "You think real good, Lieutenant."

Chaney bared his teeth in a swift grin. "I hope so."

Shortly after noon the next day, the marshal found the slow-moving pair. While Hollis kept his mouth firmly shut, Sylvester told a lengthy tale.

"He's headed east," Barney howled. "That damned son-of-a-bitch."

"How ya figger that, Barn?" Eustace Fisher leaned one arm on the saddlehorn and scratched his rump with the other.

" 'Cause he took these boys east."

"Seems like if he'd been heading east, he'd've took 'em west."

Barney thumped his chest and jabbed his forefinger toward his temple. "That's what he wants us to think. That's what he's thinkin' I'll be thinkin'. But I'm too smart. I know how that shavetail thinks. He wants me to head west while he goes east."

"Leavenworth, Kansas, is west of here," Eustace murmured to the man next to him.

"He'd never dare cross into Kansas. Not till he has to. That's Jayhawk country. Them boys got long memories. No. He's headed for Clinton over in Henry County." Barney climbed on his horse. "Come on, boys. The quicker we make it back to town, the quicker I can send a telegraph. I got me a friend in Clinton that'll hold Chaney Taggart till I get there."

Eustace remained behind as Barney led the other four men including Sylvester and Hollis back toward Rich Hill at a gallop. He stared long and hard at the tracks on the ground. With a click of his tongue, he walked his horse in wide circle. At one point he leaned far out of the saddle to study the grass at the edge of the road. Then he spat a stream of tobacco juice into the crushed foliage and followed Barney.

Even though he wasn't getting paid, he purely enjoyed watching the marshal make a fool out of himself.

The railroad bed was gravelly and sloping. By pushing the herd all night, the men had covered more than sixty miles.

Where the railroad trestle crossed the swift-running Marais des Cygnes River, Chaney called a halt. By his calculations they were about halfway to the Cass County line. He didn't know for sure whether Barney Mallott had a friend in Cass County, but he intended to act as if the marshal did.

Cass County lay directly north of Bates. Together with Jackson and Vernon they had been the battlegrounds of the infamous Order No. 11. Since all Southern sympathizers had been forced out over a decade ago, the chances of finding an honest town marshal or county sheriff were slim.

By driving his horses along beside the tracks, Chaney was trespassing on no one's land except the railroad's. Since the main offices miles were away in Kansas City, St. Louis, and Chicago, his herd would be long gone before anyone heard of his passage.

Now at noon the horses were stumbling and lagging. The men had changed mounts twice and were themselves fagged out.

Wearily, Chaney climbed down. He could feel his legs trembling under him. Never had he felt so used up and old.

Hell! He wasn't old. He just wasn't used to waging a campaign anymore. He wasn't used to staying up for forty-eight hours straight, planning and preparing, starting out at four o'clock in the morning, and then reconnoitering all over the countryside for another day and a half.

He straightened his shoulders and loosened the girth on his horse. Before he could move to his mount's head to pull the bit out of its mouth, Beth Anne was there beside him.

"Why don't you take a rest, honey? Mary Nell's making some coffee and passing out some biscuits and jerky. I'll take care of the horse."

He started to object. He really did. Then he ran his hand over his chin. He could feel the beard, sharp as boars' bristles. He could imagine it—mostly black, but with a few white hairs beginning to appear. The last time he'd chanced to catch himself in the mirror, he'd thought his cheeks looked sunken. His eyes probably looked like two burned holes in a blanket. He sure wasn't any ladies' delight.

He nodded. "I'll be first in line for the coffee."

Swiftly, Beth Anne glanced around her, then rose on her tiptoes. Her lips brushed his just a swift feather touch. He closed his eyes to hide the way her tenderness unmanned him. It always had. It always would.

While she led his mount to the water, he stretched out on the sloping riverbank. A water oak spread refreshingly cool shade above him. When she came back with coffee, he drank the first cup in one draft. Now he rested the second on his belly, which grumbled for lack of food.

He didn't have time to listen to his belly. Twenty more miles to push today. Miami Creek was his goal. In his mind he kept reviewing the plan.

Were Hardy's wagons getting through? The cook was an old campaigner. With wagons outfitted to look like drummers' goods, he was supposed to follow the back roads to Altona, then turn west to meet up with the drive at the line.

The plan was to drive into Cass County and camp for the evening and early nighttime hours. Under cover of early morning darkness, they would move on north toward Kansas City.

With good luck, Barney Mallott would be hunting all over the eastern side of the county, trying to prove how smart he was and how he couldn't be outfoxed. If the luck was bad, then Barney had located the wagons and had arrested Hardy.

If luck was terrible, Barney had located the wagons without being observed and was following their trail at a distance, pretty sure that they were leading him to Chaney and the herd.

Chaney rubbed the warm coffee cup over his stomach. It ached—more from nerves than anything else. He had to get these horses to Leavenworth. His whole world counted on it.

Beth Anne ran her hand down Chaney's horse's foreleg. Her nerves thrummed. She could feel a distinct swelling just above the fetlock. She lifted the hoof. A stone had lodged under the shoe.

"Rusty."

The hand saw the problem immediately. Pulling his pocketknife, he worked the granite loose and cleaned the rest of the hoof.

"It's bad, isn't it?" she asked, already knowing the answer.

He nodded. "He needs a new shoe. Hardy's got the spares in the wagon, but the boss won't want to take the time. And anyway, this'n can't carry no weight for a while."

"Is there a horse other than the sorrel?"

Rusty scratched his head. "Oh, prob'ly, but the boss won't want to ride it."

She shook her head. She hated to see Chaney on that horse again.

"You done been fooled, Barney," Eustace opined. "We done rode nearly to Clinton."

After sending the telegram in Rich Hill, Mallott had gotten fresh horses and ridden north and east. When his mounts were so tired that drummers' wagons loped past him, he'd signaled his men to halt. Now he looked around in helpless frustration. "Shut your mouth, Eustace," he snarled. "You don't know nothin' about nothin'."

"Then I'd still be ahead of you." The old soldier wallowed the plug of tobacco to the front of his mouth and spat. "You gone off half-cocked again. No wonder you never made nothin' but private."

"Did too." Barney reined his horse round and spurred him toward Eustace's mount.

Eustace guided his mount aside. "You never made lieutenant," he said with heavy irony. "He's probably out of the county by now."

"The hell he is."

"The hell he ain't. He headed west cross country back where he caught Sylvester and Hollis. You'd've seen his tracks if you hadn't been so damn busy tryin' to think."

Mallott's hand flashed to his gun, but Eustace was quicker. "Don't pull it, Barn. You'll never make it. I figure Chaney Taggart's no more'n a day from Kansas City. From there Fort Leavenworth's an easy lope."

Mallott's face was fiery red as he led his men galloping back to Rich Hill. He had one chance. It was a long one, but he didn't have anything to lose.

The only way to stop Chaney Taggart was to meet him outside Kansas City. And the only way to do that was to take the train.

He'd get some money from Drorsen and go alone. Let the town council pay for his ticket. He'd sneak into town and get that money back. Drorsen wouldn't ask any questions so long as the money was back. And if Barney Mallott deposited it in his name, then that was all right too.

He put his hand over the marshal's star on his chest a little regretfully. He hadn't worn it long, but he couldn't get sentimental in his old age.

He tried to concentrate on what was good about going on alone. At least he wouldn't have to contend with Eustace Fisher.

A red-tailed hawk swooped down to take a rabbit stirred up by the resting, grazing herd. The hawk was as swift and deadly as a bullet, and the kill was never in doubt. As the raptor's great wings carried it away, the small creature, stunned by the attack, hung limp from the merciless talons.

Beth Anne shuddered. She wasn't usually so squeamish. After all, this was nature's way of things. Hawks had to eat. Rabbits took their chances.

A minute later, she spied Chaney coming around the bend in Miami Creek. He'd been gone nearly half an hour, scouting along the bank searching for a more likely place to cross than the slick rock banks beneath the railroad trestle.

She heaved a sigh. Even as used to riding as she was, her muscles ached abominably and she had some sore spots in unmentionable places. With a full day and a half still to go, she could count on blisters at the end of the trail.

She wished he'd sent another man. Her husband looked

about worn slick from nearly forty-eight hours of plans
and preparations before he even began his lightning rides
across the countryside. She knew he had to be exhausted,
yet she knew a part of him was enjoying the whole campaign. Despite the worry and the danger, meeting the
challenge thrilled him. It made him feel young again.

A centaur, the half-man, half-horse she'd seen pictured
in Gayley's book of Greek myths, must have moved the
way Chaney rode the sorrel stallion. Back straight, jaw
square, head up, heels down, her husband rode as if he
still had his bars on his shoulders. As long and hard as the
horse had been pushed, it still stamped and champed at
the bit like a cavalry mount on dress parade.

Suddenly, she knew why he'd picked the sorrel and rode
it in defiance of everyone's objections. They were alike,
the two of them, in their indomitable spirit. But, oh, how
different they were in temperament.

She hoped this trip would make or break the stallion
for Chaney. Either the animal would become convinced
to cooperate and obey commands, or her husband would
have to give in and get rid of it.

Chaney galloped up to Luther, twisted in the saddle,
and gestured over his shoulder. Luther nodded in
agreement. The stallion champed and mouthed the bit.

"Let's move 'em, boys," Luther called.

Chaney touched spurs to the stallion's flanks and guided
him at a gallop around the loosely bunched horses. Again
the big horse showed his skill, snaking around the herd,
bunching them more tightly, finally strutting out ahead to
lead them across the meadow.

Beth Anne reached over and shook Mary Nell's shoulder. "Time to move."

"Oh, no. I can't do it. I'm one solid bruise from my
ankle to my tailbone."

"I'm the same. At least we'll know never to want to do

something like this again. Let the men have their way. They want to handle it without us, we'll let 'em.''

Mary Nell pushed herself up to her elbows and looked around. "Right. After this I just may put on skirts for the rest of my life."

Chaney pulled his horse aside and waited while the herd crossed. A bit anxiously, he looked around for Hardy's wagons. Though he'd left strips of rag on the railroad trestle, an arrow shaped of rocks on the ground, and another strip tied to a tree where they'd crossed the creek, he wanted Hardy to catch up with him. He didn't like to think what Mallott would do to the old cook.

And Hardy was too stubborn ever to tell something he didn't want the marshal to know. Chaney stood in his stirrups to look around. No sign yet.

The last stragglers were wading up the bank on the north side. Time to go himself. He guided the stallion down the gentle slope.

The horse dropped his head and tugged at the bit.

"Want a drink, boy?" Chaney let the reins slide through his fingers.

And all hell broke lose.

The horse bowed his thick neck and kicked out behind him. Already headed downhill, he lost his footing. Over the animal went.

"Chaney!"

He heard Beth Anne scream. Then his body slammed into the water face first. He tried to kick free, tried to throw himself aside to escape the huge animal.

His effort was futile. The horse's body toppled over on top of him, pinning his right leg between the saddle and the limestone creek bottom.

"Chaney!"

"Gawd! Lieutenant!"

"Boss!"

"Help him. Oh, dear Lord!"

The force had driven the air from his body. Automatically, he tried to breathe. Water rushed into his lungs. He choked. He had to get out from under the horse. It was writhing, struggling, kicking. The saddle broke. His thigh was crushed beneath it.

The creek wasn't more than a couple of feet deep. He twisted halfway round, got his arms under him, and pushed himself up. His face broke water. He tried to spit, tried to draw in a breath.

Beth Anne came wading toward him, struggling, her clothes dragging her back. Her face was white, her expression terrified. He didn't dare wave to her to show that he was going to be all right even though the horse was still whipsawing back and forth on his leg. He needed all the strength of his arms to pull him out from under.

A flailing hoof caught him on the back of the head. He slipped beneath the water again as everything went black.

Luther Tibbets rolled off his horse into the creek and grabbed for the stallion's head. The animal grunted, neighed, and tried to bite him. "Goddamn son-of-a—"

"Get back!" Noah Rollins had ridden his mare into the fast-moving water.

Luther stepped back, lost his footing, fell sprawling. The stones of the creekbed were polished smooth.

Rusty Huff galloped his horse into the water full tilt, splashing everything and everybody.

The stallion screamed shrilly.

Noah Rollins snaked a loop out of its coil and dropped it over the sorrel's head.

"Hurry! Oh, hurry!" Beth Anne screamed. She fell to her knees beside Chaney. Kneeling in the water up to her chin, she caught hold of his shoulders. He was too heavy for her to lift even without being pinned down in fast-moving water, yet somehow she managed to pull him up. His head lolled. She wasn't tall enough to clear his face.

Rusty rolled off his horse and waded around the flailing legs to grab hold of the tail. Heaving with all his might while Noah urged Babe back downstream, they managed to get the sorrel up.

While Noah pulled the furious, fighting horse up onto the bank, Luther floundered to Beth Anne's side and grabbed Chaney around the waist. Together they managed to get his head above water.

Rusty caught hold of his boss's legs and lifted.

Together the three of them labored toward the bank with his inert body.

Other White Oak riders had joined the melee. Two took hold of his arms, relieving Beth Anne.

To her the stream seemed wide as a river, wide as a lake. The ocean, if she had ever seen it, couldn't be wider than the stretch of water they had to cover to get her husband up on dry land.

At last they stretched him out beneath a tree and gathered round.

"Leave him on his belly," Luther instructed. "Come on, boys, head downhill." The veteran of many a campaign turned his lieutenant's head and ran a gnarled finger down his throat. Water ran out over Luther's hand. Then he straddled Chaney's ribs and pushed.

More water gushed out.

Hot tears mixed with the water on Beth Anne's cheeks. She covered her face with her hands. She couldn't breathe. Her whole world was turning black. Dimly, she felt Mary Nell's arms around her shoulders.

No one made a sound as more riders joined the circle of anxious faces. Luther pushed again. Not so much water ran out this time. Again. Again.

Chaney coughed.

Everyone let out his breath.

"Oh, Chaney. Thank God," Beth Anne moaned softly.

Luther turned him on his side. "Lieutenant, can you hear me?"

Slowly, Chaney nodded. His eyes were still closed. At last he blinked them open.

Beth Anne caught his hand and pressed it against her breast. "Chaney, say something to me. Please."

"—all right," he whispered. Then he coughed. More water ran out of his mouth. "Swallowed—"

" 'Bout half the creek, Lieutenant," Rusty said. "If we'd known you's gonna drink it dry, we'd've waited to cross."

Everybody laughed.

Beth Anne moved so she could slide her thigh under his cheek. She brushed his hair back from his forehead. To the encircling men, she said, "Let's build a fire. About half of us need to dry out."

Four of them were sopping wet. Others were damp partway up their legs. Fire was a good idea.

They scattered to gather wood.

Chaney lay with his head in Beth Anne's lap. She bent over him. "Are you all right?"

"Too soon to tell," he whispered. She watched him as he pressed his hand against his hip, then down his thigh. He caught his lip between his teeth. His face contorted.

"What?"

He shook his head.

Noah returned with an armload of wood. Dropping it, he knelt at Chaney's feet. "Want me to pull your boots off, boss?"

Chaney set his jaw. "Yeah."

As Noah's hands closed around the toe and heel, Chaney bit his lip. The boot was filled with water and tight. Noah had to work it back and forth. By the time it came free,

Chaney had broken out in a sweat. Beth Anne wiped the perspiration away with her bandanna.

"Is it sprained?" she asked him.

Chaney stared up at her with shocked eyes. "I think it's broken."

By the time Hardy arrived, they'd dried out their clothing and made Chaney as comfortable as he could be on and under everybody's saddle blankets.

Beth Anne ran to meet the cook's wagons and walked beside the one driven by Doc Gunderson as she explained what had happened. The doctor shook his head over the accident. "Is any bone poking through?"

"No. But it's crooked midway down the thigh."

Gunderson made a sympathetic clicking sound. "He's going to hurt over this one."

The fact that Hardy and Doc had gotten past Mallott relieved the entire camp. As the daylight faded, the prospect of hot coffee and a hot meal cheered them.

They set about gathering more firewood, and soon the makings of a meal were under way.

Doc Gunderson insisted on bathing Chaney's leg in hot water and soap even though the skin hadn't broken. Then he took the white oak splints he'd cut for emergencies and got down to the worst part. "Maybe you and Mary Nell'd better walk away," he suggested.

"Go on, honey," Chaney said as she was shaking her head. "You don't need to hear me holler. When you get back, I'll need you in the worst way."

She rose and took Mary Nell's hand. "If it'll make you feel better."

She walked a few steps out of his range.

Doc looked at her accusingly, but she shook her head. She had no intention of walking away. Luther and Rusty knelt and held Chaney's shoulders. Doc felt for the place. He looked into the eyes of his friends.

They were all old. Suddenly, he shook his head. "Come here, boy," he called to Noah.

Noah came.

"Son, I don't know if I've got the strength for this anymore. I want you to put your hands over mine. When I start to pull, you pull too. We'll get this done the quickest and easiest on him."

Noah nodded.

Beth Anne hid her face in Mary Nell's shoulder. Every man tensed.

"Ready," Gunderson nodded to Luther and Rusty. He looked into Chaney's eyes.

"Do it."

"Yes, sir, Lieutenant."

The four pulled together.

Chaney flung his arm across his face. His howl of agony trailed away to a sobbing groan.

Beth Anne stumbled forward and sank down behind him. Sympathetic pain racked her. She slipped her arms around his shoulders. He turned his face into her lap and held on tight.

Gunderson felt along Chaney's thigh with both hands until he was certain the bone had slipped back into place. At last he nodded. "That's the worst of it, son."

Everyone breathed a sigh of relief—

Except Beth Anne. She could feel her husband shivering. The sun was setting. His clothing was still wet. He'd nearly drowned. He hadn't had anything to eat or drink. She placed her hand over his heart as if she were comforting him. The uneven beat nearly scared her to death.

Holding her breath, tears trickling down her cheeks, she cradled his head and shoulders while Doc wrapped the leg in cotton flannel and splinted it from groin to ankle.

Hardy brought them hot coffee laced with whiskey, and then hot stew. Despite Beth Anne's coaxing, Chaney ate only a few bites. His teeth were set, and from time to time he flexed his hands. She could only imagine how much he must be hurting. And worse—how were they going to get him back home without half killing him?

Finally, Doc sat back on his haunches with his hands on his thighs. "That's as good as I can do it, Lieutenant."

"It's fine, Doc. Feels good." Chaney was lying and they all knew it. Except for the few watching the herd, the White Oak men sat or stood around waiting for direction.

When Chaney held out his cup for more, Hardy came forward with the coffeepot and the whiskey bottle. "Half and half," Chaney ordered.

He drank it down, then looked up at Beth Anne. "This is a hell of a mess."

She bent to kiss his forehead. "A hell of a mess."

"I guess you were right about the stallion."

She wiped at her cheeks. "I wish I hadn't been."

He ran a hand across the lower half of his face. His eyes were drooping. "I've got to have some sleep. Just a couple of hours—maybe three—should do me fine." He squeezed her hand. "Will you stay awake for me?"

Nothing had ever pleased her more than that simple request. "You know I will."

"Good." His gaze shifted restlessly. "Luther. Noah."

"What you need, Lieutenant?" Luther went down on one knee at his feet.

Chaney's eyes were closing, his voice trailing away. "Tell everybody to get to sleep. Tired horses shouldn't wander far. Wake at four. Just like yesterday. We'll move."

"But, Lieutenant—"

"Noah—"

"Here, boss."

"Back Luther up on point. Ride the stallion. He's a nasty son-of-a-bitch, but he'll herd 'em practically on his own." His eyes closed. His head slipped to the side.

Beth Anne, Luther, and Noah looked at each other across his limp body.

Luther shook his head. "Smartest, bravest man I ever knew."

Beth Anne covered her mouth to stifle her sobs.

Noah Rollins turned on his heel and stalked off into the dark.

Chapter Nine

"At least ride in the wagon." Beth Anne spoke slowly, measuring each word and biting it off. If she didn't, her fury and frustration would spill out in a scream.

Spots of high color blazed in Chaney's cheeks. His lips were dry and cracked. He seemed determined to kill himself. "Honey, no. Rigging a drag behind the wagon's worse for me. At least with me on the horse, I'll be able to see where he's stepping and keep him level."

"And oversee the herd as well," she all but snarled. "I didn't mean ride on a drag. I meant ride *in* the wagon."

"I'll ride your mare," he bargained. "She's like a rocking chair. And I can stop when it gets to hurting too bad."

"You shouldn't be doing any of this. You know you shouldn't."

He looked around significantly. "We really don't have much choice. It's fifty miles to the nearest hospital."

"Your leg will be crooked for the rest of your life," she wailed.

"I'll look more like a veteran then." He tried to grin. "It's been hell convincing people that I went through the war without a scratch."

She'd had enough. This wasn't anything to joke about. "No. I won't have it. I absolutely won't." She jumped to her feet and stood over him. "You can sit up on the damn wagon seat and watch for bumps while Hardy drives, but if you don't ride *in* that wagon, I'll take a gun and start a stampede, so there won't be any damned horses to drive."

Chaney blinked. He looked to his foreman for support.

Luther shrugged. "She's most likely right about the leg, Lieutenant. Doc don't have no plaster to set it. Them splints'll work if you take it easy. Curved over a horse's back, you'll come out crooked."

"Luther!" Chaney protested.

"Hardy," Beth Anne called. "Clean out a place in your wagon. We'll lift him into it. I want everybody's blankets and bedrolls. We've got to keep him still. Anybody who doesn't want his heavy coat, leave it with me. We'll use them for cover."

"Now, honey, that's not necessary—"

The men hopped to obey her orders. Chaney finally gave up cussing and ordering when he discovered no one was paying him any mind.

"I'm going to fire the lot of you," he promised direly as six of them gathered around to grasp the edge of his blankets.

"I'll hire you right back," Beth Anne promised from behind him. "Unless he divorces me. In which case I'll make the judge give me the farm and I'll need all the hands to run it."

The men tucked their heads to hide their grins. Rusty didn't even bother. He went so far as to chuckle.

"Beth Anne!" Chaney's eyes blazed. His face was unnaturally red. Already he was running a fever. She prayed it didn't go into his lungs. "When I catch you—"

She put her hands under his head. "Your leg will have to heal before you can even take out after me." To the men she said, "Ready. One. Two. Three."

They laid him on the tailgate, and Beth Anne scrambled inside to help him get comfortable. Just the act of being moved had hurt him more than he cared to admit. Moving on his own was excruciating. He found that not only was his leg hurting so much he thought for a minute he'd pass out, but his back was aching too.

He wouldn't tell his wife. She'd have something else to keep him down about, but he was pretty sure he'd done some damage just above his hips. All in all, he guessed he was pretty lucky to be alive.

Hardy had cleared out a space plenty wide. He'd spread three bedrolls one on top of the other and tucked the others on either side of Chaney's shoulders and hips, so he wouldn't jostle against the boxes and chests of foodstuffs and cooking utensils, horseshoes and smithy equipment, tack and veterinary supplies. He felt a little like a side of beef himself because the cook had done such a good job. Hardy was an expert at organizing the half a hundred different items necessary to take along on even a short trail drive.

Still protesting, Chaney crawled inside. When he finally settled down, his whole body was throbbing and wringing wet with perspiration.

At his head Beth Anne lowered herself like an Indian with legs crossed. She leaned forward and pulled the blankets up.

"Lord God, I'm hot enough to fry in here," he protested.

"You'll cool down in a few minutes," she replied.

He eased back and scowled up at her. "You've got me

where you want me. Now get on out of here. Go ride herd
if you're so determined."

She looked hurt. But she pulled out a pocket handkerchief and wiped the sweat from his face and neck. "Would
you like another drink of whiskey?"

"No." He was dying for one, but he didn't want to drink
it in front of her. She'd know he was in pain.

"Are you hurting too badly?"

"I'm fine. Get on out of here so we can get this drive
started." He closed his eyes. If he'd made her cry, he didn't
want to see the tears. He wasn't going to admit a thing.

She bent to kiss his forehead. Her lips were soft and so
tender. He could feel all his carefully nurtured resentment
melting. "Oh, Chaney," she whispered. "I hate to see you
hurting."

Her lips brushed his temple, his cheekbone, the tip of
his nose.

"Quit that," he whispered, not meaning his protest at
all.

"In a minute." Her mouth touched his.

Somehow she managed to eel her way down his left side
until she lay pressed tight against him. Taking his face
between her palms, she kissed him with her mouth and
tongue. Her passion was restrained, not the wholehearted,
excited love he was used to, but the desire was there and
all the more exciting because she held back, afraid of
hurting him. The very necessity of restraint set his pulse
pounding.

The kiss went on and on until he felt himself stirring
despite his pain. His left arm was pinned against his side,
but he pulled her tighter with his right.

They were both shuddering when she raised her head.
"Honey," he begged. "You sure can't be meaning to quit."

She kissed his chin. "I've got to take a herd of horses
to Fort Leavenworth. You lie here and heal."

She got her feet under her, stepped onto Hardy's boxes, and climbed out over the wagon seat.

He uttered a heartfelt curse as the cook released the brake and slapped the reins over the team's back.

Mary Nell caught up to Noah at the front of the herd. The sorrel had let up on his usual antics. Two hard days of constant travel, many miles at a gallop or a run, plus the fall into the creek had worn him down. Still, he laid back his ears when she guided her gelding alongside.

"If that horse is giving you trouble, you can always trade it for something else."

Noah tightened his grip on the sorrel's reins. "He's a handful. No mistake about that. But I won't take any guff. Taggart was always testing him, hoping he'd be better than he is. The only thing to do with him is geld him."

Mary Nell flushed at the language. Her comment about the horse had been a way to explain why she'd caught up and was riding along beside Noah. She certainly hadn't come to discuss it. "I guess we're in Cass County now."

He shot her a sidewise glance. "We've been in Cass since before sunup. We'd be nearly out of Cass into Jackson if Taggart hadn't been so damn stubborn. Those two wagons ought to be trotting along the road through the big towns instead of slowing us to a crawl."

Mary Nell pressed her lips together in a straight line. What had gotten his craw so full? She couldn't seem to find a safe topic. "I'm kind of glad, if you want to know the truth. Yesterday about killed me. And I know Beth Anne must be nearly dead too—"

Noah didn't reply.

"—what with all that riding and then worrying herself sick over Chaney."

"He's sure got her trained. Just like a bitch dog." Noah's

bitterness spewed out as he swept the horizon with his hot stare.

Mary Nell gasped. She looked around in alarm, half expecting the whole countryside to turn from green to brown. Then she recovered herself. "That's just not true. Beth Anne isn't anybody's b-bitch dog. She's—she tells Chaney what to do more times than not."

"Then maybe she's just playing him for a fool."

Mary Nell leaned across and caught Noah by the arm. "You take that back. Do you hear me?" She shook him angrily. Her fingernails dug into his shirt. "Beth Anne really loves Chaney. Really loves him. He's all she's got, and she's all he's got too. Neither one of them has any family. If you think because she's twenty-one and he's thirty-five—"

"That don't make a bit of difference." Suddenly, Noah smiled. "I'm nigh thirty and you're how old? Nineteen?"

She broke off her tirade. She could feel a blush rising in her cheeks. Hastily, she pulled her hand away and rested it on the horn. "Just about."

"You and me—we fit together fine." He smiled in that way he had that made the skin on her arms prickle.

She tried to act like she was mad about what he'd said. He shouldn't have said it. But it was exactly what she wanted to hear, what she'd ridden up beside him to hear. She'd just never expected to hear it. She had to say something. All she was able to do was whisper, "I don't know about that."

He put his hand over her hand. "If we weren't out here smack-dab in front of God and everybody, I'd make you know it."

As the wagon jolted and swayed, Chaney tried to brace himself against the sides of the boxes. He couldn't manage it. His splinted leg rolled; the bruised muscles around the broken bone tried to keep it steady but only hurt it worse.

He tried stuffing more bedrolls around it. The increased pressure seemed to cut off the circulation. His foot went to sleep, so he had to pull his feet out.

His back had long since become one long throbbing ache that started at the base of his spine and surged upward in waves to his skull.

How many times had he heard men screaming inside the ambulances as they clattered back from the battlefield? He'd thought they were screaming from their wounds. Now he knew the wounds were only the beginning.

How much longer?

The eastern sun shone brightly against the canvas. They'd been traveling three, maybe four hours.

How many more miles?

He tried to calculate the distance across Cass County. Twenty-five miles as the crow flew.

He gasped and reached for the top of his thigh as the wagon bed tilted up and then dropped with a crunching jolt on the other side of what Chaney calculated must have been a boulder. The pain made him want to puke. It also alerted him to the fact that he was about to piss in his pants. "God damn!"

"I'm doing the best I can, Lieutenant." Hardy stuck his homely face through the pucker hole in the Conestoga wagon. "Yuh want me to stop for a while?"

"No." The bed of the wagon tilted backward as the horses pulled the wheel over another rock. "Yes!" He shouted the word. "Yes." He whispered it. "You're going to have to stop."

"Good enough, Lieutenant." Hardy pulled back on the reins. The horses halted immediately. The wagon was still.

Chaney's whole body went limp. His mind went mercifully blank. He heard Hardy's preparations, the rumble of his voice, but he couldn't bring himself to care about any of that. He only knew that his leg and back had gone past throbbing to pounding, and the pounding echoed in his temples.

Not only was he wet with perspiration, but his blankets were damp too. The wagon was going to be unpleasantly hot in the afternoon sun. He needed to drink water.

But all he wanted was whiskey. Something to kill his pain.

"Lieutenant?" Hardy had opened the tailgate.

Chaney raised his head. "Just pull me out of here and I'll manage."

Hardy scratched his head. "We sure didn't think about that. I could've laid you crossways at the back and—"

"Just do it."

When he'd finished, Hardy uncorked the whiskey and poured an ounce into a tin cup.

"Make it three," Chaney ordered recklessly.

Hardy shook his head. "I'm sure sorry, Lieutenant. I swear—"

Chaney waved his hand. "I'm going to sell that horse to a glue factory in Kansas City."

"Now you're talkin'."

Chaney drank deeply. The whiskey hit the back of his throat like acid. He hadn't realized he was desperately thirsty. He began to cough.

Immediately, Hardy dipped water from the barrel tied to the wagon and handed it to him.

He drank, poured some into his whiskey, and drank the diluted whiskey. That was better. He could feel a measure of relief.

A rider came tearing back to the wagon. Chaney tried to straighten his body, tried to look alert. Whoever had come to see about him didn't need to see him weak.

"Beth Anne!" He stared incredulously as she galloped

past the wagon, turned the horse on a dime, and walked him back.

She was riding the sorrel stallion.

Chaney went hot and cold by turns. Anger and fear left him shaking, the whiskey and water slopping over his hand. "Have you lost your mind?"

She climbed down and came to the stallion's head. Her hand slipped beneath the cheekstrap to lead him.

"Watch out!" Chaney tried to roll off the tailgate. Hardy grabbed him by the shoulders and held him back. "For God's sake. Watch his teeth. He'll take your hand off."

She shook her head. "He's too tired. Really." She scratched the horse under the chin. He ducked his head and snorted.

"I told Noah to ride him."

She nodded. "He was going to, but, Chaney, when you're down, this is really my responsibility."

Anger boiled in him. How dared she take on something like that! She'd gone too far. He raked his fingers through his sweaty hair, trying to bring some order to his thoughts. He'd let her hire Noah Rollins because he'd been trying to make her feel good. No other reason.

Against his better judgment, he'd taken her into Rich Hill with him. When Barney Mallott had started out after them, he'd been terrified that something would happen to her.

He hadn't had any choice but to take her with him on the drive but strictly as a tagalong. He'd never intended that she should actually do work.

He struggled with Hardy, but he was too weak. The pain mounted until finally he had to give up. Then he had to swallow hard to keep from vomiting.

At last he got control of himself. With burning eyes he stared at his slender girl of a wife with her hand underneath the chin of the sorrel stallion that had nearly killed him.

"Go find Noah Rollins," he ordered Hardy through gritted teeth.

"Now, Lieutenant—"

Beth Anne tilted her head to one side. "I'm a good rider, Chaney. You've always said so."

"I didn't say you were good enough to ride a working stallion." His voice rang in the tones that he had used to command his men. "Hell! Look at me. I'm laid up here because of him."

"Jackass here leads the herd." She kept her voice even, but color mounted in her cheeks.

"J-Jackass?"

"That's what I call him. He doesn't know what it means, but I think he's beginning to answer to it. This afternoon when I called him by it, he flicked an ear back in my direction."

"Damn, Beth Anne."

Hardy snickered.

Chaney threw him a look to singe his whiskers, but the cook acted as if he'd smiled. "I'm ordering you to get another horse right this minute."

"He behaves better for me. Must be something about a woman on his back. He doesn't try to bite or pitch. He steps right out like a gentleman. I think he thinks he's protecting me."

Chaney closed his eyes. His head was buzzing. His mouth was dry. He felt helpless as if everything he said was being turned inside out.

"He's moving the herd almost by himself. I just sit on his back and let him do his work. The men ride flank and drag. We lead for a while. Then we'll take a notion to circle around and drive up the stragglers. Noah and Mary Nell move up to point."

Chaney opened his eyes. She was smiling and still

scratching the horse under the chin. He tried again. "He's a killer. You said so yourself."

"I'm doing a good job, Chaney. It's really hard work. He moves so fast and he's always snaking in and out. Sometimes I just have to pull leather."

"Damn it, Beth Anne—"

She dropped the stallion's reins to the ground and came to put her hand on Chaney's cheek. Her touch was infinitely gentle. It soothed him. "How are you feeling, Chaney Taggart?"

He hurt too badly to continue the argument. At this point if she wanted to ride, short of shooting the horse, he couldn't stop her. And his gun was somewhere else.

He opened his eyes. And closed them again. She had it on. Around her slender hips, donned backward and pulled up to the tightest notch, was his gunbelt with his service revolver positioned for a crossdraw.

It was the last straw. He couldn't even find the spit to lick his lips.

"Chaney," she whispered anxiously.

He thought about lying. He thought about telling the truth. He settled for neither. "About as well as can be expected."

"Which means like hell."

"That's right." He nodded and took a last swallow of whiskey and water and held out his cup for more.

Hardy hurried to accommodate him.

"We're taking it slow," Beth Anne said, apology in her voice.

Sighing, he took another sip and settled back. Her hand felt infinitely cool on his forehead. This drive had turned everything upside down. As his loving wife she should be sitting in a chair beside his bed of pain. That's where she ought to be.

Damn it! He needed her to soothe his fevered brow

instead of riding a herding stallion. He bit his tongue to
keep the words in his mouth. Instead, he said, "Drive 'em
hard. Get 'em into Jackson County and stop for the night.
Hardy and I can catch up."

Was his speech slurred? It could be. He wasn't used to
drinking with nothing in his stomach.

She leaned forward and kissed him on the mouth. "It
will be over tomorrow. I promise."

He kissed her back. Against her mouth he murmured
his last command. "Get off that damned horse."

She patted her husband's shoulder, stepped back, and
swung up. "As far as I'm concerned, he's not a horse. He's
a jackass. Just like someone else I could name."

To Hardy she said, "Take good care of him. Easy and
slow. We'll push the herd another couple of hours. Luther
swears we're not too far from Hickman Mills. We'll hide
out near there until daylight and then head into Kansas
City by the road."

The usually testy cook actually tipped his hat. "Will do,
Miz Boss."

Beth Anne's emotions were in turmoil as she rode the
stallion back to the herd. The horse had a smooth gait
when he felt like using it. Riding him was a pleasure that
Chaney's comments had succeeded only in dampening.

She didn't know what she'd expected when she'd gone
back to see after him. She should have traded horses with
Rusty first. What Chaney didn't know wouldn't upset him.

But she'd been so proud of herself, sitting tall in the
saddle, riding the finest piece of horseflesh she'd ever
mounted. She wanted Chaney to tell her how wonderful
she was.

A kind word, a bit of praise, would have felt good, considering that she was tired to death.

"We'll push on for another two hours," she'd told him when every muscle ached and she was fast running out of steam after too little sleep.

Chaney was unreasonable, overbearing, and downright hateful. And he hadn't thanked her.

By the time she saw the herd again, she was seething.

The stallion must have sensed her mood, because he was turning up skittish again. Suddenly, she didn't care. Leaning forward over the horn, she shouted in his ear. "Round 'em up, Jackass. Let's get these horses to Hickman Mills."

He whinnied sharply. His front hooves left the ground as if he were jumping over a high fence. He came down in a dead run. Mane and tail streaming, he swept around the herd. Almost as one, the geldings and mares raised their heads.

As his wild ancestors had done, he rounded them up, bunched them tight, set them moving. For this she gave him his head. When they were moving, she guided him to the front of the herd.

At a fast clip they left the railroad bed, crossed a meadow, and found a dirt road.

Dimly, she was aware of the White Oak men, her men, falling back. She was driving the herd too fast, but she didn't care. She wanted to get this over with as quickly as possible. Then she'd have more than a thing or two to say to Chaney Taggart.

Leaning back in comfort on the train bound for Kansas City, Barney patted the money in his pocket. Drorsen had whined and twisted. It had taken some fast talking, but he'd finally convinced the banker to give him nearly 450 dollars.

When he got to Kansas City, he'd hire some good men, not the bunch of worn-out, disloyal old—

Cursing them all, especially Eustace Fisher, he sat up straight, willing the train to greater speed.

Chaney Taggart probably thought he'd got clean away. But Barney Mallott was going to have the last word.

Beth Anne sat stiffly on the stallion's broad back. Sweat had stained his sorrel hide a dark chestnut. His head drooped and his sides heaved with the shuddering of his breathing.

On a rise above a narrow creek, she watched the herd spread out along its bank crowding each other to get to the first water they'd crossed since midmorning. This site looked like a good camping place. They hadn't crossed any farmers' fields. They hadn't gone through any wire fences.

About noon, one of the scouts had reported a cluster of farm buildings at a distance. They'd looped around them to avoid being seen.

One of the results of Order No. 11 had been that whole areas of western Missouri had been abandoned a decade before. Close as they were to the Kansas border, they could travel unobserved.

While she was deciding whether to stop here or move on another mile or two, Luther came up and put his hand on the horse's neck. He looked up into Beth Anne's dusty face. "Lord, girl, you've just about run us all into the ground."

Her lips felt stiff in her face. She was so thirsty she had to swallow twice before she could speak. "How far are we from Hickman Mills?"

The foreman looked around squinting into the rays of

the lowering sun. "Can't tell for certain. Not more'n two or three miles, I'd reckon."

"Then we can stop here for the night." She made her tone positive, even though it really was a question.

Luther pulled off his dusty hat and slapped it against his thigh. "I'm here to tell you we can. If you drive us another mile, some of us'll start rollin' over dead."

Noah Rollins came up behind him. "Want me to take your horse?"

She looked at him vaguely. She couldn't feel her legs from the knees down. She really wanted to get off the horse, to find her way to someplace private where she could relieve herself and take the time to have a good cry. Above her knees she ached. Her spine felt fused to the bottom of her skull.

But all the pain and suffering had been worth it. They'd come within a couple of miles of Hickman Mills. Kansas City was only a little farther. Leavenworth lay across the Kansas River, maybe twenty-five miles beyond that. The drive was almost over.

Despite the exhaustion and discomfort, she was proud of herself. She didn't want to embarrass herself by dismounting and having her legs collapse under her. She put her hand on Noah's shoulder.

He looked up. She could see awareness of her plight and then concern dawn in his gaze. She tried to rise in the stirrups, to swing her leg over the stallion's rear. She couldn't do it.

His expression serious, he held up his arms. She let herself fall sideways.

In the end he had to put his arm under her knees and carry her to a grassy knoll. She was embarrassed because all the men had gathered around and were looking on.

When Noah put her down and stepped back, she looked at her crew, whose expressions ranged from surprise to concern to knowing sympathy. She tried to make her stiffness into a joke. "If you tell Chaney, I'll swear you're all lying."

They shuffled their feet and muttered to each other until Rusty gave a big heehaw. "Tell him what, boss?"

When the supply wagons slowly pulled in just after dark, Beth Anne had worked the kinks out. She had washed her face and hands in a nearby creek, drunk a cup of Luther's coffee, and eaten a handful of dried apple slices. She was walking with only a slight hitch when she came around the tailgate of Hardy's wagon.

She waited while the hands unloaded Chaney from the wagon. When he was stretched out with a cup of hot coffee liberally laced with whiskey, she took his hand, but he didn't look at her. His skin was dry and warm but not burning. He probably had a little fever.

Before she could ask how he was, he looked at Luther. "How far are we from Hickman Mills?"

" 'Bout a mile and a half, Lieutenant. We sent one of the scouts to find exactly where we are. He was back in half an hour."

"Any trouble?" The question was directed to Rusty.

"Ain't seen a soul all day, Lieutenant. Just like drivin' 'em to the back pasture."

As Doc Gunderson checked his leg, Chaney lay still, his eyes closed, his right hand wrapped around the coffee cup on his chest.

Doc ran a finger underneath the splints. Instead of reporting to Chaney, he looked to Beth Anne. "He's swollen pretty bad, Miz Taggart."

Chaney's eyes popped open. His gaze cut sideways toward her. "It'll do fine."

She could see the blue bruising above and below the

bandages. Another day would be agony. "Maybe we better take you into Kansas City to the hospital, honey."

"No!" Anger and frustration doubled the volume of the word. "No! Hell, no!"

"Hardy could take you directly to the hospital." She drew back out of his reach as he made a grab for her. "Or the hotel. That's a better idea. You could go to one of the big hotels—"

"Why don't *you* go to one of the big hotels?" he snarled. "Like a woman should. You've embarrassed just about every man on this drive. I think it's about time you learned your place."

The pool of silence spread around them. Doc's hands went still. Luther bowed his head. Hardy and Rusty disappeared into the darkness.

If Chaney had slapped her, he could not have hurt her more. In fact, she almost wished he had slapped her. The pain would have been less intense.

He drained the cup defiantly.

She rose unsteadily. "You're running a fever and hurting enough to die. And you're drunk. I'm going to walk away and leave you to think about what you've said."

"I'm not drunk."

She turned on her heel and stalked away.

"Beth Anne."

She broke into a run. Her only hope was that she could get to someplace where she could cry without bumping into a damn tree.

Chapter Ten

"I heard what he said to you."

Beth Anne nearly jumped out of her skin. Noah Rollins's deep voice coming out of the dark had taken her by surprise. He hadn't made a sound when he'd walked up on her. She tried to spring to her feet, but her legs were too stiff.

Her cry of alarm stopped him in his tracks.

"Don't get all excited." His voice was low and soothing, the same tone she'd heard him use with skittish horses. "I brought you some dinner."

She drew a deep, calming breath and waited for her heart to settle down. Surprisingly, she hadn't wept as she'd expected. The hurt had been too deep. Instead, she'd leaned back against the tree and made excuses for Chaney. All the while, a tiny part of her mind had congratulated herself that she was sitting calmly rather than giving way to childish sobs.

If she were a truly mature person, she would sit up and

eat. Unfortunately, the mention of dinner failed to spark her appetite, and the last person she wanted to deal with was Noah Rollins.

Why couldn't he have been Mary Nell? Knowing Luther's loyalty, he hadn't told his daughter what Chaney had said. Her friend was probably tucked safely in her bedroll, dreaming the dreams of the loved and appreciated.

She cleared her throat. "I hope you brought some coffee."

"Brought the pot." Noah dropped down beside her. She could see his teeth flash white in the dark. "Hardy made it up fresh. And he piled the plate with enough for two people. He wanted you to have enough."

"Hardy's known me a long time." She accepted the hot cup gratefully. The dew had fallen and her skin felt chilled. "He's a good friend."

She drank a swallow and then another. It put heart into her. Maybe she was hungry after all. "Is there some pie?"

"Only about a quarter of one." Noah pressed the plate into her hand.

His fingers touched hers, guided her to the tin fork. "The pie's on your right."

"Thank you."

She took the first bite. It was actually huckleberry cobbler still warm. She ate another bite, then poked around with her fork and found the beans and the cornbread. Her mouth watered. Her tastebuds awakened. Her stomach growled.

She began to eat, taking her time, resting and recovering. The warm food comforted her. Quite suddenly, it dawned on her that Noah Rollins was sitting beside her, the man who'd tried to terrorize her on her own land.

And Chaney was laid up with a broken leg and fever.

Her hand began to shake. When she put down the fork, it clattered in the plate.

"Want some more?"

"No." She hoped her voice wasn't shaking. "You can leave me now. I really want to finish this and roll up in my bedroll and get some sleep. We'll leave before dawn."

"I wanted to ask you a question." The intensity of his voice gave her a good idea what he was going to ask.

She sighed. How much more could one human being be expected to put up with? "Look, Mr. Rollins, I appreciate your bringing me this food. I appreciate your helping me out of the saddle this afternoon. I appreciate all you've done on this drive. But I'm dead tired and I've had about all I can stand."

"I just can't figure out why you'd do it."

"You don't have to figure anything out. That's my job. My husband was drunk and in pain. He wasn't thinking straight. I can't be mad at him under those circumstances. A man's liable to say anything. He'll get around to apologizing to me."

In the meantime, she wished Noah Rollins would go away. She thought about trying to get to her feet. As weary and stiff as she was, she knew she'd stumble and probably fall over. While she was trying to decide what to do, he spoke again.

"That's not what I meant. I can sort of figure out why you married him. You were in danger and you had to take care of yourself. You'd lost everything. This was a chance to get it back."

"What are you talking about?" She leaned forward. He was talking as if he knew who she was. Quite suddenly, her exhaustion left her to be replaced by excitement. "What did I lose?"

He made a rude sound. "Don't give me that. You know."

"No. No, I don't. What's my name?"

"Come on, Beth Anne."

"No, my last name?"

"Beth Anne Taggart." He hesitated for just a second. "Beth Anne McNeil."

Cold chills skittered up her spine. She set the plate aside. This was more important than food. She could feel the goosebumps rising on her arms. "Did I know you?"

"Bethie, I'm Noah." He put his hand on her arm.

"I—I don't know—that is—I know your name. But did I know you? Did you know my family?"

"Sure. White Oak was the McNeil place. The Rollins place was on the other side of the Marais des Cygnes."

"The McNeil place?"

He still sounded disbelieving. "Sure. Our families were great friends. You were always tagging along after Josey and me."

"Josey!" Her heart give a great leap. She reached for Noah, caught him by his shirt. "You knew Josey?"

"Your brother. Sure. He was my best friend. Say, you don't remember anything, do you?"

She wanted to cry, but she didn't let herself. "No. Not much. Do you know my brother? Oh, where is he?"

Noah was silent for so long that she knew the answer.

She took a deep breath. "And my father and my mother too? What happened?"

"Your mother died a long time ago. I think she died not long after you were born." Noah put his hands over hers and drew them together. "Your father's gone too."

She couldn't let this rest. She wouldn't. Had Chaney known this? Had he refused to tell her? "What happened?"

"I imagine they were shot. Josey and Oliver, your father. My folks and I were supposed to meet your folks just east of the county line. When you all didn't come, Pa and I rode back. All we found were—er—bloodstains. The house was empty. We didn't know what happened to any of you. To tell the truth, Beth Anne, until I rode in here and saw you, I thought you were dead too."

She felt again the pain in her hands. Tears stung her eyes. She blinked them back. "This was a long time ago. I've been with Chaney ten, no, eleven years. How can you be so sure I'm Beth Anne McNeil?"

"I'd know you anywhere." He lifted her hands to his lips and kissed them, first one and then the other. "Ten years ago, I'd already made up my mind you were going to be my wife, just as soon as you were old enough."

"Oh, Noah." She shivered and pulled her hands from his and put them on his cheeks. For a moment love and loss overwhelmed her. She could almost remember him. But not really. And she didn't know him now. "You thought I was dead. And I nearly was. Someone tried to kill me too. And Chaney Taggart found me."

"I felt the scars on your hands."

"Who tried to kill me? Who killed my father and brother?"

Noah's jaw tensed under her palms. He opened his mouth.

"Beth Anne!" Mary Nell called softly in the dark. "Where are you, girlfriend? I've got a plate of food for you and your bedroll all laid out in the tent."

Beth Anne couldn't let the moment slip away. "Who tried to kill me, Noah Rollins?"

"I don't know," he admitted. "We were all ordered out. There were looters. Jayhawkers came over from Kansas. The army—"

"Beth Anne!" Mary Nell's voice was closer.

"The army—"

He took hold of her wrists and brought them down from his cheeks. "You'd better go. Mary Nell'd whup me for sure if she knew I was out here with you."

She heard the laughter in his voice and something else. "Mary Nell would?"

He shuffled his feet like a big boy. She wished it weren't

so dark so she could see his face. "Uh-huh. She's got her hooks into me good."

"Beth Anne—where are you?"

She had to answer. "Here. I'm coming." She stepped back. "We'll talk after we deliver the herd to Fort Leavenworth."

"Sure thing." He remained beneath the tree while she walked back toward the wagon.

Beth Anne heard the screech owl. She rolled over on her back and stared at the stars through the open flap of the tent. The owl called again. Another answered farther away.

She concentrated on going back to sleep. The night was silent, with no breeze to ruffle leaves or click branches. Occasionally, a horse would stamp or snort.

She turned over on her side. Moving her head off the saddle, she pillowed it on her hand. Again she concentrated on going to sleep. She frowned. Beneath her palm she could feel a faint vibration.

Horses' hooves.

She closed her eyes. Hoofbeats moving at a trot. She rolled over flat on her stomach and pressed her ear as well as her palms against the ground. She was not mistaken. She could feel the movement and hear it.

"Mary Nell." She put her hand on her friend's shoulder. "Wake up. I'm afraid we might have company coming."

She was pulling on her boots when Rusty Huff came blundering through the dark. "Miz Taggart!" he called, trying to keep his voice low. "Miz Taggart!"

"I'm awake, Rusty." She crawled out from the tent.

"The nighthawk done spotted 'bout half a dozen riders coming south. They look like they're aimin' right fer us."

"Get everybody up and mounted. Saddle the sorrel for me."

"I've already done it, Miz Taggart. We figured you'd be needin' him."

"Bring him to Hardy's wagon." She pulled the button up tight under her chin to hold her hat on and ran into the darkness.

Hardy was harnessing the mules. She located him by the sound of his cussing.

"Drive south and east to the road," she instructed. "When you get to it, don't stop. Head north and west for Kansas City. I'll meet you there at the Coates House Hotel, if I can."

"Yes, ma'am."

"Beth Anne!" Chaney had wakened. His voice sounded hoarse. "Hardy!"

She clutched the old cook's arm. "Hardy, don't fail me."

"You can count on me, boss."

"Beth Anne!"

She climbed up on the seat of the wagon and leaned in. "I'm here, Chaney."

"What's happening?"

She could see his face as a white blur in the darkness and his hand as it groped for her. She might have known he would have heard the stir. "We're getting ready to move out."

"Something else is going on." He lay silent for the space of a breath. "Horses," he whispered. "Coming in a bunch. Trotting."

"I don't hear anything," she lied.

"Goddamn it. You do too." He struggled to reach her over the boxes.

She moved her hands back so he couldn't grab her. "Chaney, I don't know who's coming. They might not have

anything to do with us. They might not even know we're
here. But most likely they do. I've got to be ready.''

"You—You—" He was helpless.

"Chaney, I have to go.''

"Oh, God. Beth Anne. Don't do it. The horses aren't
worth it. Nothing's worth it. Please.'' His voice was hoarse.
She could swear he was trying to smother a sob.

"Chaney. I love you. Don't worry. Hardy's going to take
good care of you.''

"No.'' He pulled up on his good knee. He was panting
from the exertion. "Don't you dare. Stay with me. Hardy!''

The cook climbed up on the wagon seat. "We're ready
to move, Lieutenant.''

"Help him get back down,'' Beth Anne said. "He can't
be thrown around like that.''

"No. Goddamn it. I'm still the boss of this outfit!'' He
raised his voice.

Rusty rode up with the sorrel in tow.

"I've got to go.'' She jumped down. "I love you, Chaney.
See you in Kansas City.''

"No!''

"Now, Lieutenant.'' Hardy climbed back through the
canvas opening. "Let's get you down and comfortable.''

"No. No! Goddamn it. You stop her. You hear me,
Hardy? You stop her or you're fired.''

The sorrel pranced and whinnied at the sound of Chaney's voice. Beth Anne put her hand on the sorrel's nose.
He snuffled, then lipped her palm. She straightened his
forelock and ran her hand down the center of his face.

"What horse are you riding, Beth Anne?'' Chaney called.
"Answer me. Don't you ride that man-killer. Ride your
mare. For God's sake!''

Rusty handed her the reins. She pulled them over the

big stallion's head and climbed into the saddle. "Let's go," she whispered. "He can beat me later."

She was surprised to hear Rusty laugh.

Noah Rollins with three of the hands waited in the clump of trees where he'd talked to Beth Anne only a few hours before. Their calm self-assurance communicated itself to him. These men might be old enough to be his father, but they were absolutely fearless.

The riders had slowed their approach, almost a sure sign that they were coming after the White Oak herd. Uncertain of the exact location, they were separating into two groups and approaching slowly.

"I spot a couple over on the right." The taut whisper came from Saul, whose nerve and skill Noah was coming to recognize and be grateful for.

"Want us to go after 'em?" Rusty suggested.

Noah didn't know what to answer. "Can you do it without making any noise?"

"Pretty hard with two," came the reply. "One's easy, but two make it tough. What y' think, Saul?"

"Let's give it a try. Leastways, if we don't get 'em quiet, we'll slow the whole troop down while they figger out what happened." He made a sound that might have been a chuckle.

"Might even stop the rest of 'em cold. A man gets discouraged when he don't know what's happened to his friends."

"Do it then."

As Noah watched, they silently slipped from their horses.

The White Oak herd was on the move now. He could hear the dull thunder of the stallion's hoofbeats. He could hear the snorting and stamping as they began to move. It sounded like thunder to him, but the two mounted intruders on the right pulled up short and listened as if they were trying to figure out what was happening.

That was their mistake. Two figures rose from the ground behind them. One man was dragged from the saddle without a sound. The other gave a shout. It ended in a strangled gurgling noise.

"My God," Noah whispered.

"Saul sure ain't lost his touch," one of his companions observed.

"Yeah, but Rusty's slowin' down," came the reply.

Beth Anne had learned much from riding the stallion the day before. The best thing to do was keep a firm grip with her thighs, a light grip with her hands, and let him do his work. When she'd tried to guide him yesterday or turn him to catch up strays, he'd fought the bit.

He would do things his way. Stubborn as the devil himself.

The White Oak men had learned the same thing. While the stallion did the work, they stayed back and out to the sides, loping along.

Rusty said it was "like ridin' to church."

Snorting and whinnying, nipping and snaking around, the sorrel headed the strays back where they belonged. If a horse, mare or gelding, tried to escape, he went after it like a coiled spring.

Beth Anne had learned to feel when and where he was going. The mighty muscles beneath her thighs would bunch and knot. Just to sit on his back was exciting. To ride him was a challenge. He was all power, all hard-driving male animal. A prince among horses moving surely and strongly through the darkness. His kind acknowledged his supremacy. Two hundred obeyed his every wish. She wondered if two thousand would daunt him.

Behind her she heard noise. Shouts. Then horses galloping, coming hard. Whoever was back there in the darkness had finally figured out that the White Oak herd was moving. The chase had begun.

She grasped the horn with her right hand and tightened the reins with her left.

"Now, Jack!" she shouted, leaning forward in the saddle. "Jack o' Diamonds! Go!"

The mighty muscles bunched in his hindquarters. The stallion leaped forward. At a dead run, he swept around his herd and shouldered his way into the lead.

A sudden fear made her scalp crawl. They were running so fast. Their speed plastered her hatbrim back against her crown. She could hear the thunder of two hundred horses behind her. If he went down, they would be trampled.

But he wouldn't fall. She knew it. Nothing could bring down the sorrel. "Go," she yelled in his ear. And the wind blew the words back into her mouth. "Go-o-o-o-o!"

Noah Rollins with his three men watched the knot of riders gallop by. Already they were straggling out as men lost heart for chasing a herd of horses over unfamiliar territory.

"One at a time," he ordered his men. "Just ride up on the hindmost and knock him off his horse."

"I could shoot him just as easy," the man called Saul suggested.

"He didn't do anything," Noah snapped back. "He's been hired to make that Rich Hill marshal look impressive. He's mostly for bluff. Just knock him off and ride on to the next one. By the time they find their horses, we'll be in Kansas City."

Saul muttered something but didn't object.

"Everybody with me?"

"We're with you, Rollins."

"Then follow me." Noah clapped his heels to Babe's sides.

They didn't have far to go to catch up to the first man. Noah drew his pistol. Reining the mare close, he jabbed it in the fellow's direction.

"Hey?"

"Drop off."

"No." The man tried to spur away, but another rider was on his other side.

"Off!" Noah shouted, brandishing his gun in the man's face.

The man pulled back on the reins. Without further argument he slid over the saddlebow and back over the horse's tail. He went down, rolled, and came out sitting up.

With a wild laugh Saul spurred his mount past Noah and on to the next fellow.

In the wagon Chaney ground his teeth and cursed Hardy. When the cook paid no attention, he fell to cursing his own leg and Barney Mallott. The sorrel stallion came in for his share too. Chaney declared that he should have gelded the jughead the first time he tried to scrape his rider off on a fence.

Hardy passed back a new bottle of whiskey. "I don't know 'bout that, Lieutenant," he remarked conversationally. "That horse is turning out pretty good with Miz Taggart on his back."

Champing on the cork with his teeth, Chaney wrenched

it out of the bottle. "You're fired, Hardy. Pack your things the minute we get back to White Oak."

" 'Bout time I headed for Californey," the cook replied.

Chaney turned the bottle up and drank until he choked. The wagon creaked on through the night.

" 'Course, Miz Taggart might need me," came the laconic voice. "Maybe she'll hire me back. She can't cook fer ever'body an' train horses at the same time."

Chaney cursed bitterly and took another drink. His head was buzzing from the whiskey. He was acting like a jackass. *Jackass.* She was calling that horse that had cost him a mint of money Jackass.

His broken leg had changed everything. He still couldn't believe that he was lying in the back of a chuckwagon, heading away from a fight. His wife. His twenty-one-year-old wife that he should be happily getting with child was riding somewhere in the dead of night on a loco stallion.

He should have paid the dollar a head to Barney and the Drorsens. This was all his fault. He took another drink. All he could think of was his wife—and that he had never felt so helpless in his life.

Sweat wet Barney's shirt between his shoulderblades and under his arms.

He could hear the herd ahead of him. He could smell their dust. More important, he could see riders, dark silhouettes on the right and left. They'd dropped back, most likely to keep the stragglers bunched.

And to look out for him. He eased up on his horse, thinking to let his own men catch up with him. A quick glance over his shoulder sent a ripple of anger through him.

Those bastards! More than half of them had dropped out on him. He'd paid them good money too. He'd paid them more than they could make in a week. Too much, if the truth was known. They'd held him up. A lot of Drorsen's money that he'd earmarked for himself was gone.

It galled him to think he'd wasted it.

He considered breaking off the chase and waiting until the herd ran itself out. But that might be too late. They were better horses than anything he had.

Damn Chaney Taggart! He always got the best of everything!

He let his horse drop from a gallop into a trot. The herd swept on. The riders up ahead disappeared into the darkness. Where were his men?

He cast another glance over his shoulder. A knot of riders had formed and slowed to a trot maybe fifty yards behind him. The man in the lead rode a pale horse.

Suddenly, he knew. He remembered that gray horse, remembered that rider. Those were White Oak men who'd knocked his men out of the saddle or driven them off. And they were coming for him.

Drawing his gun, he twisted in the saddle. Too dark for a good shot. Take what he could. He snapped off the shot. The gray horse stumbled and went down head first.

That'd hold 'em!

With a grin of satisfaction, Barney spurred his mount viciously into the darkness.

Noah jerked up on the reins as Babe stumbled, but she was already collapsing. He flung himself from the saddle, slamming to the ground as her whole big body carried by her speed flipped over and crashed down on her back.

His forehead struck a rock. He rolled over; then for a minute he was truly dead to the world.

"Noah. Hey, son. Lord, God. Come on, boy." Saul's scratchy voice came from far away.

Noah could hear Saul slap his cheek, but he couldn't feel it. Stunned, he sprawled on his stomach, trying to suck in enough air to keep from losing consciousness.

"Noah!" Saul slapped his cheek again.

He rolled his head and tried to speak, but his efforts came out in a grunt. Saul slapped his cheek.

"For God's sake, stop knockin' him around." Another man dropped down on Noah's other side.

"Just tryin' to bring 'im to." Saul's voice sounded apologetic.

Noah swallowed and managed to draw a deep breath. "I'm all right," he whispered. "Just prop me up."

They obeyed him, one on each side while the others leaned over him.

"Anything broken?" one asked.

"I don't think so." Noah began to test his limbs. Other than a sore shoulder and a sore hip, everything felt together. He could feel the blood running in a hot trickle down the side of his face. "Somebody take my neckerchief and tie my head up. It's dripping in my eyes."

A general sigh of relief passed among them. Saul chuckled. "Why, sure."

Still dizzy, Noah sat with bowed head while the old cavalryman folded the cloth and wrapped it around his forehead. When the knot was tied, Noah blinked rapidly several times. When his vision seemed to clear, he held out a hand. "If somebody'll just put me on my horse—"

Nobody moved. Nobody spoke.

Noah raised his head to bring his eyes into focus on the pale gray mound only a few feet away. "Babe," he whispered.

Again the silence. They were all cavalrymen. Their lives were spent working with horses and appreciating good horseflesh. Saul rose as if he were a hundred years old. "I don't think she's gonna get back up, son."

Noah closed his eyes. Babe was his horse. She was just about all he owned. He tottered to her head. She lay as she had fallen on her side. Her neck arched, her nose tucked down, as if she were about to raise her head.

"Babe—"

She didn't move.

Dropping down on his knees, he saw the dark stream that trickled sluggishly from the hole in her breast.

"Aw, Babe—"

He was going to cry. He hadn't shed a tear since his mother died. He was hurt and shocked, he reasoned. He was exhausted. As he ran his hands over her neck and face, he told himself she was only a horse.

Grief welled up in his throat in a huge terrible choking ache. He'd never asked anything of her that she hadn't given willingly. He shouldn't have ridden her tonight. He'd ridden her every day since the drive started.

He tried to cover the sob with a cough. He'd ridden her to her death. She had run like a three-year-old and taken a bullet in her chest.

He closed his eyes against another sob.

Saul put his hands on his shoulders. "Come on, son. You can ride my horse. I'll climb up behind Buck. We're both lighter than you."

He wrenched himself out of the older man's hands. "Send somebody back for me," he growled. "I've got to strip my saddle off and b-bury her."

"Son, you can't bury an animal this big. Hurt like you are. If you want us to this bad, we can catch up with Miz Taggart. She can send a detail back to do the job for you."

Noah could stop the tears with anger. "I'll take care of her, damn it! Just get on. Send someone back with another horse."

The first rays of the morning sun lightened the horizon. Shadows had become shades of gray. Noah faced them, daring them to argue further.

Saul tried once more. "Son, you look like hell. Why don't you come on with us now? I promise I'll come back with you if no one else will."

Noah touched his hand to his face. He could feel the dried blood crackling on his face. His head was throbbing, but he wouldn't leave her. "I've got everything I need in my roll," he declared. "Even to a shovel. My daddy's kit from the war. Just send someone back for me."

They debated among themselves. At last, Saul nodded. "Head on out, boys," he called. He put his hand on Noah's shoulder. The light was stronger. The blood on the ground made a dark circle. The saddle was broken. Only the bridle and bedroll could be salvaged.

"We'll hurry," he said. "Why don't you just sit down, son? Over there by that tree? Some of us'll come back soon as we can."

Noah didn't answer. Instead he bent to unbuckle the cheekstrap and gently slip the bit from between the mare's jaws. He didn't look around as the four rode off.

Chapter Eleven

Morning light was just turning pinkish orange when Mary Nell came riding to find Noah Rollins. Saul and Rusty Huff led the way. Besides a saddled horse, they brought heavy shovels and a pickax for breaking up the ground.

Noah sat beside the body. His forearms rested on his drawn-up knees. His hands hung limply between them. His head was bowed. He'd salvaged what little of his equipment was still usable and piled it beneath the tree.

They could see his pitiful attempt to dig the grave. The tough roots of the prairie grass had kept him from doing more than scratching out a shallow trench.

When he raised his head, Mary Nell's heart turned over at the sight of his face. Even shaded by his hatbrim, it looked ghastly. Bruised, swollen, streaked with dried blood, a bloody filthy rag tied round it, it looked like nothing human. His clothing was torn. Black circles rimmed his eyes.

She swung down off her horse and hurried to his side.

Pulling her saddlebag and canteen from the saddle, she dropped to her knees. "Noah, sweetheart. I'm so sorry."

He stared at her dully as she uncorked the canteen and handed it to him. "Careful. Hardy put some whiskey in it. I'm not sure how much. It could be pretty powerful."

Noah nodded grimly before he tilted it up. She saw his Adam's apple move once, twice, three times. When he'd finished, he closed his eyes and handed the canteen back to her.

"I'm just restin' a little," he muttered. "I'll get it dug."

"It's all right." She patted his arm before she opened her saddlebags. "Saul and Rusty volunteered to come back and help you bury her." She handed him a wrapped bundle. "Here. Eat these. You must be starving to death. Hardy sent some flapjacks wrapped around brown sugar and dried apples."

Noah looked once at the mare's body. Rusty and Saul took up positions on either side of the bare spot that he'd managed to scratch out. Rusty raised the pickax above his head and brought it down with a mighty thunk. The blade stabbed through the tough grass roots and into the soft loam beneath. It would break up the ground in a hurry.

"I really appreciate this," Noah said to Mary Nell. Dutifully, he took a bite of the food. He seemed to choke. His eyes watered. He took another drink from the canteen.

His gaze flickered toward the two men, then sternly skimmed away. "I didn't want to leave her out here. She deserves better."

"Of course she does." Mary Nell untied the neckerchief from his forehead. She caught her breath at the sight.

"It doesn't hurt much," he said in an apologetic tone.

Quickly, she poured a little of the whiskey and water onto a clean rag and began to wash the dirt and grime from around the wound. "It doesn't look too bad," she

said even though it looked terrible. "I think it's more of
a bruise. The skin is just sort of split."

"Tie it up," he muttered. "I want to help them."

"In a minute. Let Rusty get the ground broken. Does
your head ache?"

"Some," he admitted.

"A lot, I'll bet." She rose on her knees to get closer and
to see the rest of his head. Her hands trembled as she
pushed back the lank strands of blond hair. She was sure
he was grievously wounded.

With her back between them and Saul and Rusty, she
looked down into his face. "Oh, Noah. I was so scared
when you didn't come back. I about tore a patch off Saul
for leaving you. Daddy thought I'd lost my mind. And I
had."

He raised his gaze. "Didn't they tell you I was all right?"

"They didn't know." Her voice was low and angry. "For
heaven's sake, you'd had your horse shot out from under
you. They rode off without finding out whether you had
a concussion or something broken on the inside. You could
have bled to death before we got here."

He searched her face. Amidst the wreckage of his own,
his eyes glowed. "You cared what happened to me?"

Suddenly, she realized what she'd said. She sank back
on her heels and looked into the saddlebags again. She
could feel her face getting hot.

"Now where's that lint? I know I put it in here." Her
fingers closed over the roll of bandage, pushed it aside,
pretended to search a minute longer while she got herself
under control.

"You came back here at first light to take care of me.
You called me 'sweetheart.' "

"I—I don't think I said 'sweetheart.' "

"I heard 'sweetheart.' "

The color that had begun to ebb from her cheeks

returned. She pretended to root for the bandage roll. At last she allowed herself to find it. "Bend your head."

Obediently, he did as she ordered.

She rose up again and began to wind the gauze. When she was finished and had it tied off, he caught her wrist. "You do care about me."

His eyes were sorrowful and pain-filled, but raw emotion was stronger than either of those. He looked like a starving man who'd been offered a chair at the banquet. "Mary Nell?"

She tried to make light of it. "Of course, I care for you. I care for everybody at White Oak."

He didn't let her go. His hand tightened. "Would you have come out here for Saul?"

She closed her eyes. "If anyone needed me to go, I'd—" She couldn't say that. It wasn't the truth. Now was no time to start lying. "I came here for you. I wanted to take care of you and be sure you were all right."

He released her wrist as if it were hot. His gaze dropped to his lap.

She waited a minute. The seconds ticked by, counted off by the thud of Rusty's pickax and the crunch of Saul's shovel. At last she asked in a low voice, "Was I wrong to come?"

"Oh, no. God, no." He shook his head, though the movement must have hurt him. "I told you how I felt about you."

Happiness like a warm spring gushed through her. She poured more water onto the rag and tipped his head up. With infinite gentleness she washed his face—his blue-veined eyelids with their pale blond lashes, his straight nose, his high cheekbones, his firm lips and chin.

He was all hard lines and sharp angles. He'd compressed his mouth into a straight, tight line as if somehow that could control the pain. His cheeks were covered by several days' stubble. As she washed it, the dirt and grime came off and the blond hair turned to gold in the morning sunlight.

We'll have such beautiful children, she thought.

Had she spoken aloud?

His lips relaxed. A small smile lifted their corners.

A chill ran up her spine. Had he read her thoughts? Had he been thinking the same thing?

When he spoke, his voice seemed huskier somehow. "I don't know how to thank you. The words aren't enough. The water's cool. It feels good. I guess the only thing better than having you bathe my face would be having you give me a bath."

She broke off abruptly. The moment of absolute tenderness between them had passed. He was back to being smart-alecky again. She rocked back on her heels. "I think you need to get up and help Rusty and Saul."

His mouth closed tight. He nodded. "I guess I do. I'm not the kind of man you need anyway. I spoiled it, didn't I?"

She pretended to root in her bag.

He set his heels and pushed himself up in one strong movement—and immediately swayed and fell over.

She scrambled to get her arms around his shoulders and steady him. Exasperated with herself, she helped him stretch out on the ground. His face was bathed in perspiration. "Oh, Noah. I was wrong. You need to lie here. I'll go help them."

"I'm not going to let you dig," he snarled.

She patted his hand. "I'm not going to dig. I'll just shovel the dirt they've broken up. I've been shoveling in the garden and in the stables for years. You finish your breakfast and drink all that water."

Before he could argue, she joined them. Noah sat up and pushed himself carefully to his feet. After he'd walked a few steps, however, he sat back down again. His pallor made his condition clear. He couldn't do the work.

In under an hour, the three of them had a hole dug deep and wide enough to tip the mare's body into. As the body fell, Noah bowed his head. Mary Nell could see his lips move.

Quickly, Saul and Rusty covered Babe's body over. Noah stood and watched until the horse was completely covered over and the earth mounded above her. Then he stumbled away.

When it was all decently done, the men mounted their horses. "You think you'll be needin' us, Mary Nell?" Rusty asked.

"I don't think so," she replied. "Go on back and help Beth Anne move the herd. Noah and I'll make straight for Kansas City. We'll meet you at the stockyards."

"Good enough." With a tip of their hats, the two men rode away.

Noah had seated himself with his back to a small tree. He'd drawn up his knees and rested his arms on them. His hands were clasped loosely.

She sat down beside him, close enough so their shoulders touched.

"She's been with me since I was fifteen," he said softly. "Papa bred her dam to a stallion from the Shirley plantation down in Jasper County near Carthage. The Shirleys had just about the best horseflesh in the southwest part of the state.

"I remember riding with him when he led his two best mares down there. Nearly fifty miles we traveled. Spent the night beside the road. I couldn't believe how much he paid Mr. Shirley. But the next spring we had two of the prettiest foals."

His eyes were warm as he looked backward into the past

when everything seemed so hopeful and a boy could see his future stretch before him.

"Jed—" He picked a stem of sweetgrass and stared at it as if it were magic. "My big brother Jedediah got the colt. It was his right. He was the oldest. And he was gonna get married soon. I got the filly."

He swallowed. "That was damn near fifteen years ago. Lots of water under the bridge since then."

"A war—" Mary Nell agreed. "Where's your brother now?"

"Don't know." Noah tossed the grass into the air. It tumbled end over end as it wafted away. "Dead I guess. Or gone to Californy. I hope he's there. He never did get married. All that Order No. 11 business came about. Haven't seen him or that black stud in more'n a dozen years."

"But your father had you."

"I didn't have Pa. When we had to leave the farm, he just didn't have the heart to start over. He went fast, and Ma too. I took the mare and drifted over Kentucky way. There wasn't anything left here. No friends."

He swung his head in Mary Nell's direction. Hectic color burned in his bruised face. His eyes looked hot. She wondered if he had a fever.

"I made my living off that mare's back. Breakin' horses. Herdin'. More'n half the time she's the reason I got the job I got. My bosses were always trying to buy her off me. Sometimes they'd pay me double to work for them and stay around while they bred her to their studs." He bit his lip. "They'd pay *me* for *her* services. It was just like she was a whore."

Mary Nell didn't know what to say. He shouldn't be talking like this to her. On the other hand, she wanted desperately to know everything about him.

He must have realized what he said, because he shook

his head. "I must be sicker than I thought. I can't believe I'm saying things to you."

"It's all right." She could feel his pain. He was regretting what he'd done to his mare. "You both survived."

"Thanks to her, I did better than survive. The horsefarms are always looking for new blood, good blood, with papers like Babe has. Had." He shuddered, then went on. "There weren't so many horses left in Kentucky with the Army paying fancy prices.

"Then there weren't so many men. They'd gone off and enlisted. A boy on a fine mare could find work."

"How many colts did she have?"

"Ten. No. Eleven, I guess. The last one she had a hard time with. I had to get a doctor for her. When it was born, he said she'd had her last one.

"I'd never thought about her getting old until that minute. And then I looked at myself. I wasn't a boy anymore."

"Why'd you come back here?"

He looked at her keenly. She kept her face calm although she knew she was being tested. Her heart stepped up a beat.

At last he looked away. "I was looking for Beth Anne."

She flinched. The name was like a knife in her belly, but she couldn't let him see. "I knew it. The way you looked at her."

He nodded. "I'd known her when we were children. I was her brother Josey's best friend."

"Josey? She asked me about Josey. Do you know what happened?"

"We heard the shots, Pa and me. We rode over, but when we got to White Oak, we were too late. There wasn't anybody there. Just a lot of blood all over."

"Oh, heavens. Did you tell Beth Anne this?"

"Some of it."

Mary Nell sighed. So much trouble, so many problems,

and now the past coming back to bother her. How was her friend bearing up under all this? "How'd she take it?"

Noah looked away. "I—I guess I said more than I should have."

The silence fell between them. Mary Nell hung her head. What should she do? What should she think? More important, how should she feel toward this man? If he had come back for Beth Anne, he couldn't have her anyway. She worshiped Chaney Taggart.

Mary Nell got to her feet, made a show of dusting the seat of her pants with her hands. "It's not too far to Kansas City, but I guess we'd better be getting a move on."

He didn't protest.

She led a pretty black mare over so the left stirrup was hanging only a foot from his face. "Can you climb aboard?"

He nodded and grasped the leather. Holding the reins, she put a hand under his arm. All she did was steady him as he stood under his own power. Once his hand was around the horn, she handed him the reins.

His other hand closed over hers. He leveled his blue-eyed gaze at her with a solemnity that stunned her. "I came back to find Beth Anne," he said. "But I didn't expect her to be here. I didn't expect to find her waiting for me. I came looking for a new life. And the person I found was you.

"After this drive is over, Mary Nell Tibbets, we've got some serious talking to do." With that, he mounted in a smooth fluid motion.

She mounted her horse and they headed north after the herd.

Before they'd gone very far, he guided his mare over so his knee fitted into the back of hers. He put his arm around her shoulders.

His kiss, tender with promise, melted her insides. When

she thought she'd die for lack of air, he raised his head. His face was lighted by the first genuine smile she'd ever seen there. He steadied her in the saddle.

"Now. Let's get on the way. Kansas City can't come too soon for me."

At midday, Beth Anne called a halt above a small creek. Stepping down from the saddle, she stretched her stiff limbs and washed her face and neck with the water from her canteen. Lord, she was tired. She was almost afraid to sit down, for fear she wouldn't be able to get up again.

Thank heaven, they were on the outskirts of Kansas City. Tonight would be easier. With comfort in mind, she sent a man ahead to rent rooms for the night at the Coates House Hotel. "Rent four. One for Chaney, one for Mary Nell, one for Noah Rollins, and one for me." She shrugged apologetically. "Chaney needs rest and undisturbed sleep. And I'd be worried all night long that I'd turn over and bump his leg. And then I'll be getting up early to take the herd to Fort Leavenworth."

"That's the ticket." Luther nodded approvingly. "You girls need a bed to sleep in. It's a rotten shame we had to bring you along, but Chaney and I both knew we couldn't leave you for Barney to find."

"No, we couldn't have stayed behind," she agreed. From her saddlebag she pulled a small packet of raisins and peanuts Hardy had wrapped up for her yesterday. "And as things turned out, thank heaven I was here. Tonight I'll have a bath and some clean clothes, so they'll know I didn't steal our money when I take it to the Bank of Kansas City."

He frowned. "You can sleep as long as you want, girl. You can depend on us to take care of everything."

Her jaw set. "Until all the money including the sale of

those horses is in the bank, I'm not going to relax. Barney Mallott's tried everything short of murder. The only reason he hasn't tried that is because he hasn't been able to catch up to us."

"We'll take care of it," Luther insisted.

She smiled at her old friend as she offered him some of her food. He shook his head. "Understand me, Luther. I'm going to see this through. Chaney's going to know at the end of this that I'm his partner, not just his wife."

"Now, Bethie, he knows that."

She pinched her fingers together around a good-sized bite and carried it to her mouth. "Does he?"

"I hope to tell you he does." Luther smiled at her fondly. "Even when you were a little girl, you had him jumping through your hoops. You don't have anything to prove to him or anybody else."

She smiled. Then her expression turned regretful. "I hope he's all right. He was running a fever when I took off. But we've run so far ahead of Hardy's wagon, I can't take the time to go back. I think the most important thing is to get this herd into the stockyards."

Luther rumbled something unintelligible but said no more.

She ate the rest of her food, gazing at the herd. They were beautiful. The cavalrymen and mounted infantry who got them would have some of the best horseflesh around, and the best-trained.

"Luther, did you ever hear of Oliver McNeil?"

His whole body stiffened. His head snapped round. "Where'd you hear that name?"

"Or Josey McNeil?"

Luther looked away. A deep frown line appeared between his eyes. "Never heard of him," he stated positively. "Never heard the name before."

"I've heard he was my brother. Was Oliver my father?"

He snatched off his hat and slapped it against his thigh. "That dad-blasted Noah Rollins. He's been shootin' off his mouth. I knew when he rode up he was trouble—"

She waited for him to finish his conniption fit. When he pulled his hat back on his head, she held out her hands, palms down. The white scars on their backs stood out clearly in the noonday sun. "Luther, can you tell me what happened to me?"

Instead of rage, his eyes filled with tears. "I ain't gonna say a word, Bethie. Except that we loved you from the minute we got you. Me and Chaney. Particularly the lieutenant. I never did see any man take care of anybody the way he did you."

"I needed taking care of?"

"Yes, ma'am. You sure did." Luther wrinkled his face and snuffled hard.

"But you won't tell me about it."

"No, ma'am." He mounted his horse and rode down into the herd.

She couldn't help but notice that she'd ceased to be Bethie to Luther. In the last two sentences, he'd addressed her as ma'am. Something had changed. She wasn't sure what, but her insides knotted painfully as her dreams, Noah's story, and her own imagination combined to conjure a terrible picture of what must have happened to Oliver and Josey McNeil.

Barney Mallott's eyes burned. He ground his boot heel into the dirt as he watched the White Oak horses being driven into six big corrals in the Kansas City stockyards. He licked his lips. Two hundred head of prime stock worth 2,600 dollars.

That goddam Chaney Taggart had all the luck. Tomorrow they'd be in Fort Leavenworth.

Twenty-six hundred dollars!

That was his, by damn. He deserved it. If he couldn't get the money that Taggart had pulled out of the bank, he'd get this. He'd worked too hard. This was his last chance in more ways that one. He had to have this stake. He couldn't go back to Rich Hill now.

He'd convinced the Drorsens that they ought to tax Chaney for those horses. Who'd have thought that Chaney would take all his money out of the bank? That was just like that weasel. He never forgot or forgave a thing. Who knew where that money was? He'd probably buried it somewhere.

And who'd have thought that Chaney would drive his horses all this distance?

Barney had expected the lieutenant to try to ship them from Vernon County. He'd been a jump ahead of Chaney Taggart there. And he'd managed to round up that bunch of bums and cowards from Cass County.

But Chaney'd still got away.

He ground his boot heel some more.

He couldn't find Chaney. But he could see that sassy wife of his. His eyes narrowed.

She was the key to the whole thing. He knew it. If he could just get his hands on her, Chaney Taggart would pay everything to get her back.

He watched Beth Anne, his stare eating her alive. The way she rode that horse made him sizzle. She acted like she was as good as a man. That and all that red hair just dared a man to take a whip to her backside.

The Coates House Hotel wasn't grand. It was clean and they served family-style meals at five-thirty and six-thirty. It catered to cattlemen and cattle buyers, and occasional trail bosses.

Though women aplenty were seen moving up and down its halls, it almost never registered a lady. To have reservations for two ladies for separate rooms had caused the management some confusion.

The Taggart party had reserved four rooms on the first floor. They'd also requested two baths. One for the ladies and one for the gent with the broken leg. The second fellow could bathe at the end of the hall with the other folks.

When Chaney had arrived before the others, he had refused to let them take him to his room. Obviously agitated and hurting like blazes, he wanted to see his wife. He was worried sick about her.

"Lieutenant," Hardy begged, "it'll be a lot better if we get you settled—"

Fortunately, at that moment he spotted her through the open door. "Beth Anne!"

In the act of tying the sorrel to the hitching rail, she raised her head.

"Chaney!"

Less than twenty-four hours had passed since they'd said good-bye, but he hadn't slept a wink. He'd given up on the whiskey before he'd run out of it. "Beth Anne—"

He held out his arms.

She ran across the lobby and dropped to her knees in front of him. "Chaney."

Despite the dozen men standing and sitting about the big room, she kissed him and hugged him with all her might.

He kissed her back, feeling her body tremble. Then he hid his face in her hair. He could smell the dust and sweat. He tried to tell himself he was imagining things, but her body felt smaller and more fragile than ever. All the impressions infuriated him. His temper was the only thing that kept him from crying. He wanted to yell at her for working so hard, bawl her out for sending him on to Kansas City in relative comfort while she worked herself to the bone.

When she pulled back, her eyes were wet. "We got through," she told him hoarsely, taking both his hands in hers. Kneeling at his feet, she reminded him of a child who'd done a good deed expecting praise. "They didn't catch us. Oh, Chaney. All two hundred of our horses are in the corrals. I think we only lost one animal. Someone shot Noah Rollins's mare out from under him." Her words fairly tumbled out.

"He's sick about it, but we'll replace her. He can have his pick." She laughed with joy at the miracle. "We made it through. Can you believe it?"

He could believe it, and for a minute a stab of pure jealousy threatened to overcome him. He knew what he should do. He should say wonderful things to her. He should tell her how fine and brave she was. He should tell her how much he loved her.

Instead he said, "I see you're still riding that damned horse."

She almost tumbled backward. As if he'd slapped her, she had to throw her hands out behind her to catch herself. A bright red color flamed in her cheeks. Mouth compressed into a thin tight line, she scrambled to her feet. All the joy disappeared in a flash.

She looked in the direction of the horse. "You were right about him after all. He's one of the best horses in the state. Maybe in the whole United States. He's got stamina and speed. He's smart as a whip."

"I'm selling him tomorrow," Chaney interrupted her.

Her head snapped back around. For an instant she didn't answer. He thought he'd won. Then she looked back at the horse. "If you do, I'll buy him back. He's mine if you don't want him."

"Say, Miz Taggart," Hardy interrupted. "They've got

the rooms ready. Why don't you go on back and get started on your bath?''

Chaney shot him a look to melt steel, but Beth Anne bestowed her most dazzling smile on the old cook. "I think I'll do that." She signaled to the clerk. "I'll have my bath as soon as you can bring it in. And we need someone to help Mr. Hardy carry Mr. Taggart to his room. You do have separate rooms reserved for the four of us, don't you?''

"Yes, ma'am." The man's hand slapped down the bell beside the registry. "Theodore, show Mrs. Taggart to her room right away.''

Beth Anne smiled blindingly at the clerk and at the bellboy. She nodded to Hardy. "Will you take care of Jack? He's graduated from Jackass to Jack.''

Her eyes skipped across Chaney like a drop of water on a hot griddle. "In fact, I even called him Jack o' Diamonds once last night.''

Her back was so straight and her manner so reserved that the bellboy suddenly remembered his manners to bow in front of her. "Right this way, ma'am.''

In the bathtub with the door locked and steam rising around her, Beth Anne allowed herself a storm of weary tears. She could always tell anyone rude enough to ask that she'd gotten soap in her eyes.

He'd been mean as a grizzly bear with the toothache. He was in pain and half drunk. She had tasted the whiskey when she kissed him. She'd smelled the whiskey on his clothes. He must have spilled nearly as much as he'd drunk. But had she drawn back in disgust?

She had not.

She'd kissed him and hugged him.

Before he'd jumped all over her, she'd been about to

turn it all over to him. When he'd blazed away at her, she'd been about to say, "We'll take the money to the bank right now. Then we'll have a nice meal, get a good night's sleep, and in the morning we'll ride up to Fort Leavenworth. Luther can hire a buggy and we'll have a pleasant trip."

It could have been so wonderful. Now she didn't ever want to see him again.

She hid her face behind the washcloth and sobbed.

Every muscle in her body, every bone in her body, was so sore and he was so mean.

She couldn't believe he'd talked to her the way he had. She'd tried everything she knew to make him feel good. He didn't have a single thing to complain about. She hadn't lost a single horse. More than that, she'd told him the stallion was great.

She tried to concentrate on the stallion. Of course, he was still a stallion and would always be cantankerous, but she actually thought he liked her. The last few times she'd walked up to him, he'd reached out his nose to greet her. He'd nuzzled her and turned his head into her while she patted him and praised him. She'd started calling him Jack instead of Jackass. Whenever she said the single syllable, he flicked his ear back. He was smart and becoming more civilized by the day.

Which was more than could be said for Chaney Taggart. She twisted the rag in her hands and at last flung it into the bathwater in disgust.

This bath was supposed to relax her. Instead, she was sitting here getting madder and madder.

She soaped herself all over, slipped under the water, and then stood up. The hell with her hair. She'd wash it tomorrow when she had settled down.

She dried herself so hard she scraped her skin. Instead

of putting on her one nice dress, she put on another pair
of pants, a shirt, coat, and wide-brimmed hat.

She'd find Hardy and get that money in the bank.

She made a special effort to stomp really hard past Chaney's door. She hoped he heard her leave.

Chapter Twelve

William T. Stoneleigh, president of the Bank of Kansas City, Missouri, took only a quick look inside the strongbox that Doc and Hardy lugged in. After that he bowed and scraped as if Beth Anne had worn the finest dress in Kansas City.

He ordered tea and coffee along with a selection of sandwiches and cakes to be served to her from a silver tray. With Hardy and Doc standing behind her, she watched every certificate, every coin, every bar being counted twice.

The various deposit slips were made out in triplicate; a passbook was issued for her.

"Of course, I'll come to the Coates House myself first thing tomorrow to get Mr. Taggart's signature on everything," Stoneleigh crooned. "And, of course, he'll be issued a passbook as well. Usually we only issue the one, but since you are making the deposit in person—" He looked to her for confirmation.

"That's exactly right." She smiled at the same time as

she wondered what Chaney would say about all this. He'd probably throw another fit, but she would have her own passbook. It nestled in the breast pocket of her shirt as if it belonged there.

Stoneleigh was anxious to demonstrate the bank's services. "Don't trouble yourself about tomorrow's business. The Army pays in script, which we'll be only too happy to cash for you and deposit any way you choose. No matter how late, we will accommodate you."

He looked benignly at the scruffy cook and the old doctor. "I'll remember either of these gentlemen. All one of them has to do is knock on the door at my house. I'll come directly. In the Bank of Kansas City, the depositor is to be served. Will that be satisfactory?"

Beth Anne had just polished off the last of the French pastries. She had to smile around the last bite with her cheeks puffed out a little. She hoped she hadn't made herself look like a greedy pig, but after Hardy's cooking everything had been so pretty and tasted so good.

She felt a little guilty because she'd planned to take one back for Mary Nell. The counting had taken so long that she'd eaten them all.

She touched her napkin to her mouth, then rose with as much reserve as she could muster. "Everything seems perfectly satisfactory, Mr. Stoneleigh. I'm sure I've made the proper choice."

She extended her hand.

He clasped it, then gestured to his teller, who passed him a leather envelope stamped with the seal of the bank in gold and buckled with a gold buckle. He bowed over it as he placed it in Beth Anne's hands.

"Whenever you're in town, the Bank of Kansas City stands ready to provide any and every service."

"Thank you," she said, wondering what other services there might be.

He bowed and followed her to the door. "Banking from around the state is remarkably easy. Kansas City is really only a short ride by train from almost any town, and of course all the express cars have guards. If you have a large deposit, feel free to telegraph us. We'll send a special messenger and guard by train to collect it."

"Thank you," she said again, uncertain what to say about that. "I know my husband will be as pleased as I am to know that our money will be so safe."

"As a church," he assured her, bowing again.

Outside, the three looked at each other. Doc grinned.

Hardy scratched his head. "I'm sure glad I got to see that. I ain't never seen a man get that low down to the floor before and still keep walkin'."

Beth Anne chuckled in agreement. "He didn't seem to mind that I had on men's pants either. I've always heard money talks, but I didn't know how much until today."

They laughed again. Hardy and Doc climbed on the wagon. Beth Anne handed Doc Mr. Stoneleigh's papers buckled with such loving attention into the leather envelope. "Take these to Chaney."

"Wait a minute. Where you goin'?" the old man asked in surprise.

"I'm going down to the stockyards. My job's not over yet."

"Miz Taggart—" Hardy began.

She silenced him with a look. "I want to be ready to head 'em out in the morning."

With that, she galloped off into the darkening night.

Chaney stared at the envelope. He could feel his ears turning red.

"She's got it all taken care of," Doc told him with a tone of pride mixed with amazement. "I never saw the beat of the way she talked to that banker. We looked pretty seedy when we walked in, but when he saw the color of our money, he sat up and barked."

"Then she did such a nice job of talkin' to him." Hardy picked up the story. He had remained next to the door, his expression critical. "She had him wagging his tail before he knew it."

"She sure did a good job," Doc agreed.

"Seemed like she was dee-termined to get it all done," the cook added. "Like maybe she thought *some*body might not think she could. Like maybe *some*body didn't want to give her any credit for doin' all she's done."

Neither Chaney nor Doc had ever heard Hardy talk so long. Doc scratched his head, but Chaney dropped his gaze to the leather envelope. He rubbed his thumb over the shiny gold seal.

Hardy reached behind him to open the door. "Let's go, Doc. I don't know 'bout you, but this old bird's dead for sleep. I got plenty o' room in the wagon if you want to bunk with me."

Gunderson smiled at Chaney. "Get a good night's sleep, Lieutenant. The banker'll be over in the morning for you to sign everything."

Without moving Chaney murmured his good nights. Gunderson closed the door.

"You might as well stay here," Mary Nell insisted.

"I'm not sick." Noah looked around warily.

She wondered if he'd ever been in a hotel room before. "The room's already paid for." She pointed to the copper bathtub. Steam rose from the water. Two towels and a washcloth were folded on the stool beside it. "So's this."

When he started to protest again, she held up her hand. "Believe me, Noah, you need this."

He hung his head. "I must smell pretty bad."

"We both do." She strolled to the door. "That's why I'm going next door to take mine."

As she sat to pull her boots off, she heard Noah's hit the floor. The walls were so thin she imagined she could hear the rustle of his clothing as he pulled it off.

Careful so he wouldn't hear her, she undressed and slipped into the water. It rose up around her shoulders, so hot she shivered in delight. From her waist down every muscle felt strained. She was sure she had blisters on her inner thighs, but when she looked, she was only a bit red.

Next door, Noah grunted as he sank down in the tub. The water splashed.

She could imagine him ducking his head beneath the surface as more water splashed.

Then she covered her mouth to stifle a giggle. He began to whistle.

The sound was so sweet. He sounded like a boy. Even though he seemed so much older, eleven years wasn't so much when she thought about it. He was the kind of man she'd always planned to marry. St. Louis and ladies' finishing school faded.

The water sloshed some more.

She tried to imagine his naked body. She looked down at herself in the water. The slipper bath was comfortable for her to sit in, but she was short. She only had to draw her knees up a little bit above the water's surface.

Noah was tall. Long-legged and long-armed. His body must be folded nearly double, but he was whistling away. A familiar tune drifted through the thin walls—"Auralee."

She shivered again. Was he thinking about her? She wondered what would happen if she made a loud splash.

Would he suddenly be silent?

Next door he set up a great deal of splashing. He must be climbing out of the tub.

She could imagine him standing up on the cotton rug beside the tub. The water running down his body, down his chest, down his lean belly, down his hard horseman's thighs. She wondered how his chest looked with its yellow hair. Was the hair around his sex blond too? The whistling changed to a mixture of singing and humming.

Auralee. Auralee.
Maid with golden hair.
Hum . . . hum . . . hum . . . hum *I love you*
And I always will.

Closing her eyes, she choked on her own embarrassment. She could feel herself getting hot, aching low in her belly.

She was a decent girl. He was a drifter. Her father had always reared her in security. She'd never been alone or hungry. If she followed her heart, she might know those things.

She knew that she'd never had a chance to talk to a young man until he appeared. They'd shared the night beside the grave of his horse. He was serious-minded. His feelings and loyalties ran deep.

Her father couldn't say he didn't come from good stock. He was a friend of Beth Anne's. His father and her father had been friends.

She caught the edges of the tub and stood up. The water splashed loudly.

Abruptly, the humming and singing stopped.

She could imagine the snap of his head as he looked at the wall. Did he scan the shabby floral wallpaper to see if there was a hole in it? Did he grab his towel and wrap it around his body?

She took a deep breath. "Noah."

The silence was electric. The wall seemed paper thin and at the same time thick as a slab of oak.

"Mary Nell?"

"Yes." She'd started the conversation. Now what did she say? What did she say to get him to say, *"I love you. I'll come to you. I want to love you tonight and marry you tomorrow?"*

"I didn't—er—I guess I was singing pretty loud."

"No." Oh, that was so smart. She'd managed to say three words. She reached for the towel to wrap around herself and stepped out onto the cotton rug. "Noah. I liked you singing. 'Auralee's' a pretty song."

A small silence passed between them. She tried to imagine what he was doing.

"I've always liked it," he said.

She jumped. His voice was so close to her. So close to her ear. He must have moved across the room and stood right next to the wall. No, he must be on his knees beside the wall, because his words sounded as if they were aimed at her ear.

She reached out her hand and trailed her fingertips over the wallpaper. Again she shivered.

"Is there anything you want, Mary Nell?"

She wanted him to come to her, but she couldn't say that. She couldn't ask him to kiss her and hold her and— She closed her eyes. Between her legs a hot throbbing began.

Her fingers trembled as she slid them down her belly and into the hair at the joining of her thighs. She closed her eyes. "Noah," she whispered. "Noah."

"Mary Nell?" His voice was hoarse now, deep and froggy, like a man who'd slept a long time and waked up not quite knowing where he is. If he were to start singing "Auralee," he'd probably sing it several steps lower.

"N-Noah." She called his name in her normal voice, but not without a stammer.

"Is the door to your room open?"

She looked at the knob. The key was in the hole. She could open it with a few quick steps. Her father would kill her. He was a drifter. She could have a baby. He'd never said he loved her. Her conscience recited all the usual objections. Her body and her emotions sang different tunes.

She wanted Noah Rollins more than she wanted a stainless reputation, an education in St. Louis, a rich and prosperous life.

"Yes," she whispered. Then louder, "Yes, Noah. The door's open."

She barely had time to slip her arms into her shirt before he came through the door. The rush of energy forced her back a step. He was so beautiful.

His hair was dark gold, slicked back against his head. Because he hadn't shaved in nearly a week, the stubble on his cheeks could only be called a beard—bright gold.

He hadn't bothered to button his shirt, which stuck to him where his body was damp. He'd pulled on his pants and buttoned the two lower buttons, but the top button was undone. The golden hair spread across his chest and arrowed down his flat belly.

She swallowed hard to suppress the gasp. She couldn't help it. Gasp she did—and reached for him.

His shirt flared wide as he opened his arms.

She took two steps. Her palms slapped against the slick flesh at his waist and slid round him. Only her shirt came between them as their bodies met.

He kissed her with possessive power, opening his mouth to cover hers, thrusting his tongue into hers, sucking at her, kissing her as if this were their last kiss instead of their first.

Her whole body clenched and burned. Somehow first

one leg and then the other circled his body. She slid her hands up through the silky hair on his chest and over his shoulders pushing his shirt away.

One of his arms encircled her waist; the other opened her shirt. As she climbed his body, he stooped to take her nipple between his teeth.

"Noah. Don't—oh, I mean—do—please, Noah. Please."

She felt his lips, his tongue, his teeth grazing her flesh. The pain made her wild. She grabbed his hair and dragged him tighter against her breast.

Noah ran his hands down her back and over her buttocks. Mouth and hands both engaged, he carried her to the bed. Instead of throwing her down on her back, he sat down of the edge of it, holding her on his lap.

She opened her eyes. Before all control left her, she had to search his face, to figure out—if she possibly could—how he really felt about her.

He must have read her mind because suddenly his hands flew away from her buttocks. He spread his arms wide as if to say this was her play.

She closed her eyes with a sigh. When she opened them, they glowed hot. "I guess I must want you more than anything else in the world. I can't think what's right or good for me. All I want is you."

He shook his head. "I'll go away rather than hurt you."

"The only way you can hurt me is if you go away," she replied. "That is, go away forever."

He smiled then, his blue eyes warm. "I'm not leaving. I've come home and found more than I ever dreamed possible."

"Then let's begin here." She slipped her hands between their bodies and unbuttoned his pants. He was hard and ready and big.

Her expression must have given her away because he chuckled. "You're making me feel like a champ. I can't help but like it, but believe me, you won't be hurt. Oh, maybe a little, right at first, but not much."

"If you say so." She leaned forward to wrap her arms around his neck. Her breasts brushed against his chest.

He gasped at the caress. "Mary Nell, you make all the right moves without anyone ever telling you. Lie down now and I'll show you how it's done."

They stretched out together side by side. He touched her breasts, kissed them, caressed them, then moved down her belly. He blew hot breath into the curls at the top of her thighs.

The pleasure was tantalizing and growing more painful in its intensity. She wanted him to love her, to make her feel complete.

Now was the time for him to act the stallion. He pushed her knees up. She felt his tongue between her legs. She moaned with embarrassment and pleasure.

"Ready?" he whispered.

"Ready."

His fingers came first, touching her, sliding into her. They made her squirm and gasp. His thumb circled and pressed against the nerves that throbbed and tingled. She dug her heels into the bed and pushed against him.

He kissed her breasts and pressed her down with the heel of his hand.

"Please, Noah. Please."

"What?" he asked, his voice breathy in her ear.

"Please—er—I'm not sure."

"I'll tell you, if you want."

"Oh, yes. I want it. I do."

"Put it in—like the stud puts it in the mare?"

She could feel herself flushing hot. It was so intimate. It was embarrassing. It couldn't be right or good.

"If you don't say it, I won't do it," he whispered. His thumb flicked over her. His fingers moved in her.

"Oh, no." She was dizzy with embarrassment and with wanting him. "Oh, no. P-put it in."

"Like a stud?"

"Yes, like a st-stud."

He kissed her mouth, her neck, the slope of her breast. He moved over her and parted her legs.

She raised her head. He was so big. He really was a stud. But he slid into her. She could feel herself stretching. He came to the barrier.

His eyes met hers, his face like a mask. Only a muscle throbbed in his jaw. She whimpered in anticipation.

"Say it," he groaned.

"Stud," she ground out.

He pushed into her, and with only a couple of thrusts, the whole world exploded.

Later, she lay with her head on his shoulder, her body still joined to his. She felt wonderful. She felt sleepy. She felt gloriously happy. She tried to remember exactly what had happened. "It seems like an awful lot of work went into that one little thing," she mused. "Just all that and then"—she snapped her fingers—"it was all over."

He chuckled. His chest vibrated under her ear. He pulled his leg up and cocked it over the back of her thighs. "Didn't you like all the things we did before—" Snap.

"You know I did. I loved everything. But it was over so fast. Just—" Snap.

"The next time, I'll take longer," he promised. He put his thumb under her chin to tilt her head back. "You made me wait too long. I couldn't wait and make it better for you." He kissed her nose. "Want me to do it again?"

She pushed up on her elbow. "Can you?"

He lay back chuckling again. "Maybe."

"I'll bet you can't."

"If I weren't bruised and all beat up—"

Instantly, she was sorry. She'd completely forgotten that he'd been hurt. That he probably had a concussion. She started to get up, but he pulled her back down.

"No. I'm teasing. I can but I don't think I should. You're going to be pretty sore."

She hadn't thought about that. Experimentally, she shifted her hips. To her embarrassment he slid limply from her followed by a gush of warm liquid.

"Oh, dear. Oh, I'm so sorry."

He put his hands on either side of her head when she tried to get up and clean them up. "Don't be. It's natural. It'll happen every time. Let it alone for now. I want to say something."

"But—"

"Important," he added sternly.

She settled herself against him.

He took a deep breath. "I want us to get married tomorrow morning."

She popped up like a jack-in-the-box. "You do?"

"Sure do. I want you to be my wife. I don't have much." He chuckled a little sadly. "Actually, I don't have anything except a job. I don't even have a good mare anymore."

"Oh, but you'll have one. A very good one. Your pick. Beth Anne promised."

"And I can have the job?"

"Yes. I'm sure you can."

"Your father might be mad."

She laid her head back down on his chest. "He'll probably be glad that I've found you. He never wanted me to go away to St. Louis to school."

He held her tight. "I can't believe you're agreeing to this. You're more than I ever hoped for."

She pushed herself up on his chest, kissing the hollow

beneath his Adam's apple, his chin, and then his lips. "There's just one more thing I want to hear you say."

He returned her kiss. "I know. I do love you, Mary Nell Tibbets. And I'll be your husband with all my heart for the rest of our lives."

She smiled. "I love you too. Now turn me over and show me you can do it again."

Chaney sat in his hotel room, staring at the cooling bathwater.

With the help of a Chinaman who did that sort of thing, he'd stripped and bathed with his broken leg propped up on the side of the tub. With the hot water coursing over him and the Chinaman's clever fingers massaging his muscles, he let himself relax instead of trying to block the pain of his broken leg.

He moaned as the man's hands opened his mind to the feelings that tormented him.

He had acted like a perfect bastard toward his wife. Luther should have cold-cocked him when he'd first opened his mouth to criticize her.

He needed to apologize to her, and he hoped and prayed she'd accept the apology.

Beth Anne would enjoy the bath as much or more than he did. She was so small, so delicate. She'd done a man's work. She'd done *his* work. She'd turned the stallion into a horse to be proud of, something he hadn't been able to do.

When she came, he would make everything right with her. He would have her bath ready. He planned to watch her climb into the tub. She'd always liked the compliments he'd paid her when she bathed at home.

He'd watch her bathe her breasts and arms. Then he'd roll up his sleeves and wash her back. He'd do for her what the Chinaman had done for him, except his massage would turn into a caress. He'd make love to her, apologize to her, admit that he was an idiot.

He'd had it all planned. But the minutes had stretched into hours.

As evening darkened into night, he realized she wasn't coming back to their room.

He came to his feet between the crutches Doc had brought for him. He wasn't used to managing them. Hell of a thing to go through a war without so much as a bruise and then have his leg broken by a bad-tempered horse.

He got as far as the door. In front of it, he twisted and fumbled and cursed before he figured how to prop his crutch against his side while he turned the doorknob. Then he had to step back out of the way to open it.

He was sweating when he finally stepped out into the hall.

The sight he beheld made his blood run cold.

From the door next to him, a man stepped out. Noah Rollins's hair was slicked back. His shirt was out of his pants and his feet were bare. Chaney had never seen a grown man scamper before, but scamper Rollins did down the hall to the next room.

There he paused, placed his ear against it, drew back, took a deep breath, opened it, and walked in.

Chaney closed his eyes. He recognized that strut. Noah Rollins was going into that room to please himself with a woman. Like a stone Chaney stood. His heart flopped in his chest.

Beth Anne, was all he could think. He didn't know where his wife was. Could she have been so angry that she'd come back to the hotel and registered in another room? Had Rollins seen her come in?

He waited. Like a fool he stood there with jealousy racking him, waiting for someone to scream, waiting for Rollins to come out.

He'd go down the hall and find out. He took one step. Then stopped.

Square in the middle of the hall of the Coates House, he stopped. His whole body began to tremble. He didn't have to think twice. He knew he was afraid.

He didn't want to know if Beth Anne was welcoming Noah Rollins. He didn't want to walk into that room and find his wife in bed with a younger man, a man who wasn't broken and barely able to move. A man who wouldn't criticize her best efforts.

Chaney Taggart negotiated an about-face and clumped back into his room. Balancing on his good leg, he jabbed with his crutch to slam the door behind him.

Arranging himself on the bed, he turned off the lamp. Lying on his back, he prayed he hadn't lost her completely.

"You're my man tonight, Jack. Why don't you give me some loving?"

Beth Anne rested her arms on the sill of the half door of the sorrel's stall.

The stallion nickered deep in his throat and nuzzled her hand.

She smoothed his blond mane and rubbed his velvety nose. "I don't have a thing for you to eat. I should have saved you an eclair or whatever those little things with all the cream in the middle were."

Jack swung his head up and down as if he understood her.

"Of course, I could go back to the hotel. I really don't need to be here with you. You've got it all under control and you probably need your sleep."

She looked at the fresh straw piled high in the empty

stall beside the stallion's. The straw would be a better bed than she'd slept in since she left home. She checked it. Clean, sweet-smelling, probably just brought in today.

She made a nest for herself in it, arranging it so she had thickness beneath her hips and shoulders.

"Good night, Jack," she called.

He nickered softly.

A moonshadow skipped down the shedrow, rocking from side to side, bobbing ever nearer as a man might stride along.

From his stall Jack heard the crunch of boot heels. One ear pricked forward, catching and locating the sound. He didn't open his eyes.

Men were always walking around outside the buildings they stabled him in. They yelled to each other and frequently cursed him and his kind. Mostly they walked during the day, but sometimes they walked at night.

As the man drew nearer, his step slowed, grew lighter as if he were sneaking. Jack opened his eyes. One step, two. He thrust his head over the half door.

In the next stall he could hear the woman's soft breathing.

He liked her fine. She patted him and talked to him, brought him treats, and didn't try to rein him around when he knew how to manage his herd.

The man's bulky body was silhouetted in the doorway.

Jack thrust his head toward the body and snuffled. A stranger. He'd allow the woman in his circle. He'd tolerate the men who worked for her.

But never a stranger. He bared his teeth and snorted.

The man paused. His odor was rank. Sour sweat and gases that exploded from both ends of his body and left their traces in the fabric of his clothing.

Jack snorted again. *Be warned. Go away.*

The stranger drew his gun and stepped into the shedrow.

Jack whinnied. Whirling in the stall, he kicked the door with all his strength. Shod hooves splintered the wood and shattered the quiet of the night.

Beth Anne sat bolt upright. Her heart thudded in her chest as the stallion stamped and whinnied his challenge, then kicked the stall door again.

She sprang to her feet, disoriented in the dark, but alert and alarmed, ready to meet the intruder.

In the tackroom at the other end of the shedrow, Rusty Huff rolled out of his bunk. Like magic his gun came up with him. His army training stood him in good stead. Throwing the door open, he yelled, "Halt! Who goes there?"

The stranger cursed and ran away into the night.

Chapter Thirteen

"Mrs. Taggart took care of everything exactly as she ought to," William T. Stoneleigh informed him. "A wonderful lady. Why, I don't know of another woman, particularly not someone so young, who could have conducted herself better."

Chaney smiled and nodded, keeping his temper tightly in check. The Coates House Hotel parlor was deserted. At least no one was around to hear that his wife had conducted his business.

He shifted his splinted leg propped on a footstool. It was still throbbing like a toothache. "You're right about that. I'm lucky to have her."

A hard lump was gathering in his stomach. Beth Anne was succeeding in everything she tried. She hadn't put a wrong foot forward. While he was proud of her, he was also irritated. He should have been the one to do all this.

Of course, he was glad that she deposited all that cash

and gold. He would tell her so just as soon as he caught up with her. She'd never stayed away from him before.

As the banker brought forth all the documents to be signed, Chaney couldn't keep his expression pleasant.

Every scrap of paper bore Beth Anne's signature on the line above his own. This wasn't right. He considered making the banker go back and recopy them. But then he'd have to hunt up Beth Anne and get her to sign all over again, below his name.

Still, this was all Stoneleigh's fault. The man should have had better sense than to let a wife sign like that.

When the banker placed the new account passbook on the table in front of Chaney, he had to clench his fists to keep from cursing. The passbook had the account number written in India ink at the top of the first page. In thick black permanent characters, he read Number 009311-2. The 2 raised his heartbeat a notch. He was being given the second passbook. His wife must have Number 009311-1. It was his money, for God's sake!

"I believe that's everything for now." Stoneleigh looked in his briefcase, then smiled at Chaney. "When we can be of service, as I told Mrs. Taggart, we stand ready. For deposits of sizable amounts, we'll gladly send a messenger and a guard by train to collect them. The same is true for withdrawals. We'll gladly—"

Chaney stopped listening. She'd gone straight to the bank he had mentioned only in passing, opened the account, deposited the money. Of course, she'd saved him the trouble when he was exhausted and in pain. He had to keep his mind on what was best for him. But he was furious.

"The first favor you can do me, Stoneleigh, is tell the hotel clerk to have a gig brought round for me."

"A gig?" The banker's eyes opened wide. He stared at the splinted leg propped up stiffly on the footstool.

"As soon as possible," Chaney added.

"Er—certainly." The banker cleared his throat. "Would—that is—the bank would be happy to provide a driver."

"No, thank you. I've a notion to drive after my wife. She'll be delivering the herd to Fort Leavenworth. It'll travel fairly slowly. I should be able to catch up to her in a light gig."

"But, Mr. Taggart—"

"I don't drive with my leg, man. Tell them I need a gig."

He pushed the rented horse hard. By the middle of the afternoon, probably less than five miles from Leavenworth, he caught up to the herd. By that time, his leg propped on the gig's dashboard was throbbing like a sore tooth.

Feeling desperate, he scanned the hind-enders, hoping to see Beth Anne, even though he reasoned that if she was riding the sorrel stallion, which she most likely was, she would be at the front.

He slowed down, reluctant to drive among the horses and disturb their peaceful meandering. Impatiently, he waited for a place where a more or less level field would allow him to pass.

The first person who spotted him was Luther, riding drag, not the usual position for the foreman, Chaney noted. Galloping back to the gig, his former sergeant hitched his horse to the back of it, climbed aboard, and took the reins from Chaney's hands.

"Lord's sake, Lieutenant, that leg'll never heal."

With a groan of relief, Chaney maneuvered himself into a more comfortable position. "It's my herd," he growled. "I may be broken up, but I'm not ready for the trash pile yet."

Luther threw him a less than curious look. "Maybe you ought to think real serious about what you're sayin'," he remarked to no one in particular. "Nobody's suggestin' that you're ready for the trash pile."

"She's taking too much upon herself." Chaney shrugged. No use trying to talk around the subject with his foreman. The man was his oldest friend, but he'd spoiled Beth Anne from the first.

"Not any more than she wanted," Luther suggested mildly.

Chaney stared straight ahead.

Luther let his gaze drift over to the right flank of the herd. "See that?"

Chaney followed his man's nod. Noah Rollins rode there astride a fine black mare, one of the best in the herd. Jealousy shot through Chaney like a splash of vitriol. Then he relaxed. Beside the man, rode a woman—Mary Nell— not Beth Anne.

Scowling, Chaney looked inquiringly at Luther, who merely grinned.

"I guess I'm not going to have to come up with the money to send her to school in St. Louis."

"The hell you won't. You can run the so-and-so off," Chaney snarled angrily. "I'll fire him today. Give him his pay and send him on his way."

Luther shook his head. "Why would I want you to do that? She'd just leave with him and then I'd lose her. She's my pride and joy. I want to see her married to someone who'll take care of her."

"Your daughter can do better than a drifter," Chaney argued.

"Maybe. Maybe not. He's a good worker around horses. One of the best I've ever seen." He looked squarely at Chaney. "He could take over as foreman in a few years."

Chaney reared back, staring in amazement at his old

friend. What he saw was a man whose hair was iron gray where it had once been dark brown. A man whose beard was grizzled and whose neck was sunburned and crêpey. A man whose shoulders were more bone than muscle.

Luther had never been one to put on flesh, but the drive had worn him down until he looked ready to drop in his tracks.

Chaney wondered how many of his men looked the same. He'd been so busy nursing his broken leg and cussing Beth Anne for her muleheadedness, he hadn't looked recently.

Hell! He remembered the face in the mirror last night. He looked just about as bad. Guilt stabbed him. If he'd paid the dollar a head and dealt with the town council later, they'd all be a lot better off. He was too hardheaded for his own good.

Humbly, he reached out and put his hand on his old friend's knee.

Luther smiled a little sadly at him. "I'm fifty-seven years old, Lieutenant. I married my Marlee when she was thirty-seven. You know that. We didn't never expect to have a baby—being as how we'd waited so late. We were happy as young'uns." His voice choked in his throat.

He cleared it and went on. "Havin' Mary Nell killed Marlee. And just about broke my heart. Toughest trade I ever had to live with. But she's turned out so fine. And now that I've ridden with him, I see he's a real good man."

"What about St. Louis?" Chaney reminded him.

Luther nodded. "I know. I know. But St. Louis was the place to send her so she'd meet a real nice feller. As I look at them ridin' along there together, I know she's met a real nice feller. I'm seein' the future."

"A future with Noah Rollins," Chaney snorted.

"At least they'll be right here at White Oak for me to see after if they need me." He cast a knowing glance in

Chaney's direction. "Maybe our babies'll grow up together just like their mamas did."

A roan mare stopped to snatch at a particularly appetizing clump of prairie grass. Instead of either Mary Nell or Noah turning aside to drive her forward into the herd, they let their horses halt too.

While their own mounts dropped their heads to graze, Noah put his hand on the cantle of Mary Nell's saddle. She leaned toward him, slipping her arm around his waist. His hat had dropped back on his shoulders, the way he usually wore it. It concealed what went on between them as she stretched up in the saddle. It went on for nearly a minute, while the mare finished her tidbit and trotted on to catch up with the herd.

Neither Chaney nor Luther could doubt that they'd exchanged a kiss.

Luther chuckled. "Don't that make you feel old?"

Chaney snorted again. Reluctantly, he nodded. It made him want Beth Anne here beside him. So he could kiss her.

Leavenworth was the oldest town in Kansas. It was also a stronghold of both the U.S. Army and the hostile Jayhawkers.

The White Oak men kept their hands near their pistol butts as they crossed the bridge over the Missouri River.

The town lay off to the right of the bridge along the road that led to the old landing. While the men drove the horses straight toward the fort, Luther turned Chaney's buggy down Esplanade Street toward the Planters Hotel.

"You can take it easy here, Lieutenant. This is liable to take some time."

Chaney clenched his fists in frustration. "Damn it, Luther."

His foreman tied the reins to the hitching post. Instead of asking why Chaney was damning somebody, he came back to his side. "Let's get you down and in a chair on the porch."

Once in a rocker, Chaney watched people hurry past to see the herd of remounts coming in. Prime horses ambling down Metropolitan Avenue to the gates of the fort brought the citizens out in force.

Besides a post office and all sorts of decent businesses, Leavenworth boasted a bordello and a saloon. It was a place for people who offered recreation for the soldiers at Fort Leavenworth, one of the oldest military posts west of the Mississippi.

A herd arriving meant men being paid off. Those men had money to spend before they rode back where they came from. Leavenworth citizens were eager to help them spend it.

Several of the women from the bordello hurried out in garish taffeta dresses and feathered hats to wave and preen in front of the men.

Beth Anne, riding down the center of the street on the stallion, could feel their stares.

One gravel-voiced woman called to her, "Hey, honey, why don't y' go back home? Yer crampin' yer man's style."

Beth Anne stared at the creature, trying to see what a man would want from her. The harsh light of the early afternoon sun picked out wrinkles and pockmarks under the cracked powder on her cheeks. Her shiny red dress had a deep square neckline without a scrap of lace to conceal her flesh. Her blowsy breasts that spilled over the top of her corset were enormous mounds freckled and blue-veined.

Before Beth Anne's stare, the woman's eyes dropped. She raised her shoulder and turned her attention to Rusty, who was riding swing and about to pass under her balcony.

"Hey, cowboy, I'm right here when y' get paid off. Name's Mabel."

Rusty grinned and touched the brim of his hat.

Shaking her head, Beth Anne touched the reins to the stallion's neck. He broke into a lope. The lead mare followed and the herd picked up its pace. With a sigh of relief, she saw Saul trotting back to meet her and lead her around to the back of Fort Leavenworth, where the herd could be penned.

Through the open door of the Overland Saloon, Barney Mallott watched the herd trotting past. He nursed his beer and cursed softly. Two hundred dollars that should have been his. Never mind that the Drorsens expected their cut. He should have gotten the credit.

Now he'd have it all, plus a lot more. He'd been studying. He was kind of glad he hadn't been able to snatch Taggart's wife in the stables last night. He had come up with a new plan.

He drained his mug and motioned for the bartender to fill it up. No need to save money. He was going to get more in just a few days. Lots more.

Chaney Taggart realized that Luther was right. He didn't have the strength to go on to the fort. He excused himself by telling himself that this was Beth Anne's play. Let her make it.

His leg was a throbbing wound from ankle to waist. Inside his boot, his foot was swollen and hot. While his foreman made the arrangements, he sat blessedly still, waiting for the various aches to ease off.

"You can sit on the front porch for free or stretch out inside on the chaise longue for two bits," Luther called.

"Inside." Chaney tried to maneuver himself to get down. In the end, Luther and one of the men sitting in rocking chairs on the porch had to help him up the stoop.

The parlor was cool and dark after the hot, bright day. Chaney lost all dignity as he tumbled onto the chaise. Luther bent and picked both legs up together. Chaney let out an agonized hiss as the sidewise motion twisted his thigh.

Luther patted his boss awkwardly, then left him to hold a whispered conversation with the desk clerk. Details taken care of, he came to stand over his boss. "I'd better get on down there."

Chaney had closed his eyes. He didn't bother to open them. "Do what you need to do," he muttered. "Help her if she needs it."

Under his breath, he added, "She probably doesn't."

Luther's footsteps retreated. Chaney drifted away into a pain-filled dream.

"How'd you like the looks of that herd?"

The two brothers leaned back in their chairs on the porch, rocking solemnly, their feet on the rail.

"Looked like it ought to bring top dollar," came the reply.

"I take it that's the owner." The older of the two tilted his head back toward the parlor. "Someone's going to have to bring him his money. Lots of chances 'twixt here and the bank."

"I don't think so, Frank." The younger one shook his head. His lids drooped lazily over his sapphire blue eyes. "I don't need money so bad that I'd rob a cripple. Something like that, if it got around, would just ruin a fella's reputation."

The older chuckled. "You're right, Jesse. Forget I said anything."

"Let's just rear back and wait until a whole one comes along."

The sight of all her beautiful horses trotting through the gates into the Army's pens made Beth Anne sad. Many of them she'd raised from colts. She'd been in the stables when they were born. She'd trained them personally. Now they were passing into the hands of someone else.

Would the men who rode them respect them or would they abuse them?

Several young men in blue uniforms stood with their arms draped over the top rail of the pen. She noticed them punching each other and pointing. They looked like young men excited to be picking out their horses. Did they know how to ride? Or were they men from the cities who'd joined up without really knowing what they were getting into?

"Taggart." A short, plump man in blue with epaulets on his shoulders called from the archway that led into the interior of the fort. "Where's Mr. Taggart?"

She walked her horse over to him. "I'm Beth Anne Taggart."

He frowned before he remembered he was supposed to be an officer and a gentleman. "I'm Major Hiram Durky, ma'am. Right pleased to make your acquaintance."

"Good afternoon, Major Durky." She swung down and offered her hand.

A pair of deep lines appeared between his eyebrows as he took it. His stare took in her dusty trousers, her man's shirt and vest, her battered hat. She could almost feel his distaste. This gentleman didn't recognize her as a lady.

Dismissing her as inconsequential, he passed his gaze

over her shoulder to the men herding the last of the horses into the pens. "I don't see Mr. Taggart."

He wasn't going to deal with her unless she insisted. She supposed she shouldn't be surprised or irritated. "My husband broke his leg the first day of our drive."

"I'm sorry to hear that." The major looked genuinely sympathetic. "Er—will he be coming—er—that is—who's representing him?"

"I'm delivering the horses in his stead." She pulled an envelope from her saddlebag. "Why don't we get on with the sale? We've delivered the horses as our contract calls for. Actually, we're a day early."

"Um-hum." The major did not actually brush past her, but he walked quickly in the direction of the pens. She had to catch up to him. As he spotted Luther, his mouth broke into a relieved smile.

Beth Anne stopped. Folding her arms across her chest, she waited.

Durky hailed Luther, who dismounted. The two shook hands. Watching their brief conversation, Beth Anne was pleased to see Luther shaking his head, protesting, shrugging, and finally pointing back at her.

At last the officer gave up. His brow so deeply creased that his eyebrows met in the center of his forehead, he came back to her. His tone was accusing. "Seems your husband's back at the boardinghouse in Leavenworth."

"He's had a hard trip," she explained. "Now, Major Durky, why don't Luther and you get together and count and inspect these horses? I can assure you they're exactly what you've stipulated. The counts can be made and everything settled between us."

"These are your husband's horses," he argued desperately. "I can't authorize money to be passed over to just anybody."

Luther came up behind the major. Rusty and Doc Gunderson and Saul joined him. When Noah Rollins and Mary Nell walked over, the major scanned their faces for support. "This is highly irregular. Mr. Taggart's name is on this contract."

"Mr. Taggart's laid up," Doc Gunderson explained patiently. "He shouldn't ought to've come as far as he did. Miz Taggart'll sign for him."

Durky's attitude became belligerent.

"I'm not authorized to hand anything over to anyone except"—he consulted his papers—"Chaney Taggart."

"She's his wife," Luther confirmed mildly. "She's bossed this trail drive."

The others muttered agreement.

Durky crossed his arms over his chest. "I can't turn money over to a woman even if she is his wife."

Noah Rollins's jaw clenched. "She'd be the boss if her husband had been killed on the trail?"

"He wasn't," the man insisted stubbornly.

"Chaney Taggart really isn't able to come over here and conduct business." Mary Nell stuck her two cents in. "And even if he was, he isn't here right now. You've got your horses and you've got the boss who drove 'em here. And why can't you turn the money over to her?"

"Yeah. Pay her off and let us get the hell outta here," Rusty growled.

"Yeah," Saul agreed. "Pay the boss."

The major's ears turned red. "Miz Taggart, surely you must see—"

"She did the work," Mary Nell interrupted him. "She's the boss."

Durky looked at the hostile faces. He looked at the horses in the pens. At last he shrugged. "I hope I don't get demoted for this."

Beth Anne flashed him a reassuring smile. "You're buying some of the best-trained horses in Missouri or Kansas. How can you get demoted?"

While the horses were being counted and inspected, Mary Nell put both hands on the top rail and looked up into her father's eyes. "Daddy, we have something to tell you."

Luther sighed. His gaze shifted to Noah Rollins hovering at Mary Nell's shoulder. Luther had known it was coming, but he didn't think it would come so fast. At least he hoped she'd wait until she was eighteen. But when had age ever mattered?

He swung his leg over the top rail and stepped down a little awkwardly. More than his bones were telling him he was getting old.

Mary Nell took his arm and led him away from the pen. She was smiling at him, her lower lip trembling. He thought about her mother. Even though he couldn't remember much about what Marlee looked like, he wished she were here. So many times in the past seventeen years, he'd wished for her. But again, he'd have to handle it himself.

Noah Rollins retreated several paces. He'd folded his arms and pulled his hat down tight on his forehead. One hip slouched to the side. His eyes were narrowed against the setting sun. His mouth was set in a tight line.

Luther eyed his prospective son-in-law. He looked every bit a hardcase, but Luther remembered that behind all that anger and resentment was a very brave man. He remembered Noah charging into battle against Barney Mallott's gang. He'd been new to White Oak, yet he'd backed Luther's play. Luther had backed Chaney, and Noah had backed them both.

"Fire away."

"I love you, Daddy." His daughter looked toward Noah, who straightened out of his slouch. "I—I—Daddy, Noah and I are— We want to get married."

She spoke in a rush, running the words together. The sentence died away as she ducked her head.

Luther looked across to Noah, whose scowl deepened. "Well, now."

"I know you planned—that is, I planned to go to St. Louis, but that was before I met him."

"You haven't known him very long," Luther pointed out even though he'd seen Marlee on the street and decided that she was the woman for him.

Mary Nell threw a quick glance over her shoulder. She swallowed hard as she looked back up into her father's face. "I love him, Daddy."

Luther put his arms around her. He'd always felt free to hug her, but over the top of her head he saw Noah stiffen. He felt a wave of resentment at the fellow's action. Mary Nell was his little girl.

Careful, Luther, careful, he advised himself.

He wanted to be able to hug her if and when he wanted to, but he wanted his son-in-law to like him. If he could handle this just right—

Still with his arm around her, he held out his right hand.

Noah stared at it. His eyes widened. Then, hesitantly, he stepped forward. Hardly daring to hope, he took the hand of his father-in-law to be.

Mary Nell gave a little gurgle of happiness. Keeping one arm around her father's waist, she transferred the other one to Noah's hand. "My two men," she smiled up at both of them. "I'll have to work extra hard to keep you two happy."

Noah's face had a stunned look as if he were about to collapse with relief.

"We want to get married right away, Daddy. In fact, we'd like to get married right this minute. There's the chaplain here at the fort. We could go right now."

Luther raised his eyebrows. *So that was the way the wind blew.* "Don't you want to wait and have a wedding at White Oak with Beth Anne and Chaney?"

For a second she looked guilty as if she suddenly realized what she was about to give up. Then she shook her head. "We can do that too. Let's do it and surprise everybody. When we get back, we'll have a party."

"Is that what you want, son?"

Noah shrugged as if he couldn't picture a surprise party. "We want to get married right away."

Luther hugged his daughter again. Her smile was lighting up the whole place. "Then let's do it. Just as soon as the count's finished, we'll sneak off if you want. I'll tell the boss we're going to take care of business and we'll see her back at camp."

Mary Nell grinned. "Then it's settled. Come on, Noah. Let's earn our pay, so we'll have something to get started with."

Beth Anne decided that Major Hiram Durky had gotten over his concern about buying the horses from her. While the animals were being inspected and counted, he called for a table and chairs in the shade of the fort's wall. Ostensibly, they were for him to put his ledgers, pens, and ink on.

However, a young private served them coffee and donuts while the ledgers were stacked on a stool beside his chair. While the refreshments weren't up to the standards of the Bank of Kansas City's, the coffee was excellent and the donuts were edible when she dunked them.

"Yes, I'm a career man," Major Durky informed her.

"This is my third post. But I like it here. It's safe. It's comfortable. My last assignment was Fort Gibson in the Oklahoma Territory. Now, that was a bad post. The stories I could tell." His face sobered for a moment. "Why, one time—"

She didn't want to hear any of those stories. Nervousness that had been trembling in her belly now began to zing along her muscles. What was taking them so long? Was this unpleasant man going to play some kind of trick on her?

She clenched her fists, then carefully straightened out her fingers along her pant legs. She didn't know enough to deal with men like him. She was only a girl, after all. Maybe he thought he could take advantage of her. Would she have to order the White Oak men to drive the horses from the pens and take them outside of the fort?

Would Chaney have to be brought here tomorrow to deal with this stupid man?

She forced herself to smile pleasantly as if she'd paid attention to Hiram Durky's reminiscences. "But things are better here."

"Oh, yes." He brightened at her words; then his face fell. "Looks like they're getting finished, Mrs. Taggart."

"Good."

Actually, if she had only known, the time had been relatively short. The horses had been counted and only cursorily inspected. Because of Chaney's reputation, the veterinarian had only looked at a few that had been roped out of the herd as examples of the rest.

The time had come for her to collect the check.

Luther came to tell her that Mary Nell, Noah, and he had some business to take care of. The other White Oak men mounted their horses and trotted off to the south of Leavenworth where Hardy had set up a camp and was probably cooking dinner.

Major Durky received the tally sheets. His mouth pursed as he looked over them. He scanned them as if his command depended upon their accuracy.

Finally, he laid them down on the table. "I don't like the idea of giving this check to you," he said baldly.

So he hadn't gotten over his dislike of the idea. She hadn't come this far to back down. "I assure you that I'll carry it directly to my husband."

"Many men wouldn't want their wives to be burdened by handling all this money."

She leaned forward, her forearms crossed on the table. "Major Durky. Believe me, I don't want to be here. For reasons too long-drawn-out to explain, I had to come on this drive. When my husband broke his leg, we had two choices: turn back and lose the contracts or continue with me in charge."

"Well, you've got a foreman—"

"I'm the boss."

He pursed his mouth even tighter. "You're an impertinent young woman."

She sat up straight. "How many horses did we deliver?"

"Two hundred and six." He begrudged her the triumph.

The thrill that went through her was almost too great to contain. She hadn't lost a single head. Not one. "Then I'll take a check for them."

He sighed.

The private removed the food and drink. While Beth Anne watched carefully, the major made out a check for 2,678 dollars. He rocked the blotter back and forth to absorb the excess ink. With reluctant care he tore the paper seemingly one perforation at a time.

Finally, he passed it over to her.

She stared at it. A sense of accomplishment swept over her. She wanted to cheer, to jump up and down, to wave the piece of paper around her head. If Major Durky had been nicer, she'd have shared her joy with him.

Instead, she rose, conscious to keep her back straight, her head high, her voice cool and precise. "Thank you, Major Durky. I speak for my husband when I say everything is satisfactory."

He too rose and inclined his head. "I hope he recovers. The Army likes to do business with him."

The private brought the sorrel stallion forward. He snorted and pawed the ground.

Don't move, Jack, she begged silently. *Act like Jack o' Diamonds. Don't you dare take a notion to behave like a jackass.*

The stallion stood still. Then nodded his head as if he understood.

With studied grace, she put her foot in the stirrup, grasped the horn and cantle, and pulled herself straight up. While her mount stood like a tree, she swung her leg gracefully over his back, found the other stirrup, and settled herself into the saddle.

Looking down into the man's face, she took in a look of grudging approval. She couldn't resist smiling a superior smile. She touched two fingers to her hatbrim and rode away.

She could imagine the check folded in the breast pocket of her coat. She'd done it. All by herself she was carrying a check for over two thousand dollars—money for the new horses, money to maintain the farm.

For the second time in two days, she was the one on whom everyone depended. The fortunes of her husband, her men, her farm rested in her hands.

She trotted sedately down the road until it wound through a grove of trees. Then she swept her hat off her head and heeled Jack hard in his ribs.

"Eeee-yah!"

The sorrel stallion took off like a thunderbolt. They left a trail of dust rising behind them and the echo of her yell of triumph.

"Eeeeeee-yah!"

Chapter Fourteen

At full dark Beth Anne looped the stallion's reins through the ring on the hitching post. The Planters Hotel in Leavenworth was mostly dark as well. The only lights glowed dimly from the front parlor and a window on the second floor.

She supposed the entire house was asleep. A really considerate person would have waited until morning, but she couldn't wait that long when she found out her husband was in Leavenworth.

The sale of the horses had almost been forgotten in the excitement of Mary Nell's announcement. Her best friend, the friend she knew better than anyone else in the world, had hugged her, hugged her again, then asked shyly if Beth Anne would be her bridesmaid.

Clearly she remembered how she'd flashed an uneasy glance at Noah Rollins. Even though she'd made her peace with him, that didn't mean he could marry Mary Nell.

As she tried to make sense of what was happening, Mary

Nell had handed her a bouquet of day lilies from the walk in front of the officers' quarters.

The White Oak men gathered in the base chapel. Noah and Mary Nell stood before the chaplain, their faces glowing with happiness. Still that hadn't been enough for Beth Anne. Only Luther's serenity had put her fears to rest.

If Luther was pleased with his new son-in-law, then Beth Anne was satisfied.

The only fly in the ointment was that Chaney wasn't there when they had so much to celebrate. Then she'd found out from Luther that Chaney had followed them to Leavenworth.

She shivered with anticipation. All the trouble was over and done. Tonight she would sleep in her husband's arms.

Directed by the night clerk, she tiptoed into the cozy parlor. At first Beth Anne thought the room was empty. No one was sitting in the chair by the light. Then she heard a muffled cough and a faint groan.

A man's boots sat neatly beside the couch—her husband's boots. She'd found him.

Chaney lay in the shadows. His breathing was heavy. He'd slumped until his chin rested on his chest. One arm had slipped off the couch and trailed along the floor.

A wave of love and sympathy swept her as she knelt beside him to lift his hand and lay it across his chest.

He stirred, groaned, rolled his head on the scrolled back. She winced as she thought how stiff his neck was going to be when he woke.

Poor Chaney. She lightly touched the splint. His foot was badly swollen. It needed to be higher than his heart. He needed to be flat on his back in bed with pillows propping up his leg.

Barely a week had passed since Barney Mallott had ridden out to White Oak to try to force them to pay a dollar a head. How her husband had suffered for his stubborn refusal to be blackmailed! His righteous refusal to give his money to thieves! Principle versus practicality. Did two hundred dollars pay for all that he'd gone through, all that she'd gone through?

She shook her head. Hardheaded didn't begin to describe Chaney Taggart when he knew he was right.

How she admired him! Without his leadership she would probably have paid the dollar. Now that he'd shown the way, she knew she never would.

"Beth Anne."

She glanced up hastily. "I'm here, Chaney."

He rolled his head to face her, then groaned as the muscles and ligaments pulled. "Honey." He blinked like a barn owl caught in the lantern light. "Aw, honey—"

He reached for her, his strong arms encircling her shoulders. He pulled her to him. She went up willingly into his arms, across his chest. Their lips met in the prickly growth of nearly ten days' beard.

"Honey. Honey. God, I'm glad to see you." He kissed her and kissed her and kissed her. "I've been so scared."

Warmth inside her turned to heat and then to fire.

"Beth Anne. Bethie." His tongue bored into her mouth as if he'd never kissed her before. His mouth engulfed her lips. At the same time his hands moved over her back from shoulders to buttocks.

She squirmed.

He hardened beneath her belly.

A faint warning sounded in her brain—concern that he'd hurt himself, that she'd hurt him.

But she wanted him. Wanted him so desperately. All the tension, all the frustration rolled itself into a tight, painful ball in her stomach. She couldn't stand it another minute. She wanted his love to make it all go away.

He forced his hand roughly between them, pressing hard against her mound. The pressure should have been painful, but her body reacted as if he'd scratched an itch. The more painful the scratching, the more she wanted to be scratched.

He raised his good leg and levered her into the space between his thighs.

"I'll hurt you," she said.

"You'll hurt me a hell of a lot more if you don't get those pants peeled down."

She knelt and went through the necessary motions to push her clothing down around her knees. She would have stood except that his hands reached beneath her shirt and camisole and grasped her breasts.

She gasped, clenching her jaw tight, while hot liquid wet the tops of her thighs. He was twisting her nipples, pulling them. He pushed her breasts tight together and squeezed them.

Groaning, gasping with pleasure, she managed to hook her toe over the end of the couch. Her boot slipped off and she pulled one leg out of her pants.

He groaned. "I'm behind you. This damned leg." He pulled his hands away from her breasts to unbutton his pants. He bucked up and pushed everything down until his clothing hung on the top of the splints. "Damn," he whispered. His face contorted. "Damn."

She started to get up, but he grabbed her hips. "Not on your life. If I don't have you, I'll just about die right here and now."

She reached for him, guided him to her opening. "I don't think I could have stood up anyway."

With a chuckle he pulled her down on him, sheathing himself in her in one exquisite brutal thrust.

She made one more plea for sanity. "We're in someone's parlor."

"If they stay out just a minute more, we'll be through,"

he predicted. His hips bucked up. His hands pulled her down.

She rode him like the sorrel stallion, her arms at full stretch, the heels of her hands in the hollows of his shoulders.

Shaken by intense desire, they pushed together, straining. She twisted and writhed above him, taking him deeper, then deeper still.

He ignored the protests of his leg in his need to drive upward higher into her.

Her whole body was shuddering as she set her teeth. "Now," she whispered. "Now, Chaney."

"Now!" He was gasping with every movement. Then he arched and exploded.

She could feel the hot wetness flood her. The muscles of her sheath clasped and pulled upward. She could feel movement deep inside her. Inside herself she was opening to receive him.

We're making a baby, she thought.

And then she couldn't think anymore. All the tension went out of her. Her arms went limp, unable to hold her. She collapsed. Her cheek sank to Chaney's chest. Beneath her ear she could feel his heart beating, not staggering and missing as it usually did, but with perfect rhythm.

"I think we got it right this time," she whispered.

He patted her backside before wrapping his arms around her and holding her tightly. His chest heaved beneath her as his breathing calmed. "Nope. That was close, but we'll have to keep trying."

"I love you." She didn't actually say the words out loud. Her lips moved against his chest.

He made the softest whisper of a laugh. His mouth touched her hair. "I love you."

She didn't hear the words. She felt them warm and gentle against the top of her head. She closed her eyes, thinking this was about as close to heaven as she would get here on earth.

Perhaps they slept. Beth Anne couldn't be sure. She only knew that she felt as if she had blinked her eyes and when she opened them, the lamp was smoking its chimney.

With a groan, she pulled herself off Chaney and had to hop around the room to get her leg into her pants and her boot back on.

He opened his eyes, grinning like a contented cat as he reached down and buttoned himself back to decency.

When they looked fairly presentable, she went to pay the room rent on the parlor and to ask the night clerk for some food. The man's eyebrows rose when he took in Beth Anne's disheveled appearance. His mouth twitched in a cynical grin as he swung the register around for her signature. With a flourish she signed "Mr. and Mrs. Chaney Taggart" and plunked down a quarter eagle gold piece. Two bits persuaded the man to bring a tray with sandwiches and cake.

When he arrived, she was sitting decorously in a chair in front of the tea table drawn up in front of Chaney.

"The coffee's all gone," the clerk said defiantly. "But I guessed you might want some fresh milk. You all must be pretty thirsty." He exchanged a manly leer with Chaney, who lolled back against the maroon velvet chaise.

When the man left, Beth Anne indulged herself by fussing over Chaney, helping him prop himself up, and passing him half a sandwich. He smiled at her as she took the other half.

She thought at that moment that even with his clothing stained and travel-worn, his face unshaven, his hair rumpled, he looked incredibly handsome.

Tomorrow she'd drive them both back to Kansas City

and stay in a hotel for a week or more so he could rest. His leg would be stronger then and they could drive home slowly. They could practice making babies every night if they wanted to—until they got the job done.

With those thoughts in her mind, she reached into the pocket of her coat. "I have a present for you."

His eyes flicked to the folded piece of paper and then back to the sandwich he was preparing to take a bite of. "Keep it."

His curt tone had the same effect as a spray of cold water in her face. She blinked and jerked back. "What?"

"I said, 'Keep it.'"

"But—"

"You've earned it. It's yours."

She set her plate aside untouched. She mustn't lose her temper. They were both tired and he was hurting. She must keep cool. She must use the common sense she'd discovered she had in abundance.

She'd learned a lot of things on this trip. One of the most important was that when she spoke with authority, when she displayed her confidence, the men did what she said. Because her orders were reasonable and she didn't ask them to do anything she wouldn't do herself, they obeyed her. She'd gained confidence in herself. The very last vestiges of Chaney's little girl had disappeared. She was Taggart's wife. She knew she could act like one.

"It's not *mine*." She struggled to keep her voice even. "I think it's ours."

He stuffed another bite of the sandwich in his mouth.

She'd never seen him eat like that. What was he doing? Was he so angry he couldn't control himself? "When you had your accident, I took over as I should have. We've always worked together."

He swallowed with an effort and reached for the milk to wash the lump down. "You took over."

She spread the check on the tray in front of him. He couldn't help but see it. He had to reach over it to set his glass of milk down. He was really angry. He sounded as if he were sneering at her.

"You couldn't ride," she reminded him, trying to keep her voice low and even. *A soft answer turneth away wrath.* "If we were going to get the horses to Kansas City, someone had to ride the stallion—"

"The stallion! The stallion!" He set the milk glass down so hard it slopped over on the tray.

She snatched the check away just in time to save it.

"I told Luther and I told you to get rid of that animal." Chaney's words were hurried. Unreasonable anger flushed his face. "He was a mistake. I admit it. I thought I could break and train him. You called him an outlaw and you were right. His badness went too deep. Bred in the bone."

"I think he's better than you give him credit for." Beth Anne knew she shouldn't argue. She didn't think even Chaney believed what he was telling her. "Don't be angry because I could ride him."

Chaney's ears turned red.

She wished fervently she could take those words back.

"Since I've been laid up, he's not the only thing you've been riding."

She blinked. *What was he talking about?* "Chaney, for heaven's sake—"

"The sale was over hours ago. Were you and Rollins able to find yourselves someplace private? Is that where you've been? Is he checked into some hotel down the street?"

She folded her arms. "As a matter of fact, he is."

Chaney spat out some words she'd never heard before. "You know he's courting Mary Nell," he thundered. "He's playing you both for fools."

Where was he getting all this stuff? "Mary Nell's with him."

Chaney bolted upright. His splinted leg hit the corner of the tea table. Beth Anne had to grab it to keep it from rolling across the floor. "Damn him! Luther'll kill them both. You ought to be ashamed of yourself."

She took her time answering. Rising, she moved the tea table out of Chaney's reach. Over and over, she kept making excuses for him. *He's ill. He's hurting. He's out of his mind.* At last she cleared her throat. "They got married this afternoon. Luther gave her away. He was really happy about them."

Chaney frowned. A flash of uncertainty crossed his features. Then he set his jaw. "I saw him. I should have gone down the hall and caught you both."

She sank down in the chair. "And when did I do this?"

"Last night," he sneered. "I saw him."

"Did you see me?"

"He was headed for your room."

She felt light-headed, a curious floating sensation as if she'd somehow left her body and was watching this from the doorway. "I wasn't in my room last night."

His mouth straightened. "Of course you'd say that."

"You can check with Rusty if you want to. We had a prowler in the stables. He didn't see me, but I wouldn't have known about the prowler if I hadn't been there."

The silence grew in the room. Thick and almost as tangible as her hurt. She hurt so badly that she couldn't remember another time in her life when she'd needed to cry more. But her eyes were dry. She'd not only grown up. She felt like an old woman.

At last Chaney let out a long breath. The angry red color began to seep out of his cheeks. "Oh."

"Is there anything else you want to ask me?"

"What were you doing in the stables?"

She put her hand to her forehead. She didn't see how

she could take much more of this, but she was determined to stick it out to the bitter end.

"Taking care of business. Just like you would—if you'd been able. Being sure nothing was bothering the herd. Checking on the stallion."

She'd said the wrong word.

"You were acting like a damned fool," he accused. Sparks flared in the depths of his dark eyes. "I wanted him sold with the rest of the herd. I gave strict orders."

"Well, I didn't hear them." She crossed her legs and pulled her arms in tight across her chest. "I have to have something to ride back."

"Damn it, Beth Anne. You didn't listen to me."

She lost her temper. It didn't really matter since he'd lost his long before. "No, I didn't listen to you. I truly didn't. What I did do was ride him until the insides of my legs and my butt were raw from ankle to the middle of my back. I started out by calling him Jackass, but—by damn— by the end of the drive, I was calling him Jack."

She rose, so agitated she couldn't sit still. Four paces across the parlor—four paces back to stand over Chaney. "And yesterday in front of the major, he behaved like Jack o' Diamonds."

He opened his mouth.

She held up her hand. "And we didn't lose a single animal. He's a great stallion. He kept the whole herd in line. Never let one escape. We'd sweep around that herd a couple of times every hour. Then he'd carry me right up through it to the point. I've never ridden anything like that in my life. I'm just glad I was able to ride him."

She knew her face was red. She'd raised her voice so high they must be hearing her in every room in the hotel.

Chaney's color darkened again. She knew how he hated to lose, but his next remark took her by surprise. "You really took it upon yourself when you put my money in the bank.''

"Oh, for God's sake! I put *our* money in the bank," she snarled. "You were carried into the Coates House Hotel like a dead body. Would you rather I'd left it in Hardy's wagon overnight? It could have been stolen. Barney Mallott was probably prowling around. If he'd found it, he might have killed Hardy to get it.''

His eyebrows drew together. He folded his arms across his chest. "You signed the card all wrong.''

"Chaney Taggart!" She couldn't believe what she was hearing. According to him, she hadn't done a thing right since he'd started this whole terrible mess.

"My signature should have gone first. I know that banker probably laughed himself sick at the idea of a woman knowing what a person had to do to open an account and deposit money. You probably embarrassed him.''

She let out her breath in a fierce snort. "I didn't hear him laugh once while he was serving me refreshments and we were sitting there watching them count the money three times.

"When everything was counted and deposited, he filled out all the papers. Someone had to sign for them.''

"It should have been me.''

"No. No.'' She stamped her foot. "No. It should have been the one who made the deposit. What difference did it make who signed for it? I was there. You weren't. And anyway the accounts are in your name.''

"And yours.'' She'd never heard such a nasty tone in his voice.

"That's enough. That's more than enough.'' She threw the check down at the foot of couch. "I've listened to all that I'm going to. Here's your money that I've ridden back to deliver to you.'' She started for the door.

"Come back here.''

"I'll find someplace else to sleep the night."

"Don't be a fool."

She swung back to face him. Her fingers curled like claws. It was all she could do to keep from flying at him. "If I'd camped with the men outside Fort Leavenworth, I'd probably be having a good time right now. We'd all be sitting around campfires, swapping stories. We might even be l-laughing."

"Come back and sit down." Now he was trying to get her to sit down, after he'd driven her off.

Her voice was breaking. She cleared his throat. She was not going to cry. Not now. Not ever again. "I wouldn't be here listening to someone eat me out blood raw. Doc w-would have gotten out his medicinal whiskey and passed it around. And I'd have had a good, long, strong swig and I'd be feeling fine right now. As a matter of fact, that's what I need. And—you know what? I'm going out to find it."

With that, she slammed out of the parlor.

"Beth Anne," he thundered. "Beth Anne. Come back here."

She was out on the porch before she realized she didn't really have any place to go. She couldn't disturb Mary Nell and Noah on their wedding night, and she didn't want the men to know that she and Chaney had been fighting. She didn't want to be embarrassed, and, above all, the men should think that Chaney was wonderful.

Even when he wasn't.

She wrapped her arms around herself. She was dog-tired and the night was cold. She was going to have to sleep somewhere. She supposed there was a barn in back of this place. Chaney's horse and gig must be stabled somewhere.

The door creaked behind her. The thud of his crutches made her feel guilty. She'd argued with an injured man, her husband, who'd been in constant pain for four days now. No wonder he'd gotten so mixed up in his thinking. No wonder he'd growled and snapped at her.

"Beth Anne." Of course, his tone wasn't apologetic. He was right to think of her as a child. She'd lost her temper. "Come back in the parlor and finish your supper. We've disturbed the house long enough. I'll sleep on the couch. You take the daybed in the corner."

She was so angry she could hardly breathe, but she didn't want to sleep in the barn. She didn't deserve to sleep in the hay with the horses. She didn't deserve to sleep on a daybed in the corner either, but it looked like all she had. With these thoughts in her mind, she allowed him to lead her back in, even helped him maneuver through the doors.

She took his crutches and helped him put his feet up and stretch out. Calm, cool, and collected, she handed him his plate, mopped up the milk, and poured him some more. Finally, she seated herself across from him.

Grinning as if he'd won, he settled back. "Go on now. Eat your supper like a good girl. We'll get everything straightened out tomorrow."

She gritted her teeth so hard she was surprised one or two didn't break off. What she really wanted to do was throw the plate at his head. Instead, she took a bite. The bread was dry and the roast beef tough, but her stomach rumbled.

When they'd finished, she pulled off her boots and coat. She wished for a bath, but the clock in the hallway had struck the half hour after midnight. She was exhausted and the daybed was made up with clean sheets.

"You can go ahead and undress," he suggested.

"No, thank you," she said stiffly. He wasn't going to get his way in everything. "We're in the parlor. Someone might come in. I've been wrinkled for so long, I'm used to it."

Like a good wife, she covered him with a blanket and turned off the lamp.

"Don't I even get a kiss?" he begged plaintively.

She bent over and kissed his forehead. "Good night, Chaney."

"Good night, little girl."

Little girl. She was so angry she could die.

Barney Mallott rubbed his eyes. A grin spread across his face.

Taggart's wife was riding out all by her lonesome. He couldn't believe his luck. He'd just been standing out back of Maisie's place relieving himself when she'd ridden past.

The sun wasn't even halfway up and there she was walking that big sorrel stallion out of town. The direction she was going, he guessed she was heading back to Kansas City.

Without the lieutenant.

Barney buttoned himself up and hurried to get his horse. He figured they'd sold those horses for a pretty penny. He didn't guess she was carrying it on her. More than likely, she'd given it to the lieutenant, but he'd pass it on over to Barney if he didn't want his honey messed up.

Barney wouldn't kill her. He didn't mind killing somebody. He'd done it before plenty. But folks got pretty riled up if a man killed a woman. On the other hand, people stayed mighty quiet about some woman spending too much time with a man. They didn't want it to get out and mess up her reputation.

So the lieutenant would pay up if he knew what was good for her. And he'd be on the way to California with what he should have had a long time ago.

The lieutenant had acted high and mighty a long time. Now was Barney's turn. As for Taggart's wife—Hell! She might like it. A lot of women did. They just didn't want to say they did.

He reined his horse into the trees. He didn't want her

to turn around and see him coming after her as she crossed over the bridge into Missouri.

He'd wait until he got closer to Kansas City. No use wrestling with her and giving her more time to try to get away.

"Morning, ma'am. You're out early on this fair day." The language was cultivated even though the deep voice had a Midwestern twang.

Beth Anne didn't quite know what to say. She had encountered her first problem with being alone on a public road. What would she do if she caught up to someone, or someone caught up to her? Should she stay well behind them, ride along with them, or hurry on ahead?

These two strangers looked presentable enough. But how did she look to them? She was a woman alone, wearing men's clothes and riding what she considered to be one of the finest horses in the state. How safe were the roads in Missouri?

Even as she considered all these questions, she returned his smile. "Good morning. It is a nice day."

Jack was cantering along at a faster pace than their mounts.

The older man, the one who had spoken, had kind eyes. He tipped his hat. "We're bound for Kansas City, ma'am. We'd be glad of your company."

She slowed a little. She was tempted. She truly was. But the younger man was almost too handsome for his own good. His bright blue gaze had a steely quality. As it slid over her, she felt uncomfortable. "I do appreciate the invitation."

"We're pretty harmless," the older man continued. "Sometimes Jesse here gets a little wild-eyed, but our mother raised us right."

While she hesitated, the one called Jesse spoke. His tone had a sarcastic edge. "That's a great horse, ma'am. You surely wouldn't want to get knocked in the head for him."

She stared at them. She could be making a terrible mistake. Their horses were good, almost as good as Jack. But she bet he could outrun them.

"No, I wouldn't. I thank you kindly for the invitation." Both smiled.

"The name's Frank James." The older man introduced himself. "This is my brother Jesse." Both men eyed her steadily as if their names might have meant something to her, but she was a stranger to central Missouri. She smiled and nodded a little apologetically.

"I'm Beth Anne Taggart. Mrs. Chaney Taggart," she added.

"Pleased to meet you." They both seemed to relax.

"You're the lady that brought that herd of remount horses through town yesterday, aren't you?" Jesse asked.

She shifted in the saddle and frowned. She didn't relish the idea that they might think she was carrying a lot of money. "Yes. Er—my husband broke his leg. That was the reason I was leading them instead of him. We spent last night at the boardinghouse. He'll be along soon."

She looked over her shoulder hoping to give the impression that Chaney was right behind her. At the same time, she thought about galloping ahead, but she didn't dare. With all her heart she regretted the impulse that had brought her out of bed so early determined to ride back to Kansas City and take the train home to Rich Hill.

She'd acted like a fool. She hoped she didn't have to pay for doing so.

"Good-looking horses," Frank commented. "Must have brought a pretty penny."

Her heart stepped up its beat. They were going to rob her. "I let my husband take care of all the finances."

"I don't think I'm going to get to do that. I've been engaged more than a year now, and Zee—she's my lady—pretty much keeps up with everything." Jesse remarked with a laugh. "She's got the brains. For which I'm purely lucky."

"When are you getting married?"

"Next year. The house is all paid for and—"

The miles passed quickly. As they got closer to Kansas City, Beth Anne was glad to be with the two men. The road became more crowded with vehicles. Horses, mules, oxen. And men. So many men. Farmers with loads of produce, teamsters with huge loads covered over and tied down with tarpaulins, businessmen driving fine black carriages.

She noticed that occasionally one of the drivers would stare fixedly at Jesse. When he noticed the look, the man would hastily drop his gaze.

She followed the stare and saw Jesse grin.

"You must be someone famous," she suggested curiously.

"Not really, ma'am," he replied. "At least not yet."

Frank cleared his throat loudly.

Here and there a woman rode beside her man. Occasionally children sat in the back. She didn't see a single woman riding alone on horseback.

"I'm really grateful to you both for inviting me to ride with you," she said at last. She was thoroughly convinced that she had taken a foolish chance riding this way. No matter how provoked she was with Chaney, she should have waited for him.

"You don't need to thank us, ma'am," Jesse said. "We didn't do anything. What fella wouldn't rather ride down a long road with a pretty red-haired gal than just plod along with this old stick-in-the-mud?"

Frank laughed. "Or tear around with this crazy coot?"

"I hope you haven't taken yourself out of your way."

"Which way would that be, ma'am?" Frank asked.

"I'm going to the Coates House Hotel down by the stockyards."

Frank looked at Jesse. "Well, that's a coincidence. We're going right by there."

"I think you're just saying that to be nice." She didn't believe them for a minute.

"Are you calling my brother a liar, ma'am?" Jesse's handsome mouth spread in a wide grin. He pulled his coat back from his hip to reveal the walnut butt of a Colt Peacemaker.

She widened her eyes and shrank sideways in the saddle. "Oh, never, sir. Never."

"That's good. 'Cause we were going right straight by there. We've got cousins over in Lee's Summit that we're on our way to visit."

"I'll be stopping at the Coates House Hotel." She smiled. "It's not grand, but at least the sheets are clean and the food's not too bad."

"Let's get you there." Jesse touched spurs to his horse's flanks.

The big bay gelding broke into a trot that quickly changed to a gallop.

Not to be led by a gelding, which he despised on principle, Jack bowed his neck and followed. With Frank galloping along at a more sedate pace, Beth Anne Taggart and Jesse Woodson James ran their horses the last mile to the hotel.

The bay was strong and half a hand taller than the sorrel, but his rider was heavier. And the sorrel ran for pride. Nostrils flaring, neck snaking out, he cut the wind away before him.

Although Beth Anne hadn't intended to make a race, the stallion's excitement and determination communicated itself to her. Almost without realizing what she was doing, she bent low over her horse's neck and stood in the stirrups to take her weight off him.

As they blew by Jesse's gelding, Jack laid his ears back and bared his teeth. The gelding faltered a half a stride and the sorrel left him with a frisk of his flaxen tail.

Beth Anne began to worry that she wouldn't be able to stop the horse at the hotel, but he quickly lost interest in the race when the gelding had been passed. He slowed to a gallop and then a bone-jarring trot.

Jesse caught up with her. "That's some horse," he said admiringly. "What's his name?"

She laughed. "He was bought as Jack o' Diamonds, but I call him Jack. Short for Jackass." She patted the sweaty neck. The stallion flicked an ear back as if he understood. "He's stubborn and nasty-tempered. He's the one that broke my husband's leg."

"But you ride him."

"He behaves for me." She leaned toward Jesse confidentially. "I think he considers me a different kind of mare."

"I could use a horse like that."

"Come down to White Oak Farms east of Rich Hill in Bates County. We'll have some of his get in two to three years. We've already got his first crop. We'll sell you a great horse."

"I might just do that," Jesse said. His gaze passed admiringly over the stallion. "Just might."

Chapter Fifteen

Chaney woke without pain that morning. He took it as a sign that he was healing. He turned on his side and looked for his wife.

The daybed was empty. She'd probably gone to see about their breakfast. He stretched and sighed. His feeling of utter contentment made him smile. Even with a broken leg, their lovemaking had been satisfying. She was the greatest wife in the world. Beautiful and smart, a great rider, a partner in the farm.

What's more, he had to admit that she'd been the one who'd made this drive a success.

He hadn't even looked at the Army check. Suddenly, he wondered how much money he'd gotten. How many horses had they been able to sell?

He hung his head over the side of the chaise and searched till he spied the piece of paper nearly hidden behind the back leg of a table.

He could wait for her to come back and fish it out for

him. Then he changed his mind. He could get it himself. He didn't want to wait. He wanted to know right now. Maneuvering carefully, he worked his way off the chaise and around the end of the table. There, with one arm hanging onto the table, he balanced on his good leg, bent at the knee, and lowered himself until his fingers could grasp the paper.

He'd broken out into a sweat when he raised himself and limped back to the chaise. Dropping onto it, he unfolded it.

He stared at it for a full minute. "Two thousand six hundred and seventy-eight dollars," he read. "Two thousand six hundred and seventy-eight." He shook his head incredulously as he did the math. "We didn't lose a single horse."

He couldn't believe it. They had expected to lose some head in the cattle cars if they'd shipped by train.

He couldn't believe it.

"Beth Anne!" he thundered.

He waited, looking in the direction of the door, smiling, expecting her to burst in through the door. What a surprise he'd have for her.

"Beth Anne Taggart!"

His smile faded just a little. Then he heard footsteps. She was coming. He smiled again.

The door opened. "Beth—"

The hotel manager stood in the doorway, an irritated expression on his face. "I'm going to have to ask you to leave, Mr. Taggart. At the Planters we're a cut above the riffraff that stay in the other—er—establishments."

"Where's my wife?"

"How should I know? She rode off early this morning. And I'll have to ask you—"

"Rode off?"

"Bold as brass in those trousers. I don't hold with women dressing up like men and riding astride."

"Where'd she go? In what direction?"

"Northeast out of town." The man nodded curtly. "And good riddance, I say. She's already paid the bill, but you owe me another quarter, since my night man served the two of you a meal."

Chaney didn't hear the rest of it. He dropped his head into his hands.

The check crackled.

Jack laid back his ears and shied when Beth Anne tried to lead him into the relative darkness of the stable. Still excited from her victory over Jesse James, she made an exasperated sound.

"Come on, you silly boy. Don't start going crazy on me. I know there are some strange horses in there, but you're the best of anything around."

She caught his bridle by the cheekstrap and led him through the door.

He snorted and shied again, half-rising on his hindlegs.

"Jack—"

"Hold that damned horse down or I'll shoot him."

She gasped. A rod of steel stabbed into her back just below the right side of her rib cage.

"Oh, God." Panic froze her in her tracks. Someone had a gun to her back. "Don't shoot," she begged.

"I ain't gonna shoot anybody or anything if you do like I tell you." The gun stabbed again for emphasis.

Jack snorted and champed at the bit.

"Hold that damned killer or I swear to God I'll shoot him right between the eyes."

He might be going to shoot her horse, but his gun was aimed at her. She kept her hand through the cheekstrap while she put her free hand on the stallion's nose. "Calm down," she whispered, trying to make her voice soothing. "It's all right. It's all right."

The pressure on her back eased fractionally. She drew a deep breath.

"I haven't got any money. Ow!"

The gun barrel stabbed again. Jack snorted and stamped.

"Don't you lie to me, Miz Taggart. I know what you've got."

"Who are you?" Despite the gun in her back, she turned around. "Barney Mallott!"

He smirked. "Surprised to see me? Y' shouldn't be. Y'all cheated me outta a share of that Army money. Now I'm a-gonna take it all." He poked her again, this time in the navel.

The sorrel stallion neighed shrilly. Up he went on his hind legs, lifting Beth Anne clear off her feet. Terrified, she grasped at his mane.

But terrified as she was, Barney was more terrified. "Hold him or I'm gonna shoot him."

Jack dropped to all fours with a jarring thud. Beth Anne almost lost her grip on the bridle. "Wait. Don't shoot him. Let me put him in a stall. Don't shoot him."

Barney cowered back, waving the pistol from her to her horse.

She covered Jack's nose with her hand. "Come on, boy. Come on." Trembling in every limb, she led the stallion into the nearest box stall, where she closed and bolted the door.

Instantly, the stallion's hooves rang on the wall at his back.

Barney straightened up and resumed his belligerent stance. "Now. Hand it over."

She drew in her breath sharply, then wished she hadn't. The marshal of Rich Hill stank powerfully. Rank body odor mingled with the smell of too many horses.

She stared at him incredulously. His face was dirty, greasy with sweat, the lower half covered in grizzled stubble. His clothes likewise were filthy and stained. Only the marshal's badge on his chest glinted, reminding her that he still might convince others of his authority.

"I don't have anything to hand over," she replied, keeping her voice calm and flat. Barney was a bully. He'd gain strength if he thought he frightened her.

His lip curled in a sneer. He prodded her again. "I want the money you got for them horses. I know you've got it. The Army wouldn't give it to nobody but you."

She stepped back against the door of Jack's stall. The stallion's head bumped against the small of her back. He snorted and snuffled at her shoulder. Highly agitated, he kicked back again. One of the boards at the back of the stall splintered. Again the stable rang.

Barney retreated. He looked at the stallion uneasily. His gun wavered.

"Marshal," she said in her sternest voice, "they didn't give me any money. I don't have a cent on me." She couldn't keep a tremor from rising at the end. Every muscle in her body was quivering. She felt as if she might fly apart in the next second. Actually, she had almost twenty dollars, but she didn't think it would be enough to make him go away.

He looked amazed. "Yer lyin'."

Jack whinnied shrilly.

She shook her head. "They gave me a check. I gave it to Chaney. It's back in Leavenworth."

She could almost feel the disappointment. Barney's silhouette seemed to shrink. He grunted. Then he stepped closer. "Yer lyin'."

"Why would I lie?"

"To save the money. To keep me from gettin' any." He

holstered his gun and reached for her. "Where is it? Yuh got it on yuh?"

"No." She slapped at his hand as it closed over her wrist. "Get away."

Jack's broad chest thudded against the stall door. His head snaked out, teeth champing for Barney's hand.

The marshal jerked her toward him and slung her across the stable. She thudded into an empty stall and fell sprawling in the straw. Rebellion boiled inside her.

She rolled over and tried to scramble to her feet. Too slow. He thudded after her and slammed his knee into the middle of her back. Stunned, she collapsed, her breath whooshing out of her lungs.

She couldn't even curse in anger or weep with shame.

Methodically, he turned out the pockets in her coat, chortling with glee when he found the twenty dollars. He flipped her over and checked the pockets in her pants and vest, even the breast pockets in her shirt. When he was done, she was trembling with humiliation and he was grinning as if he'd been handed a present.

"Looks like ol' Chaney Taggart had the right idea, waitin' fer yuh to grow up and all. I useta think he was dumb to be carryin' around a little girl."

A noise from outside the stable made them both turn their heads in its direction.

They had both forgotten that they were in the middle of a large town, in a public place. She opened her mouth to scream. He slammed his fist against her jaw.

Barney had a time hauling her unconscious body over his shoulder. By the time he had her positioned to carry, he was grunting with the effort. As sweat poured off him and he quivered in both limbs, he carried her up the ladder to the loft. There he dropped her unconscious body in the hay and listened.

Noise! Hoofbeats, boots, the mutter of men's voices. At least two people had brought their horses into the hotel stable. And no one must even suspect that she was up there.

He stripped off his sweaty handkerchief and stuffed it into her mouth. Then he used hers to tie it tight across her face so she wouldn't spit it out.

He flipped her over on her stomach and tied her hands behind her with his suspenders. He reasoned he had to tie her real tight. Otherwise, the elastic might stretch enough to let her get her hands out.

She stirred. He flipped her back over and jerked her belt from around her waist. Her eyes were open by the time he got her feet tied.

He drew his gun again and aimed it at her chest.

The long minutes ticked by until at last the men went away.

"Now," he said as he settled back on his haunches and wiped his sweaty forehead. "Now we're gonna wait. Just you and me."

Chaney sat in the buggy, his leg propped up on the dash. He hugged Mary Nell, who had climbed up beside him and introduced herself as the new Mrs. Rollins. He hadn't had any choice but to offer his grudging congratulations to Noah. Part of his uneasiness came with the perverse realization that he owed his wife an apology for doubting her faithfulness.

"You fellas deserve bonuses," he told them, his voice ringing with sincerity. "A man can't have any better friends. You sure came through for me." He took a deep breath. "I want to thank you too for keeping my wife from getting herself killed."

"Glad to do it, boss." Luther grinned like a boy.

"I'll take that bonus right now," Rusty called. "There's a woman over there in Leavenworth I'd like to make the acquaintance of."

Everybody laughed.

Only Hardy looked around. "Where's Miz Boss?"

"Er—" Chaney didn't want to tell them the truth. "She—er—she decided she needed to get that check in the bank in Kansas City. She's got the bit in her teeth and I don't know how I'm going to rein her in."

Some of the men frowned. A few chuckled a little uneasily.

"Don't be mad at her," Mary Nell chided. "You owe her a world of thanks. We all do."

A slow flush crept over his cheekbones as he scanned the faces of the men gathered around him. He nodded curtly.

"You did thank her, didn't you?" From her new status as wife, little Mary Nell Rollins dared to ask the question. She slipped down out of the buggy to slide her arm around Noah's waist.

Chaney's flush deepened. "Well, sure."

His old friends Luther and Doc Gunderson were frowning. Rusty shook his head and stared at the horse's rump. Hardy muttered something under his breath.

Noah Rollins raised his eyebrows and whistled softly between his teeth.

"Well—she—I—that is—she should have known— Of course I was grateful."

"But did you tell her?" Mary Nell was like a terrier with a rat.

"She didn't need to be told that. I gave her credit for

what she'd done. I told her she could keep the money.
She tried to give it to me, but I wouldn't take it."

"Aw—Lieutenant." Luther shook his head.

"A man's got his pride." Chaney defended himself.
"She's been acting like she's gone crazy. Opening bank
accounts and selling stock and— It'll take me weeks to get
everything straightened out."

"Now, Lieutenant—"

"That's an awful thing to say," Mary Nell interrupted.
"All your money is safe. It's not in the bed of Hardy's
wagon about to be dumped in a creek or stolen. Your herd
sold for top prices."

Chaney shot her a fierce look, but she thrust her chin
out at him. "She about killed herself to get everything
right. And all you do is criticize her." She looked around
her. "And in front of us."

Chaney clenched his hand over the back of the seat until
the knuckles showed white. "I'm going to do what she
asked me to do in the first place. I told her I was going to
get rid of that killer horse that she's been onto me about."

"Goddamn," Hardy muttered to no one in particular.
Rusty stumped at the ground with his boot.

Noah Rollins grinned. He draped his arm around his
wife's shoulder as he purely enjoyed Chaney's discomfi-
ture. "I'll take that horse off your hands. He sure has
proved his metal. 'Course I don't know how that'll set with
the boss lady. She thinks Jack was the real reason we got
all the way to Leavenworth without losing a single head."

More than the others' scolding, Noah's sarcasm hit Chaney a blow to the jaw. He let his hand drop to his side.

Mary Nell put her hand over it. "Chaney," she said
softly, "she stopped calling him Jackass and started calling
him Jack. She really loves that horse."

The silence weighed heavy in the circle as they all
watched Chaney come to terms with himself.

At last, he raised his head. His face was red, but his tone was apologetic. "Fellows, I've been a damn fool. I've got to go find my wife and beg her pardon. Luther, if you'll start home with everybody, I'll go back to Kansas City. I hope I can find her at the Coates House Hotel. If I can't, I'll just have to take the train back to Rich Hill."

"A couple of us ought to go with you, boss," Rusty volunteered. "We can ask around town. She might've already started for home."

"She didn't take the check. I—er—lied about that." Chaney pulled it from his pocket and smoothed it out. "Fact is, she was so mad at me, she left before I woke up this morning. Looks like she had every right to be mad. I'm just lucky to still have my hair."

He looked up at his friends. "I'd appreciate your company, Rusty, but I'm going to ask Mary Nell"—he smiled—"Mr. and Mrs. Rollins to come with me. Maybe you two can explain it to her?"

"I'll be glad to." Mary Nell looked up at her handsome husband. "We can make it a sort of a honeymoon."

Noah grinned down at her. "We sure can." Then he looked up at Chaney. "Glad I'm not gonna miss this."

Chaney ground his teeth.

Numb with hopelessness and suffering acutely from thirst, Beth Anne wondered if Barney Mallott would ever get drunk enough to pass out.

Her hands were numb from the constant pressure of the elastic in the suspenders. Her throat was dry as a desert as Barney's foul handkerchief soaked up every bit of saliva.

Her captor had left her only once during the long afternoon. He'd gone away to buy himself a bottle of gin with the twenty dollars he'd found in her pocket. Sipping regularly, he'd kept watch through a knothole over the comings and goings of the hotel.

"The lieutenant'll be back," he'd informed her. "He rented the buggy here. He'll be back. And then I'll get my due."

He nodded drunkenly now and seemed about to doze off. She thought of rolling to the edge of the stairwell and sliding over. Better to risk breaking something than to stay up here with him.

He roused and looked at her steadily. "I'm gonna tell y' all about it soon as I get that money," he said with measured care. "I'd tell y' right now, but I wanta see the lieutenant's face." He took another drink and eyed her blearily. "I ain't really mad at you, Miz Taggart."

She pushed herself up and tried to ease the pain in her wrists. His face was so wet and greasy from the heat and the gin, she couldn't tell for sure, but he looked as if he were turning maudlin. Men did sometimes begin to cry when they were drunk enough. If only he would take out the gag, she was sure she could persuade him to let her go.

"I ain't never got nothin' fer all my trouble. Chaney Taggart got it all." He took another drink and looked through the knothole.

He turned back to her with an unholy grin on his face. "And here he comes."

"Jesse, you might as well forget about that horse. Even if I would go along with you stealing him, you don't want to do it."

"Th' hell I don't. He's too much horse for a girl." Frank's brother, more than slightly drunk, smothered a belch and grinned sheepishly.

"She didn't handle him like he was too much for her.

And besides, Jess, you don't want to get a reputation as a horse thief.''

Jesse blinked his blue eyes. He'd draped his arms over the swinging doors of the Kansas City saloon from where he stared mutinously down the street toward the Coates House Hotel.

He'd had too much to drink, and now all he could talk about was the big sorrel stallion that had run the legs off Dancer.

''Jus' gonna take one more look at him.''

Frank made a grab for his arm, but his brother plunged through the doors. Drunk or sober, Jesse was greased lightning when he wanted to be. He was on his horse and trotting down the street weaving only slightly in the saddle before Frank had his own horse untied.

When Frank caught up with him, Jesse had his lower lip thrust out, his neck bowed. Frank hated to knock his brother in the head here on a public street.

Not that Jesse wouldn't forgive him for it when he sobered up, but it would draw too much of a crowd. With a sigh, Frank shook his head. He figured he was in for trouble.

''She checked into the hotel, but she hasn't come back.''

Noah's boot heels thwacked down the front steps of Coates House Hotel as he returned to the buggy.

Chaney closed his eyes against the disappointment. ''Didn't they have any idea where she went?''

''She was going to stable her horse. From there they don't know any more.''

At the mention of the horse, Chaney winced. He opened his eyes and looked helplessly around.

Mary Nell put her hand on his good knee. ''Why don't

we take you in and get you settled? Then Noah and I can go hunt for her. Maybe she went to buy a dress. Maybe she went to the bank for—er—some money."

Chaney raised one eyebrow at the mention of money. He caught the look that the couple exchanged.

"I think Mary Nell's got the right idea," Noah agreed. "Let's get you in."

Chaney shook his head. In disgust he stared down at the dusty bandages holding the splints in place. He was miserable. He was beginning to feel feverish. He was in pain. But he was frustrated to the point of screaming. He wanted to find his wife. He wanted to sweep her into his arms and apologize to her. Instead, he was going to be put to bed like a child.

He bent forward and lifted his leg down off the dashboard. He had to set his teeth against the pain as the muscles in his back, his hips, and the leg itself all racked him. He'd driven too fast today. He was too beat up to take punishment like that.

When he found her, he would check them into this hotel for a full week or more. Then they'd take the train home.

With Noah on one side and Mary Nell on the other, he allowed himself to be half-carried up the steps and into a first floor room. While Mary Nell waited outside, Noah helped him undress and stretch out under a sheet.

"Thanks a lot," he whispered as Noah handed him a full glass of water. He drank it down and then another. At last he settled back and closed his eyes.

"Be back soon as we can." The younger man's voice seemed to come from far away.

Chaney roused. "Congratulations," he murmured. "You've got a wonderful wife."

Noah grinned. "I know."

* * *

"Here's Jack all right," Mary Nell said. The stallion nickered in recognition. "Where'd she go, old fellow?"

When Beth Anne heard her friend's voice below, she kicked out furiously, bringing her legs down with a terrific thump.

She had only one chance. Barney threw himself across her body and nearly crushed her with his weight. She couldn't draw a breath, nor could she lift her legs again with his heavy thigh across them.

His face was only inches from hers, his teeth bared, his eyes promising to hurt her.

In the stable below, neither Mary Nell nor Noah seemed to pay the least attention to her effort. They talked on, discussing where she might have gone, discussing the possibility that she might be hiding from Chaney to give him a chance to think things over.

"I don't think she'd do something like that," Mary Nell objected.

"Why not?" Noah shrugged laconically. "She's got every right to be mad at him. She about killed herself for him, and all she got was a hard time."

"Just see that you don't forget that," Mary Nell told him.

"Not in a million years."

There followed a period with no talking. Beth Anne could hear them kissing. Their breathing became heavier. Mary Nell made a little squeaking sound and then a sigh. Noah chuckled and then groaned.

Barney Mallott could hear them too. He grinned into her face. His hand came up to squeeze her breast. She closed her eyes, promising herself that when she got free, she would find someone to horsewhip him.

At last Noah let out a long sigh. "I guess we'd better go

look for her. The quicker we find her, the quicker we can get checked into our own room."

"Oh, yes," Mary Nell agreed.

Beth Anne tried desperately to move again. The best she could manage was a pitiful squirm under Barney's weight.

He waited several minutes before rolling off her and crawling to the knothole. "Street's empty," he told her. "Now things are gonna get interesting."

He rolled her over on her stomach and dragged her around until she was next to a cross brace on the inside of the roof. His purpose was all too clear. He unbuckled the belt around her ankles and tossed it over the two-by-four. Before she could move, he had caught first one and then the other of her ankles and bound them together beneath the timber. She lay facedown in the hay, her feet nearly a yard above her head, unable to move.

"Now stay real still." He patted her rear. "I'll go pitch a note through Chaney's window. He'll come out directly if he cares anything 'bout yuh a-tall. We'll get this money exchanged, and I can be on my way."

She tried to make a sound, but her throat was too dry. Trussed up like a pig for slaughter, her body was too strained to do anything but groan.

She couldn't even turn her head to see him disappear down the ladder.

Breaking glass and heavy thudding interrupted Chaney's sleep. At first he couldn't be sure whether he'd dreamed the noise or actually heard it. He opened his eyes, staring upward at the same ceiling he'd seen only night before last. If he ever got back home to White Oak, he wouldn't leave it for months.

The noise. He frowned. Had he heard it, or dreamed it? He rolled his head on the pillow.

The lower left pane of the window was definitely broken. It hadn't been broken before he went to sleep. He stared at the glass on the floor. Someone or something from the alley had broken the window.

Still befuddled, he pushed himself up on his elbows. His eyes searched the Turkish pattern of the rug. At last he found the culprit. A wad of paper? Paper?

He leaned out of bed. It was beyond his reach. He stared at it halfheartedly, tempted to leave it lying where it had fallen and go back to sleep. Probably some child—

Oh, well—

He stretched farther. Took a deep breath and let it out. His fingertips brushed the paper, caught the top, tipped it toward him. It was strangely heavy. He hooked it and dragged it to him.

A rock with paper wrapped around it. Still puzzled, he opened the paper. He couldn't breath. His closed his eyes, then opened them again.

If you want to see your wife agin come to the stabel. Bring the chek. Ill trad you.
Come by youself. Dont tell nobody.

Chaney flung the sheet back and stood so fast that a wave of dizziness drove him back down. The springs creaked, but he bounced up. Not bothering with his shirt, he stabbed his arms through his coat sleeves.

The first step on the splinted leg sent a shard of pain all the way to his brain, but he never faltered. In three searing steps, he crossed the room and dropped into the chair. Gasping for breath, he managed to pull his boots on.

Then he rummaged through his grip. In the bottom he found what he sought. His old service belt with his .45-caliber Army revolver. Now he knew why he'd put it in. Standing, taking most of his weight on his good leg, he buckled the belt around his waist over his coat. It fitted against his hip like an old friend.

Whoever had taken Beth Anne would have less than a minute to hand her over, or Chaney vowed to blow a piece of him off every thirty seconds until he did.

Barney dashed into the stable and skidded to a halt. Two men stood in front of the sorrel stallion's stall. The younger one had his hand through the cheekstrap.

Barney's eyes widened. "What the hell you all doin'? Get away from that horse."

The older man stepped back, but the younger one merely turned. "Someone didn't even take the bit out of his mouth," he said. "Don't seem fair to treat a great animal like that."

Barney shook his head in a baffled way. He glanced upward, then brought his gaze back down. "Well, I was—yeah—I was comin' right now to do that. I'll take care of him now."

"Is this your horse?" the older man asked. A muscle flickered in his jaw. Tension radiated from him.

"Well, sure." Barney strode forward to push the younger man aside, but the stallion laid back his ears and snorted. "Easy, boy."

The stallion stamped and neighed.

The younger man let go the bridle and stepped aside. "He don't seem like he knows you. What do you think, Frank?"

Before Frank James could answer, the horse kicked out behind. His iron-shod hooves rang against the stable walls. Another of the one-by-twelves cracked and spanged outward.

Barney jumped back, pulling his endangered hands in against his chest. He looked upward as if seeking aid, then back at the maddened horse that snaked his head over the stall door.

"Sure he does." The sweat oozed out on Barney's forehead. It ran into his eyes as he glanced up again.

Frank James looked up too. "I don't think so, Jesse. But this gent's powerful interested in something up there in that loft. Maybe I'll just take a quick look."

"No." Barney stepped in front of the ladder and drew his gun. He pulled his badge from his watch pocket and flashed it. "No, sir. You fellows better get on about your business. I'm a U.S. Marshal and I got a prisoner up there."

"A U.S. Marshal, huh?" Jesse chuckled. "I've seen a few U.S. Marshal's badges, and they don't look like yours."

"I think that badge looks like it might be a hunk of tin somebody in some little jerkwater town might wear," Frank suggested. "Who'd you take it off, rube?"

"I didn't. Stay back!" Barney was sweating profusely now. The gin was roiling in his stomach. He swallowed, praying he wouldn't puke. These were horse thieves. He'd bet his badge on it. And he didn't have time for them. Any second now—

"Where's my wife, you son-of-a-bitch?"

Chaney Taggart, his face so contorted with pain Barney barely recognized him, leaned against the doorway. His splinted leg dragged behind him. His face was gray beneath the sweat that glistened on his forehead.

The pistol in his hand trembled, but the bore never left Barney's chest.

Both the James brothers stepped back into empty stalls out of the line of fire.

The stallion flung up his head at the sound of Chaney's voice and nickered shrilly.

"Where is she?" Chaney repeated.

Barney cringed. This wasn't happening at all the way he planned it. Inwardly, he began to curse. If those damned horse thieves hadn't been there, he could have made this thing work. Since they were, he needed to change his plans. He couldn't ask Chaney for the check in front of them. They could take it off him and ride off with the horse as well.

"I don't know." It was lame, but it was the best he could come up with. He cleared his throat and tried not to cower. "I don't know what you're talking about."

"The hell you don't." Chaney tried to put his weight on his broken leg. The pain was too intense. He settled for jumping sideways and throwing his arm over a stall rail.

Barney glanced to the side. The two thieves were eyeing the proceeding like the audience in a bur-le-que. He decided to bluff. "You'd better drop that gun, mister. I'm a U.S. Marshal."

"The hell you are," Chaney snarled. "Where's my wife? You've got about ten seconds before I blow a hole in your foot."

"God!" Barney backed away. "Don't be a fool. If you shoot me, you'll never find her."

"Sure I will," Chaney spit out each word as if he were spitting nails. "I'll just keep shooting parts off you until you tell me." He laughed bitterly. "And you'll tell me, Barney. You know you will."

"Help me!" Barney appealed to the horse thieves. "Draw your guns and save me. There's a reward for this fella."

Jesse was grinning like a cat in front of a cream pitcher. "How much?"

Frank waved Jesse back. "I don't think you'll have to shoot him, mister. I think we've both got a pretty good idea where your wife is. She'd be a little redheaded gal named Beth Anne, wouldn't she?"

Chaney let his gun sag. His left knee buckled. Only his arm kept him from falling to the floor. "Beth Anne."

Barney saw his chance. Maybe he wouldn't get the money, but he could kill Chaney Taggart. That would get him something. He pulled his gun.

But Jesse James was faster. Jesse's shot caught Barney in the hip. The .45 Colt Peacemaker fired from a distance of ten feet slammed the marshal sideways into the wall.

Oddly, he didn't feel any pain from the wound. Only from the force with which his head banged into the wall. Everything went black for a second. Then he opened his eyes. He clapped his hand against the hip. Hot blood was pouring out.

Goddamn!

Knowledge of what a wound like that had done struck him. He was done for. He'd lost. Lost. Lost. "Damn you, Chaney Taggart!"

Frank James strode down the shedrow and helped Chaney to the door of the stall, while Jesse kicked Barney's weapon away into the straw. Wounded as he was, the marshal fought the man who'd shot him. He'd kill Chaney Taggart if it was the last thing he ever did.

"Where's my wife?" Chaney looked from Frank to Jesse to Barney.

Frank carefully lowered Chaney to the straw. "Why don't you just rest easy here and I'll see what's in the loft? He's been way too interested in that."

"Damn you!" Barney screamed. "You come back here. You sons-of-bitches. This ain't none of your business."

Frank's head and shoulders disappeared through the stairwell. "She's here," he called. "Little the worse for wear, I imagine, but I'll get her down."

"Damn her too!" Barney screamed. "Damn you all!"

Chapter Sixteen

"Easy does it." Frank James pulled the filthy handkerchiefs out of her mouth.

When Beth Anne tried to speak, she found she could only croak. Her throat felt as if it were lined with sandpaper. When Frank unbuckled Barney's belt, her legs crashed to the floor.

Now she should roll over and sit up. Her brain sent signals to her limbs, but nothing happened. Her helplessness made her want to weep. The thought of weeping made her angry. She wouldn't let herself do something so stupid as to start crying after she was safe.

In the next minute, she found an excuse to cry. Frank knelt at her waist to untie her hands. He let out a low whistle before he began to work at the knots. The elastic suspenders had dug into her flesh all the time she'd been tied up. Likewise, the knots had kept tightening. Frank struggled for what seemed a long time, apologizing as he did so for taking so long.

At last the knots popped free.

Her hands fell limply to her sides. Embarrassed, she had to wait for him to roll her over and help her to sit up. Gingerly, she brought her hands around in front of her body, where she gasped at the sight of them. They were purplish blue—her fingers swollen like sausages.

Frank grabbed one and began to massage it vigorously.

"Oh, Lord," she croaked. "Oh, sweet Lord." The pain struck her as the circulation rushed back in. She let her head fall back on her shoulders as she struggled for control. Then she remembered. "Who? Who was shot?"

"Beth Anne!" Chaney roared from below. "What's wrong?"

She took a deep breath and clenched her teeth. Frank dropped her hand and began to rub the other. Despite her will, she couldn't stifle the keening cry that slipped out between her lips.

"Beth Anne!"

"She's—" Frank started to ask Jesse to come up and help him get her down. Then he looked into her agonized face.

She shook her head desperately. Chaney had enough to worry about.

"She's just a little stiff," Frank amended. "I'll bring her down in a minute."

Beth Anne nodded gratefully. Below them, they could hear Barney moaning. She remembered the shot. She'd almost jumped out of her skin when it had gone off beneath her.

"Is Chaney all right?" she managed to say between clenched teeth.

"Except for walking on that broken leg, he's fine."

"Did you shoot Barney?"

"Jesse did. He was drawing down on your husband,"

Frank added hastily. "That fat man's got a powerful hate for him."

Beth Anne nodded. "Chaney's a rich man. Barney's jealous."

"Uh-huh." Frank James laid her hand on her thigh. "We'd better put the quietus to this. Can you climb down that ladder yourself? I can carry you, but it's mighty uncomfortable."

For answer she scooted herself to the edge of the stairwell. Her legs felt all right, but she still couldn't use her hands. "You go down first. I'll climb down if you'll hold me from below to keep me from tipping."

"Will do."

On the ground at last with Frank's help, she forgot her pain at the sight of Chaney laid back in the straw. With a cry she threw herself gratefully into his arms. He squeezed her so hard she yipped. Then he tipped her face back and kissed her. He clasped her cheeks and stared into her eyes. "You're all right?"

She was conscious that the James brothers were looking on. She heard Barney Mallott groaning and whimpering in the straw, but she saw only Chaney. "I'm all right."

"What about your hands?" He gathered them up and rubbed his thumbs across their backs. "Good God Almighty! What'd he tie you up with?"

"His suspenders." She managed a chuckle. "The blood's already running back in them. They hurt a little now, but they'll be fine." Actually, they hurt something fierce, but she wasn't going to tell Chaney. When she got back to the hotel room, she could soak them in cold water. She rolled off her husband and started to get up. "Frank rubbed them for me."

Chaney pulled her against him again with his left arm. He thrust up his hand. "I'm sure obliged to you fellows.

I wish I could tell you how much, but I just don't know how. She's the most important thing in the world to me."

Frank shook his hand. "We're just glad we could be here."

Jesse too stepped forward and shook hands. He jerked his head back in Barney's direction. "What did he want with her? She's a nice lady."

Beth Anne cleared her throat. "He wanted the money from the sale of the horses." She looked up at Chaney. "He felt like we cheated him. He kept telling me you got what he should have had."

Chaney's expression darkened. He made an effort to pull himself to his feet. His gaze locked with Frank's as if he were trying to send a message. "I need to take Beth Anne back to the hotel. I'd be much obliged if you fellows would go find the U.S. Marshal. Tell him I'll meet him back at the hotel and explain everything."

Jesse shook his head. "Sorry, mister. Maybe you'd better take care of the U.S. Marshal. We try to steer clear of those fellows as much as possible."

Chaney frowned. His mouth drew down in a tight line as he studied the faces of his wife's rescuers. Recognition dawned. He blinked. His mouth quirked up.

Frank looked somewhat embarrassed.

Jesse shrugged and grinned. Pulling off his hat, he swept an elaborate bow.

"Y' all are horse thieves!" Barney dragged himself into the shedrow in front of Jack's stall. He was panting. Sweat dripped from his brow and trickled into his beard. His blood soaked into the dirt. But his eyes blazed with hatred at the four of them. "Damned horse thieves."

Chaney tried to turn Beth Anne toward the door, but she balked. She couldn't go away and leave so many unanswered questions. She stared pointedly at the James brothers. "Did you come to steal Jack?"

Jesse got a stubborn, mulish look about his mouth. He started to shake his head, but Frank punched him on the shoulder. "He wouldn't have done it. He was just drunk and jealous 'cause your horse beat his."

Beth Anne made a tsking sound like a mother scolding a bad child.

"Hey, if we hadn't come, look what would have happened." Jesse defended himself. "We saved you and him too." He nodded toward Chaney. Then he puffed out his chest. "We're heroes."

Beth Anne smiled. "You are. You really are. And heroes should be rewarded. Come to White Oak Farms. It's on the Marais des Cygnes River in Bates County. Come in about two years. You can each have the pick of our horses. From the new crop of yearlings to our best-trained riding stock. You'll have the very best because he's going to be at stud. Jack o' Diamonds."

Frank looked really pleased. "That's a fair offer."

Jesse kicked at the ground a couple of times; then he too smiled. "It's a deal. But don't you forget."

"We won't." Again Chaney tried to lead Beth Anne out of the stable.

Barney had twisted himself around and braced his shoulder against a four-by-four. The pain must have eased, because he found the strength to begin another diatribe. "Don't you sons-of-bitches walk away and leave me here to bleed to death."

Beth Anne tried to reassure him. She couldn't help feeling a little sorry for Barney. His schemes had come to nothing but his own pain. "We'll send someone back in a minute."

His face twisted into a devil mask. He didn't even look like himself anymore. "You think you've got it so good, Beth Anne Taggart! Your husband's your little tin Jesus, ain't he? Well, ask the lieutenant why he hardly never pulls a gun. Ask him why."

Her gaze flickered to Chaney's face. His expression was agonized. The pain in his leg couldn't be causing that.

"Goddamn it!" Barney screamed. "Ask him!"

Beth Anne was conscious of Frank and Jesse James as witnesses to what was sure to be unpleasant. Barney had known Chaney longer than she had. Something must have happened to Chaney during the war. Something he was ashamed of.

"Let's get out of here, Beth Anne," Chaney said desperately.

"Run!" Barney screamed again. "Run. You can't get out of here fast enough. I've got you now. I've got you."

Beth Anne put her arm under Chaney's shoulder to support him to the door.

"You got scars on your hands, Miz Taggart." Barney lowered his voice. It rolled out of his throat like the growl of a timber wolf. "I seen 'em when I tied you up. And I seen 'em when you got 'em. And you got a scar on your head, ain't you?"

Beth Anne froze in her tracks. Leaving her husband to support himself on the stable door, she turned back. "What do you know about that?"

"I wuz there." Barney leaned forward. Sweat glistened on his face. The arm on which he braced himself shuddered. "I saw him when he done it. I saw it all."

"Beth Anne—"

She motioned Chaney to be silent. To Barney she said, "What did you see?"

Now the center of attention, Barney managed a dry chuckle. "Your pa was meaner'n a spotted-ass ape."

"My father?"

"He wasn't gonna go peaceful. He kept on a-shootin'."

Her dream. "On the porch by the railing."

"Beth Anne—" Chaney's voice was agonized.

Barney's feverish stare fastened on his former commander. "The lieutenant shot him."

She wouldn't believe it. She didn't dare believe it. She closed her eyes.

Barney chuckled. "Plugged him dead center. Knocked him down like a steer at the slaughterhouse. And when you young'uns tried to shoot him, he shot you too. Plugged your brother and then shot you when you threw that little singleshot varmint rifle on him."

Beth Anne spun around. She stared at Chaney, saw the truth in his eyes, and dropped to her knees. As if a curtain had been swept back, she saw the part of her dream that her memory hadn't supplied. Across a distance of six feet and ten years, she saw it all in Chaney's eyes.

"You shot my father. You shot Josey." She held out her shaking hands.

Stone-faced, Chaney stood like a man in front of a firing squad.

"He shore did," Barney crowed.

"Shut up, you son-of-a-bitch!" This came from Jesse James. "I wouldn't believe a thing this rat says."

But Beth Anne was remembering. "The horse—" she murmured. "Your old horse with front legs white to the knees. That was Brownie." She held out her shaking hands. "How could you?"

Frank James knelt beside her and gathered her into his arms. "Easy now, Beth Anne. The war's over."

Emotions exploded as more and more pieces of the puzzle fell into place. "All these years of nightmares. All the screaming and weeping and feeling so scared. You knew why! You could have stopped them. You could have!"

Like a statue Chaney accepted the damnation she heaped on him. Then like a man condemned, he turned and walked away. If he felt the agony of his broken leg, he did not show it by his walk. Like a soldier he strode away down the alley.

Barney's malicious laughter rose, then choked off as Jesse stuck a gun barrel under his nose. "I should've done this about five minutes ago, mister. Now I'm giving you the word. Another peep out of you and you're a dead man."

Beth Anne held on to Frank's arm as he helped her to her feet and led her out of the stable. Outside in the hot bright sunlight she sank down on a weathered bench.

Frank sat beside her. Jesse came and sat down on the other side. The three didn't say a word for several minutes. At last Frank spoke. "You've got to put this behind you, Miz Taggart. That's what Jess and I've done."

"Sort of," Jesse added with a cynical tone in his voice.

Frank cleared his throat warningly. "Maybe he killed your father and maybe he didn't. I wouldn't believe anything that skunk said. And maybe if he did shoot, he shot to save himself. Any man'll do that."

"Why didn't he tell me himself? I've asked him and asked him. I've had the most horrible nightmares for years," Beth Anne whispered.

"Most likely because they were so horrible," Jesse supplied. "And you didn't remember anything from them, now did you?"

"No," she said reluctantly.

"You forgot about them when you were awake." Frank nodded. "Maybe he was hoping you'd stop having the nightmares. And then he'd never have to tell you."

She rubbed her hand across her face. "I'm going to have to think about this a long time."

The James brothers stood immediately. She looked up into their handsome faces. She rose and placed her hands on their arms. "I don't know how to say how important you've been to me today. You're strangers. But you've gone out of your way to be best friends."

"Don't mention it, ma'am," Frank began.

"You've really had a dangerous time. I don't know how to thank you."

Jesse's smile made his face angelic. "Aw, now. Don't feel obliged, Beth Anne. We've been purely entertained. Watching all these goings on has been more fun than a night at the oprey house."

She shook her head a little in wonder. Jesse James surely took things in stride. She wondered who he really was. She'd never ask. Instead, she rose on tiptoe and kissed first Jesse and then Frank on the cheek. "Just know that you'll always have a place at White Oak."

"On the Marais des Cygnes River." Frank smiled and doffed his hat.

"In Bates County." Jesse swept his before him in a graceful bow. "In two years. You can count on us to pick the best."

Chaney hadn't stopped in the Coates House Hotel. Beth Anne realized she should have been worried. She should go hunt for him, but she was too near collapse.

"I need a bath immediately," she ordered. "In your biggest bathtub. Extra hot water, extra towels. And bath salts. Green."

The desk clerk glanced once at her bruised, filthy face and twice at the expression in her eyes. "Yes, ma'am. Right away." He tilted his head to one side. "Would you get mad if I suggested a bottle of whiskey?"

"Whiskey." She took a deep breath and nodded. "That's the ticket."

She was soaking and sipping when a knock sounded on her door. She started to get up. Then she slumped back.

On second thought, why answer it? This was her room. Her room alone. She didn't want to talk to anyone.

Before she'd sat down in the water, her heart had thudded painfully. She'd gagged and retched, but she hadn't had anything in her stomach to come up. Her head was splitting. And her mind was considering one emotion after another. Burning hatred. Self-pity. Guilt. The desire for revenge. Righteous wrath.

The whiskey wasn't helping her to think straight, but at least it was numbing her.

The knock sounded again, stronger.

She wasn't going to answer that. Not until she was damned good and ready. Maybe never. Maybe she'd just sit here until she drank herself to death. Chaney Taggart could go straight to hell, for all she cared. She tipped up the glass, drained it, and poured herself another.

At the same time, she swished her left hand back and forth through the water, wiggling her fingers. They were returning to normal size, but her swollen wrists each had a bracelet of bright red flesh, turning purple.

"Beth Anne?"

She didn't even want to talk to Mary Nell. Mary Nell was happy. She was married to Noah Rollins. Noah Rollins. Beth Anne remembered him clearly now. When they were children, he'd been the one she looked up to. She'd always believed that he'd be the one she'd marry some day. He had been her brother Josey's best friend.

Josey. How clear his face seemed now. How dear. Tall, red-haired. Freckles on his nose. Smiling. Like the sun. She could remember her father too. Stern, unsmiling. He'd tolerated no nonsense from either one of them.

Just as he'd said he wouldn't leave White Oak to the U.S. Army or the Jayhawkers. He said he'd die first.

And so he had. And taken Josey with him. And nearly her.

The knocking came again. Through the door she could hear Mary Nell's voice higher and lighter calling her. Calling her name.

She wouldn't answer.

"What if something's wrong?"

She heard Noah's deeper rumble. "There's not much that a hot bath and a bottle of whiskey can't handle."

Their footsteps faded away.

She slid deeper into the tub. The water came up around her shoulders. Both wrists were under the water as she drank. Her hair floated around her.

She wondered briefly about Barney Mallott. Had he bled to death? Had someone found him and taken him to the doctor?

She didn't care about him either. He'd played his last card. But it had been a joker. Now he had nothing left, and no one would ever pay him any money.

She'd laugh if she weren't afraid she'd start laughing and wouldn't be able to stop. This disaster. This stupid trail drive to Leavenworth—along railroad tracks, for God's sake—had been because Chaney didn't want to pay Barney and the town council 206 dollars.

She could feel a laugh bubbling up in her throat. Holding her drink aloft, she ducked under the water. There she held her breath until her chest ached and all desire to laugh was gone.

Coming up, she leaned back against the edge of the tub. "Stop thinking about it," she said aloud. "Stop thinking."

She sipped and paddled. Sipped and paddled.

"Lieutenant, what the hell you doing, boy?" Luther Tibbets put his hand on Chaney's shoulder.

Chaney sat at a table in a dark corner of Ruby's. His

back was to the corner, his face to the wall. Two whiskey bottles, both empty, sat on the table in front of him. A third dangled loosely from his fingers. It was still a quarter full.

"Gettin' drunk."

Luther dropped down in front of him and shook his head. Pity for his friend twisted his gut.

Suffering had honed the little extra flesh from the bones of Chaney's face. His eyes were feverish and sunken in his head. He looked like a man in hell.

Luther turned one of the empty bottles around to read the label. "Having any luck?"

Chaney took another swig. "Not much. Whiskey's watered. Leg hurts too much."

"I doubt if you can even feel the leg."

Chaney met his friend's stare but said nothing.

Across the smoke-dimmed room, three whores in various stages of undress draped their arms around the shoulders of three men who were playing cards. Layers of cigar smoke laced with the scents of sex and unwashed bodies wavered in the still air.

Another couple were halfway up the stairs, their hands groping for the most intimate parts of each other's bodies. Luther tried to remember the last time he'd been in a place like this. It must have been a long time ago, for now the sights and scents only embarrassed him.

Chaney took another drink. He lifted the bottle to eye level. "Almost empty. Three bottles and I'm still hurting. Must be a hell of a break."

"You'll think hell of a break in the morning, my friend. This stuff in here would probably kill a goat."

Chaney drained the bottle, set it carefully on the table, and raised his arm to snap his fingers. The man behind the bar started around the end with another, but Luther motioned him back.

Chaney let his arm fall. He leaned forward on his elbows. From out of the shadows beneath his hat, his eyes glittered. "She remembered, Luther."

"Well, son. Now the other shoe's dropped. You got nothin' to be afraid of anymore."

"Nothin' to be afraid of. Nothin' to live for."

Luther felt helpless. "Aw, now, Lieutenant. It ain't like you to roll over and play dead like a whipped dog."

Chaney let his head slump forward until his cheek rested on the filthy table. He closed his volcanic eyes. "It's all ready for her. She's proved she can handle it. This trip proved it."

"Son—"

Chaney opened his eyes to stare through the distorting glass of the empties. "Where the hell's that fresh bottle?" He swung around. "Bartender! Goddamn it. I told you to keep them coming till I pass out."

Luther heaved a deep sigh and rose. He shook his head at the bartender. Then he put his hand under Chaney's arm. "Let's go, son."

"Go? Hell, no. A man's got a right to get drunk at the end of the trail." He tried to twist his arm out of Luther's grasp. The motion stirred his leg. He gasped and reached down to hold it with both hands. "Goddamn. It hurts. It hurts so bad."

Luther looked around the room. The cardplayers had interrupted their playing to see the outcome of the argument. An overblown rose in purple satin who must have been Ruby came out of an alcove. Luther gestured to his friend. "How's about your pimp helping me get him over to the Coates House?"

"No," Chaney moaned, still clutching his leg. "Can't go there. Can't go anywhere near her. Can't—" He swallowed hard, made a snubbing sound. He looked up at Luther with tears starting down his cheeks. "Can't."

A burly black man emerged from the shadows beneath the stair. Without speaking, he took Chaney's other arm, passed it over his shoulder, and put his arm around Chaney's waist. With Luther leading the way, they passed out of Ruby's.

Barney Mallott was feeling pretty weak and woozy, but he figured he was in luck. He'd wadded the tail of his shirt up in his pants and stuffed it against the wound. That seemed to slow the bleeding down to nothing.

He still had what was left of the town council's money plus twenty dollars from Beth Anne Taggart.

He'd rest here tonight. Then tomorrow he'd get himself patched up and take the train for Californey. His stake wasn't nearly so big as he'd planned, but he wasn't broke.

He was drifting into sleep when he heard footsteps. Thinking that he might get someone to help him to the doctor, he rolled over and put on his pitiful face.

"Hey, Barney. Heard you'd run out your string."

He groaned and slumped back as he recognized the voice. "No such thing." He tried to bluster. "I done tangled with some horse thieves, but I've got my eye on Chaney Taggart. Now that you're here—"

"I've come to cart you back to Rich Hill, Barney," the laconic voice went on. He could hear the amusement in it. "Eleazar Drorsen wants his money back."

"I've got it. I've got it."

"That's good. They'll use it to pay my salary. I'm the new town marshal."

Eustace Fisher bent over and plucked Barney's badge off his shirt.

* * *

Chaney woke to the sound of his body telling him that he was sick, sick, sick. His head pounded. His stomach roiled. His heart thumped and skipped. The only good thing was that so long as he lay perfectly still, his broken leg didn't hurt. Perhaps, despite everything that had happned to it, it was really, finally healing.

He sat up in bed, then dropped back immediately. Sweat poured out of his skin and soaked the sheet beneath him. He stared at the ceiling for a few minutes before his stomach settled down and he could reach for his wallet.

The first thing he pulled out was the check for the sale of the horses. He stared at it, remembering his lack of appreciation, his arrogance. He wiped at his stinging eyes. He would leave it at the desk for her.

He raised himself up on his elbow and counted out his money. Thirty-eight dollars in change, plus the coins in his pockets, some of which were silver dollars and a few gold pieces.

It was enough.

He couldn't face her. He couldn't bear to see hatred in her eyes. He hoisted himself off the bed and made his way to the door. He hadn't long to wait for one of the maids to pass by. He sent her for a bath, some breakfast, and his bill.

In an hour he was at the depot. The first train out was for Wichita, Kansas. He bought a ticket. He sat down to wait, his broken leg outstretched. Oddly, he didn't feel worried. He'd had the best ten years a man could have. He'd had the best friends a man could have and the love of the sweetest woman on God's green earth.

That would have to be enough to last him the rest of his life.

* * *

"Beth Anne Taggart. If you don't open that door, Noah's going to break it down," Mary Nell called.

"Go away."

"Not on your life. You've pouted long enough."

"I'm not pouting. I'm thinking."

"Stand back, sweetheart. A good swift kick right next to the lock ought to do it." Noah's voice sounded suspiciously loud, but Beth Anne got the point.

"Wait a minute." Reluctantly, she opened the door to the worried faces of her two friends. "I don't feel very good. I was sleeping."

"You look like you don't feel good." Mary Nell came in pulling Noah with her. "What did you do last night?"

Beth Anne pointed to the cold bathwater and the empty whiskey bottle.

Noah nodded sagely. "Feel better? Other than the headache and the flannel mouth."

"Upset stomach."

Mary Nell motioned her friend to a chair. "Noah, sweetheart, why don't you go find someone to bring us coffee?" When he was gone, she took up the hairbrush and began to stroke it slowly through Beth Anne's tangled red tresses. "So, what did you think about?"

Beth Anne bowed her head. Mary Nell's gentle brushing felt good. For more than a minute, she let the soothing effect of the strokes calm her.

"Yes?" her friend prodded.

"I thought about what to do."

"Is that so hard?"

"Mary Nell, suppose your husband had shot your father and brother down on the front porch of your home?"

The brushing paused for a second, then resumed. "It

would depend on how long I'd been in love with Noah when I found out about it."

"I remember my father clearly now. It's like Barney Mallott burst a dam in my mind. All those terrible memories have been waiting behind it. Now they've rushed out. And I can't find anyplace that isn't filled with them. I can't think about anything else."

Noah entered with the coffee. He poured them all cups and sweetened them with lump sugar. "They didn't have any milk that didn't taste blinky," he apologized. The springs squeaked beneath him as he sat down on the end of the bed. "We'll all have to drink it black."

"This is fine." She took a sip. It scalded her tongue. The pain made her want to cry, but instead she managed to smile. "And hot."

"Do you want to go home to White Oak?" Mary Nell asked doubtfully.

"Of course. I don't know anything else."

Mary Nell exchanged a relieved glance with Noah.

"Why would you think I'd go anywhere else?"

"I was afraid you might try to run away."

Beth Anne snorted. "I'm not a quitter. Where would I run to? I don't know how I can live with Chaney. I'm so afraid that I'll look at him and remember more than I remember right now."

"Do you remember him shooting you?"

"Not really." She shrugged. "There were so many men, so many horses, galloping and rearing and stamping. All I remember is Poppa on the porch shooting. I can remember his beard blowing in the wind. His beard was snow-white and long.

"We were already on the wagon when he fell. Then Josey jumped down and dragged me off with him. He pushed me under the wagon and tried to run across the yard.

"He was shooting at a man coming right for him on

horseback. Poppa fell over backward, and Josey went down almost at the same time." She looked at Mary Nell and Noah. "Maybe Chaney didn't shoot them both. Maybe he didn't shoot either one."

Mary Nell put down the brush to take up her coffee. The look in her eyes pleaded with Noah to say something.

"What happened then?" Noah asked.

"Noah! Change the subject."

"No. Let her get it all out of her system."

Beth Anne looked at him gratefully. "I only had a singleshot .22. I'd already fired it. I didn't even have any ammunition, but I had to help Josey. I crawled out from under the wagon and ran to him. I don't know why I took the rifle with me.

"This horse came galloping right at me—white stockings up above the knees." She looked at them both. "Chaney had a horse like that for years. Do you remember Brownie?"

Mary Nell nodded. Her expression was troubled.

"I never knew." Beth Anne shook her head. "I never knew. My brother Josey looked back at me. He motioned me to stay down. Then he ran to help Poppa. I ran after him. Then the horse was there and the rider, and I pulled the .22 up in front of my face."

She took a deep breath. "That's the last thing I remember for a long, long time. After that there's only Chaney."

"Whether he did it or not," Noah said, "he ordered it."

Mary Nell made a face at him.

"I guess so," Beth Anne admitted. "But he must be a good man. Otherwise, why did he pick me up and take me with him? He could have left me lying there. I probably would have died. He's all I've ever known."

She raised her fingers to the scar at her hairline. Then she dropped her hands into her lap to stare at the scars there. "What am I going to do? What's the right thing to do?"

She looked at them both. They were all young. They had never fought in a war, never been in battle. Yet they'd lived with war and its destruction for ten long years. It had shaped them all.

"What am I going to do?" she repeated.

"Don't you hate him?" Noah asked curiously.

"Noah Rollins!" Mary Nell batted at him with the hairbrush. "Shut your mouth."

Beth Anne buried her face in her hands. The question was the one she couldn't deal with.

Mary Nell's arms slid round her shoulders. "Don't pay him any mind. He's got crazy ideas about getting even with everybody who's ever done him wrong. He'll get over them."

But Noah wouldn't back down. "She's got to look at all this," he said stubbornly. "She's doing the right thing to think it over. What'd happen if she went back to the farm and found she couldn't look him in the eye? What if he made her sick every time she looked at him?"

"Noah!"

"He's right."

Mary Nell flounced down on the other side of the bed. The pooch in her lower lip testified that so long as Noah was going to argue, she would argue too. "Do you miss Chaney Taggart?"

"I guess I do. I haven't had time to think about it yet."

"Can you imagine going back to the farm and him not being there?"

Beth Anne thought about that. "Not really. Even though I know about Josey, I can't imagine not sleeping beside my husband, getting up with him, training horses with him." She looked at the two of them.

When Mary Nell had sat down, Noah had stretched his

long frame out so he was almost touching her. He could lay his head on her shoulder if he cocked it to the left. They were so much in love.

Beth Anne could feel the heat in her cheeks. She was in love like that. "I can't imagine going through life without making—er—love to Chaney."

All three of them looked away. Then they looked back and exchanged smiles as if they shared a secret.

Noah put his hand over Mary Nell's where it lay on the bedspread.

Beth Anne's fingers twitched. "I was only a little girl when Chaney shot me. I didn't remember anything from my past life. I was so badly hurt. But Chaney took care of me. He loved me like a daughter and then a sister and then a wife. He taught me just about everything I know."

She rose and walked to the window. The street outside was filled with traffic. Horses with riders, horses pulling wagons and buggies, horses and cattle being driven to the stockyard. The dust rose around them.

"I want to go home to White Oak as soon as possible," she said softly. "I expect Chaney to go with me. I can't imagine any life without him."

She stared out into the street, her mind turning over everything. So long as she couldn't come to some sort of conclusion, she had to stay in this town, in this room looking out at the dirty, dusty, noisy street.

At last she turned back to her friends. "I'm an orphan of war. But I was luckier than most orphans. I didn't know hunger or cold or brutality. I didn't live in an orphanage with strangers who didn't care anything about me. All I knew was love and security. Love and security was Chaney Taggart."

The tears brimmed in her eyes and trickled down her cheeks. She looked at Noah Rollins. "Is that so wrong?"

He shook his head. His expression was rueful and more

than a little disgusted, whether at himself or at her logic she couldn't tell. "When you put it like that, I guess not."

Mary Nell sent Noah to buy green ribbons, ladies' powder and rouge, and tortoiseshell combs.

He protested that he didn't know what to get, that he didn't know where to go, that he'd be laughed at. She kissed him full on the mouth and patted his bottom as he walked out the door.

By the time he returned, Mary Nell had helped Beth Anne into her dress. He lounged on the bed and watched in amusement while his wife braided the ribbons into Beth Anne's hair. She secured the braids with the combs. Then she powdered Beth Anne's face and used a dab of rouge on her cheeks and mouth.

"What do you think, Noah?"

He'd been grinning broadly throughout the entire process. Now he shifted a little on the bed as if his pants might be a little tight. "I think she looks like a picture out of a catalogue."

"You're ready." Mary Nell hugged her friend. "Now go down the hall and tell him what you told us. And let's get the hell out of Kansas City."

When Beth Anne was out the door, Noah rolled over on the bed and stretched out with his legs spread. "Come over here, sweetheart. I've got a powerful itch that's been needing a scratch ever since you started all that braiding and twisting and—"

Laughing delightedly, she flung herself into his arms with a great creak of springs.

"He's checked out, Miz Taggart," the desk clerk informed her. "He left this for you."

Trembling, Beth Anne tore open the sealed envelope. The only thing in it was the check. The stupid check that had caused all the trouble to begin with.

She wanted to rip it into little pieces. But she didn't. This was the future. Chaney would share it with her.

"How did he leave?" she asked the clerk.

"I think the jitney took him to the train station."

"The gentleman with the broken leg? He took the train to Wichita."

"When does the next one leave?"

The station master consulted his schedule. "In an hour. It's the night train to Salina and points west. You have to change in Topeka."

"Sell me a ticket."

EPILOGUE

Chaney Taggart sat in the lobby of the drummer's hotel in Wichita, Kansas. Hour after hour he listened to the trains rolling through. They were driving him crazy. But he couldn't stay in the room he'd rented. The four walls drove him crazy too.

His leg hurt, but that wasn't the worst of his pain. He missed Beth Anne with a gnawing ache. All he could think about was her face. She'd been beside him so long that he couldn't feel any more lost if he'd misplaced his right arm.

When he wasn't thinking about her, he was thinking and worrying about White Oak. What was going to happen to it, to his men? They needed him. He had a life back there. A life he couldn't ever finish.

He thought about Beth Anne as he'd first seen her—a wraithlike figure darting across the yard in the dust and powdersmoke. Then she'd thrown up that rifle and he'd shot before he was sure of his target.

He'd realized what he'd done when she'd fallen over backward. Her hat had come off and two braids of that glorious red hair had lashed out in the dust. He'd all but fallen off Brownie and dropped down beside her.

He'd picked up one braid, willing it to be something else, terrified at what he'd done.

Then self-loathing quickly turned to hope when she'd stirred. After that he'd fallen very quickly in love. She was the only woman he'd ever loved. He couldn't even remember if he'd ever had carnal knowledge of another woman before Beth Anne. It was as if his life began the night her father and brother had died.

Now he sat here in this chair that stank of cigar smoke and stale sweat and regarded the rest of that life. He hadn't a single idea. Not a notion. What would he do?

Nothing.

He looked around him with unseeing eyes. Then he let his head fall forward on his chest.

How long he sat there he didn't know. Someone turned out the lamps except for the one at the desk. All was shadows from which the noises came and went. Horses' hooves plodded, loped, and galloped by in the street. Wagons and buggies rattled after them. An occasional gunshot cracked the night from over on the other side of the tracks. And trains rolled by hourly with whistles and bells and great bursts of steam.

He must have slept, but how could he when he'd heard it all?

Morning light crept across the worn carpet.

He wondered if he sat here long enough would he just die? Would they notice that he was dead? He pictured himself as a skeleton in a dusty suit with a splinted leg.

A skirt appeared in his line of vision. The skirt billowed out. A slim waist, a woman's breasts, arms reaching out to him.

"Chaney."

He heard her voice. He didn't question. Didn't ask how she could possibly be here. If this was a dream, he wanted to go on dreaming. If he was crazy, he welcomed insanity.

With a groan he reached for her. She was flesh and blood. She was his.

"Beth Anne." He pulled her against him tighter than he should, but he couldn't take the chance that she'd get away. He'd walked away and never expected to see her again.

Now he wouldn't ever walk away again.

The tears started in his eyes and ran down his cheeks. They were wetting her face, her hair as he kissed her. He couldn't keep from crying, and once he started he couldn't seem to stop.

At last, she was holding him. He'd pulled her into his lap, but she was holding him.

At last he got himself under some semblance of control.

"Why?" was all he said.

"Because I love you," she answered. "I've come to take you home."

Put a Little Romance in Your Life With
Fern Michaels

Put a Little Romance in Your Life With
Janelle Taylor